Danger At The Door

Danger At The Door

By

Michelle Sutton

Other Titles by Michelle Sutton

Danger at the Door
In Plain Sight
In Sheep's Clothing
When Love Collides
Out of Time
Surprise Love

Her Innocence - Coming 2013

Tombstone Treasures

Book One: First Impressions
Book Two: First Love
Book Three: First Response

High Desert Devotion
Book One: Collette's Crusade - Coming 2013
Book Two: Serena's Something - Coming 2013
Book Three: Barbie's Breakthrough - Coming 2014

Valley of Decision
Book One: Hard Pressed but Not Crushed - Coming 2014
Book Two: Perplexed but Not in Despair - Coming 2015
Book Three: Persecuted but Not Forsaken - Coming 2015
Book Four: Struck Down but Not Destroyed - Coming 2016

Desert Breeze Publishing, Inc.
27305 W. Live Oak Rd #424
Castaic, CA 91384

http://www.DesertBreezePublishing.com

Copyright © 2009 by Michelle Sutton
ISBN 10: 1-61252-920-8
ISBN 13: 978-1-61252-920-2

Published in the United States of America
eBook Publish Date: August 1, 2009
Print Publish Date: April 2013

Editor-In-Chief: Gail R. Delaney
Editor: Gail R. Delaney
Marketing Director: Jenifer Ranieri
Cover Artist: Jenifer Ranieri

Cover Art Copyright by Desert Breeze Publishing, Inc © 2009

Dedication

To my enthusiastic friends who kept telling me to keep on writing and never give up. Thank you! You've encouraged me to keep on keeping on, and this book is the result of that effort. Thank you Desert Breeze staff for seeing merit in my work. I also want to thank my family for supporting and loving me through this process and the Lord for the inspiration.

The poem found in this book is an original work and used with permission. The author is Aida Bode. She also speaks fluent Albanian, Greek and Macedonian and is the person I consulted regarding culture.

Regarding the value of property and taxes, I'd like to thank the Cochise County recorder's office. For information pertaining to the Chihuahua's symptoms, thanks go to the vet at a local veterinary clinic who wishes to remain anonymous. Since I wrote this story over three years ago I may have forgotten people and for that I apologize. Last and best, thanks go to Tamela, my talented agent and friend.

Prologue

The door slammed behind him as lightning flashed across the summer sky. A boom echoed as thunder struck the ground. Moist summer air filled his lungs and electricity raised the hair on the back of his neck. He savored the scent and held it in like smoke from a cigarette. With a grunt, he exhaled, wishing he had something more powerful than tobacco to inhale.

The unpredictability of monsoon season shot bolts of excitement through him. It gave him energy. Made him want to go on the hunt for someone weak.

A slow grin tugged at his mouth. It had been a long time -- nearly a year -- since he could do as he pleased. How he hated being restricted like a child, and jail felt like one big time-out. Idiot guards thought they could control him. But he made sure to wish them dead whenever he was forced to comply.

After all, it *had* worked on his Momma.

If only she'd used time-out with him instead of her wicked ways.

He clenched his fists and blocked the memory, resisting the urge to smash his knuckles on the brick wall. Sporadic drops of rain pelted his head, cooling him off.

His cottony mouth made him long for a strong drink. Something with kick, like whiskey. Resisting the urge to open his mouth and let the raindrops quench his thirst, he pressed his lips together. Childhood had abandoned him long ago.

He imagined going to *Jeepers Creepers* pub and finding an easy woman to keep him company tonight. But this time he'd watch himself and make sure she didn't have a jealous husband waiting in the wings. Yeah, tonight he'd pick a gal that he could crash with until he got his life together.

There was only one woman he really wanted. She just didn't know it yet. Their reunion would be sweet, or she'd regret it. He'd make sure of that.

Soon the tangy taste of adrenaline would flood his veins. He missed the tingling sensation, the warmth coursing through him when a woman begged him for mercy. There had been many cries echoing in his head over the past few years. But none of them satisfied his craving. He imagined his first night with her. Yeah, he'd make their time together memorable.

He leaned against the rough brick wall of the decrepit jail building. Grumbling, he popped his knuckles as he waited for his ride. What was taking him so long to get there? He better not back out just because he found himself a woman with a kid.

First, he had to collect what his narc friend owed him. And if he felt generous, he might let him go without pounding his face in. Depending on how useful he'd be.

Just a running vehicle and some cash. That's all he needed to get back on his feet. And a decent job. Something low-key to avoid having his background checked. But it had to be legit. Work that would make his probation officer content. Then, when he got himself set up in a place, he'd find that brunette who taunted him in his dreams.

Sam's girl.

This time he'd get the right house.

Chapter One

Laney Cooper released a shuddering sigh.

She set the table for two one last time and ordered their favorite meal -- spinach pizza and antipasto salad -- to celebrate Sam's life.

Tonight marked the anniversary of her fiancé's death. She wanted the farewell dinner to propel her into a new year of hope, to help her move on. Blinking back tears, she lit tapered candles and dimmed the lights.

Her shoulders slumped. They had planned the perfect wedding. Images of her dress, the lace veil, and the three-tiered cake flashed through her mind. The perfect honeymoon, a two-week trip to Cancun.

Finding something to look forward to without him was proving more difficult than she'd imagined. But she'd try. He would have wanted her to.

She approached the window and moved the blinds so she could check the road. Total darkness covered the Huachuca Mountain range in Sierra Vista, Arizona. The inky blackness smothered the sky as the last bit of sunlight faded on the horizon.

No headlights snaked up the mountain. Her shoulders sagged further as she backed away from the window. Dinner should have arrived half an hour ago. She ordered the same thing every week, but tonight she'd added cannoli -- Sam's favorite dessert -- to her order. She wanted to end the commemorative meal with something sweet.

Flipping open her cell phone, she quickly bypassed a digital photo of Sam with his arm draped over her shoulder. The evidence of joy on their faces seared her heart if she lingered on the image too long. She'd delete the picture soon. Maybe after she ate.

It'd be hard, but she'd do it.

After dialing to check on her order, she squeezed her eyes shut. The phone rang numerous times before someone finally answered.

"Little Italy. May I take your order?"

She pushed the words past the lump in her throat. They didn't know how much their lateness hurt. "I don't need you to *take* my order. I need you to *deliver* it."

"Ma'am, I need your name."

She released an exasperated sigh as she ran her fingers through her bangs. "It's Cooper. My food should have been here by now. You guys know me. I order the same thing every--"

"Please hold." The bored-sounding voice cut her off. She wondered if the man had even heard her complaint. As she waited, a local radio announcer introduced a country western song. Friday nights were always busy at Little Italy, but never so bad that they'd had to put her on hold and force her to listen to music about love gone sour.

A sob crawled up her throat.

"Oh, Sam. Why did you have to leave me? What am I going to do without you?"

Silence echoed in the dimly lit room.

As usual, nothing. Even God had clamped His lips shut.

Sudden longing to visit Sam's grave one last time tugged at her need to remain cocooned in the safety of her home. When had she last visited the site? Three months ago? Six?

Yet the idea of driving anywhere sent shivers of fear skittering up her spine. The thought of getting behind the wheel of a death trap made her stomach lurch. Driving was simply too dangerous. Even riding in a cab made her nervous these days.

Baby, her longhaired black Chihuahua, yipped.

Someone must be coming. Thankfully Baby paid attention and alerted her when anyone approached her house. She didn't like surprises.

The sound of crunching gravel captured her attention and her stomach knotted. At first she thought she heard people arguing, but when she listened closer she recognized the blood-chilling sound of coyotes attacking some poor creature again. Probably someone's unfortunate pet. She rubbed her silk sleeves and tiptoed to the door, thankful Baby wasn't the cornered animal.

Silence permeated the air for several long moments. Even the coyotes had ceased their frenzied howling. Her stomach suddenly growled, making her squeal and jump. She gasped and laughed at her overreaction. No way could such a hyper vigilant nervous system be healthy.

She paused and inhaled several deep breaths. Though eager for her dinner to arrive, caution still made her pause and peer through the blinds. If only she had a sense of security like her pet. Instead, she felt cornered like the hapless animal outside her door. The past few nights she'd had strange dreams about being pursued by something sinister -- like a band of coyotes -- but she couldn't recall the details after she woke up. Worse, she couldn't shake the feeling that someone had been watching her the past few days.

She shuddered and glanced over her shoulder, and then peeked through the blinds a second time. Maybe she was just being paranoid. Wouldn't be the first time she overreacted only to discover her imagination had been running wild again.

Most of the time her anxiety came from a credible source. Like the morning she found a snake dozing on her front patio. Thankfully she'd had the good sense to shut the door before it had a chance to react to being startled. Animal control sure came in handy in those situations. She had their number on speed dial... just in case.

It was bad enough she'd found scorpions in her home when she first moved in. The pest control man had searched for them with a black light to make sure he caught them all. She shuddered at the memory and recalled the hairy tarantula in the sink last month. There were enough creepy critters in the desert to make even the bravest woman swoon.

She shuddered again. Fortunately, her exterminator came every other month and killed the pests before they could sting her or her sweet dog. Without Baby as her companion, she would become even more of a recluse -- if that were possible.

Hating her weakness, her fear of leaving the house, Laney rubbed her forehead and groaned. Maybe if she had a friend to talk to -- someone other than her pet -- she could get her life back to normal. But fear followed her everywhere these days, cutting her off from normal relationships. From love and friendship. It even smothered her faith.

You're not alone...

She sucked in her breath. Had God finally spoken to her heart after all this time?

The doorbell chimed. Her heart jolted even though she'd anticipated the sound. She swallowed hard, fighting to calm her breathing. It seemed ridiculous that she'd expected the delivery, and yet the abrupt noise still made her pulse race.

Baby whined and wriggled in her arms, trying to break free. She stroked her dog's fur, heedless of her pet's pungent need for a bath. She sighed and kissed Baby's head. It must be a new delivery boy, for her pet couldn't be soothed this time.

"Shhh... It's okay, sweetie."

But Baby wouldn't relax and struggled even more.

Laney shouted, "Just a minute!" After jogging to the other side of the house, she placed her dog in her traveling cage so Baby wouldn't scare the delivery guy. Though small, Baby sounded downright vicious when she growled, especially when an unfamiliar visitor entered her territory.

With a forced smile, Laney wiped her eyes and returned to the foyer. She peered through the peephole to make sure the person was safe before opening the door to them.

A little over a year ago a woman had been attacked in her home, which looked a lot like Laney's house. The woman had lived less than a mile away. They never caught the man, and the frightened woman soon moved away.

Occasionally border patrol would stop by and check on her because she lived on the foothills. Year round, illegals would hike over the mountain to avoid detection. She appreciated the border patrol looking out for her, but at the same time they had her scared to death, filling her mind with visions of being attacked or robbed. She would rather not know about those situations in her area.

Yep. A person could never be too cautious. She scanned the man's clothing and recognized his uniform -- especially the Little Italy t-shirt. She opened the door and motioned with a wave to usher the deliveryman inside.

The olive-skinned Adonis stared at her, unmoving on her front patio. His gorgeous, light brown eyes fixated on hers. He had a distinct Mediterranean look, mixed with Russian or Greek descent. She stared back, mesmerized for a moment by the slow grin forming on his face. He stood several inches taller, forcing her to look up.

At least the delivery guys were getting better looking. So much so, she found herself gaping when he removed his baseball cap to reveal a thick head of hair and nodded.

The man's smile grew wider. No doubt her staring flattered him. She couldn't help admiring the gleam of his straight, white teeth, and the tiny dimple in his left cheek.

Flustered that he'd noticed her gawking, Laney combed her bangs with her fingers. Her cheeks heated as she glanced away and tried to collect her thoughts.

The man shifted his feet and tucked his ball cap under his arm. His grin faded and his brow furrowed. Maybe he'd never made a delivery before and didn't know what to say. He grew serious as he scanned her face, settling on her mouth for a fraction of a second, before returning to her eyes.

"Where's Tom?" Her voice trembled, betraying her still-fragile emotions, her fear.

"Sick. He has bad cold." The corner of his mouth curved upward, and he held out the boxes containing her order. "Your food?"

"Please, come in?" she asked again and licked her lips, a nervous habit that used to drive her sister crazy. What she wouldn't do to have her sister back, even if it meant getting nagged about her quirks all the time.

The man nodded and averted his eyes as he stepped inside, then captured her gaze again. A deep, tender expression teased his suntanned face.

Warmth melted her insides. It should be illegal to heat a woman's heart with an intimate glance within minutes of meeting her.

Though the same intense look in the past -- before Sam -- would've made her desire an invitation to dinner, this man's attention made her melt on the spot. If only dating didn't require leaving the safety of her house.

After hesitating a moment, she turned and muttered, "Just set the box over there, and I'll be right back with a check."

The man nodded as he strolled to the table and set down the boxes. For a moment she watched him, fascinated by his graceful movement. So smooth, and yet so thoroughly masculine. She swallowed hard.

Admiring the chocolate color of his wavy brown hair for a moment, she quickly averted her attention. The fresh scent of his woodsy pine after shave wafted in the air, reminding her of Sam. She sped from the room before tears formed.

Looking at any man with appreciation seemed like betrayal of the worst kind. Especially today, since she'd intended to devote every minute to Sam's memory. The attraction she felt toward the deliveryman was wrong.

She couldn't be so lonely that she'd long to spend time with a complete stranger, no matter how nice looking he happened to be.

Chapter Two

After giving herself a sound lecture on the hazards of getting emotionally involved right now, Laney returned to the dining room with her checkbook. She found the intriguing man inspecting an abstract painting with an intelligent smile in his eyes.

A year earlier she'd purchased the portrait from a local artist, mere days before her life had fallen apart. The rough texture and vibrant colors reminded her so much of Sam that her throat tightened. He'd been so full of life and joy over their upcoming marriage. No one had ever loved her like Sam did.

She doubted anyone ever would again.

"Is beautiful house." The man flashed a grin.

His thick accent had immediately intrigued her but she didn't want to sound nosey, so she hadn't asked when he first spoke. Though she rarely conversed with visitors, she appraised her situation. His warm smile invited her to talk.

"You from around here?" Her voice sounded rough, like she needed a drink of water, so she cleared her throat.

"Yes. Lived in town here, and before lived in Tucson and Phoenix. Moved last month when *Tetko* -- I mean Uncle Alek -- offered work for business. He is now, how for you say... hmmm... retire? I share for business."

Huh? She cleared her throat again, so distracted by his accent that she barely registered what he'd said. Not that it made any sense. "Alek is your uncle?"

"Yes, but he not for Little Italy here now. Moved back for home country. I would cared for business now." He thrust back his shoulders in a regal posture -- proud to be related to the former owner, no doubt.

Though confused by his statement and rather poor grammar, the confidence he projected cast him in an appealing light. Like someone who could steal her heart if given the chance. But it was too soon. Even if it could work, she wouldn't let it happen.

A sparkle appeared in his eyes, lighting his entire face.

Not knowing how to respond to his sudden change in demeanor, she thought for a moment. He must have been confused by her question because she still didn't know where he lived. "I meant have you been in the United States long?"

"Ah, yes, I moved for to Arizona three years back now. With parents, for father must sponsor me. He is legal resident." He nodded as his gaze locked onto hers, caressing her face as he spoke. "My father is teacher for University in Tempe."

"Wow." Her breathy response had more to do the strong vibes

he radiated than his confusing answer.

She must have looked dazed and confused, because he continued, his lower lip curling until his face formed an adorable frown.

"I am sorry. English I speak is very bad."

For only living three years in the USA, his speech wasn't that awful. No doubt she'd be illiterate in his country. She opened her mouth to encourage him, but the words stuck in her throat.

The sudden sound of Baby's sharp yip-yips jerked her back to reality. "Settle down, Baby," she called over her shoulder. Her cheeks heated. "Sorry if her barking bothers you." At least Baby wasn't singing. *That would surely scare him off.* Laney smiled at the thought.

The man offered an endearing, broad smile in response, once again displaying his perfectly straight teeth.

"Is cute." He winked.

She ignored the rapid hammering of her heart as she tried to work out what he'd meant when he said he moved to America with his parents.

"Do you still live with your parents?" Please say no. But then again, why should she even care?

He laughed, deep and husky. "No. Have my home."

"What's your first language?" Laney tried to sound casual as she glanced away and wrote him a check, pretending his throaty voice hadn't flustered her. Her hand trembled as she signed the bottom with extra flair. She peeked through her bangs, hoping he wouldn't catch her watching him with such avid interest.

Guilt swelled into a lump in her throat. How could she even think of another man tonight? She was supposed to be honoring Sam, not flirting with the delivery guy.

"I had speak Macedonian and Greek language."

"Hey, Macedonia is near Albania." She smiled, proud of her head for geography.

"Yes!" He laughed. "Many people not know where country is. Was Yugoslavia many years back."

"I went to elementary school with a girl from Yugoslavia."

He cleared his throat. "I speak very good Greek. Not so good English. I had studied languages at University before I finish and changed program for Business Administration. Is better for work, and how you say... career. Now have permanent resident hmm... how you say this? Oh yes, status. Have permanent status. Soon I must apply for citizenship papers."

His dimple grew more pronounced when he held out his hand to shake hers. "Name is Bullion Trajkovski. Trajkovski is like Smith for you Americans. In English say Bow-john like name sounds...B-O-J-O-H-N, but I say called me Bob, please. Is much easy for say American name. Think like SpongeBob, no? Good friends called me Bo-key." He winked and chuckled like it was the funniest thing he'd ever said.

Tearing the check from her checkbook, Laney then held it out to him, ignoring his offered hand. Touching any part of him would be disastrous. He exuded as much charisma as a foreign actor and she worried she wouldn't be able to let go.

And what a strange name. Bullion. Made her think of chicken broth. But Boki sounded too much like hokey or pokey. "Nice to meet you too... uh, Bob."

He nodded and tucked the check in his pocket. Then he clasped his hands together as if waiting for her to continue.

Baby let off another string of yips.

"I'll be there in a sec, Baby," she yelled. "Stop your barking, will ya!" With a smirk, she rolled her eyes and added, "Mercy, sometimes that dog really gets on my nerves. She just doesn't know when to shut up."

"*Kuche's* name Mercy? I thought you say name is Baby."

"Her name *is* Baby. Mercy is just an expression. My name's Laney, by the way." She offered a swift nod and dodged his extended hand again.

"Ah, yes. Is much pleased to meet Laney." Bob looked thoughtful for a moment, then smiled. "Is beautiful name. Never heard name from my country."

"Laney? Oh, it's short for Elaine. But nobody called me that except my mother, and she's been gone for..." Laney cleared her throat, trying not to cry. "For almost three years now."

"She move?"

"No, she... died." The tears pooling in her eyes threatened to spill over onto her cheeks. "In a car accident... with my dad and sister."

"Is very sad. I am sorry. Is all you family parents and sister?" He swallowed, and his eyes glistened as he searched hers.

She nodded. For a moment she believed he understood her pain. Sniffling, she reached for a tissue, dabbing her nose as she nodded. "It's all right. You didn't know."

He shifted on his feet and offered a tender smile. After a moment, he sighed and rubbed his eyes, and then glanced away. "Is very sad," he whispered.

Wiping her tears with her fingers, she choked on a laugh. "Look at me. I'm never this weepy. Especially not with someone I don't even know."

His face grew somber, and he gently touched her arm. "Is okay for feeling sad."

Glancing at his hand, she stiffened and he removed it from her arm.

"You have... hmmm... how you say, *romantic* dinner?" He gestured toward the table with a broad smile. "Is very beautiful."

Laney blinked back fresh tears. A lump formed in her throat, and she coughed into her hand.

His expression softened further, and he leaned toward her, this time without attempting to touch her arm. "So sorry. I say something more for make you cry?"

She shook her head and covered her mouth with her hand. Taking a step back, she frowned as she attempted to pull herself together. "I'm... I'm dining by myself. It's just.... My fiancé died a year ago. Today."

"So sorry. Is very sad. What fiancé name?"

"Sam. He was a new surgeon in town. We were going to get married when... Oh, why am I telling you this? You have other places to go." She offered a nervous laugh as she wiped her eyes and tried to brush off the pain.

He frowned. The puzzled look on his face made her heart warm.

"Thanks for delivering my dinner, even if you *were* late getting here." Goodness, now she sounded like a nag.

"So sorry. I could not find street and have short people for work. Is very hard for see number on house." He shifted his gaze, as if nervous. "Is last stop for me. I stay for you company? Help cheer up?"

His offer appeared sincere, but she couldn't accept. "No, that's okay." She dismissed him with a wave. A few more minutes in the same room with Bob and she'd start thinking about wanting him instead of honoring Sam's memory. She had to stick to the plan, and that didn't include a sexy man with a dreamy accent.

"You must get light. Help for see house number."

"Yeah, I suppose." She sighed and opened the cardboard pizza box. Peering at her dinner, she frowned. "Um, wait a sec. I ordered a spinach pizza, hold the onions."

Hesitating, she opened the other takeout container and examined the antipasto salad. Her heart plummeted. Nothing was going right. "Same here. I always order 'hold the onions'. This salad is really loaded with them."

Her stomach chose that moment to growl. She choked on tears. Her dinner was ruined. She despised onions. They made her gag. The last thing she wanted tonight was to gag on her dinner.

"I can't eat any of this." She sniffled and flicked her wrist in a shooing motion. She turned her face away, but her voice still broke. "Please, just take it back."

"I am so sorry. I not see note say for no onions." Holding the slip, he moved until he stood in her line of vision. He showed her the receipt. The order contained a circle with a slash before each item, followed by the word onion.

Was the guy totally clueless, or just playing dumb to gain her sympathy so she wouldn't complain to the owner? Surely he had to know what that symbol meant. She heaved an exasperated sigh and grabbed the paper from him.

"Look, here." She pointed at the slip. "That symbol means no, or hold the onions."

He squinted at the paper, and his eyes widened. A horrified look appeared in them. "It is! Symbol for none. I make mistake, so I must fix *jadenje* -- I mean food -- for you. I thought say more onion. Here is check." He thrust it at her. "Please, take back. I come back in one hour and have right order for you. Yes?"

Tears filled her eyes again. She hated being so emotional and glanced at the clock. A groan escaped her lips. It was almost seven. There was no way she could wait that long.

If she ate dinner even a minute past eight o'clock, she'd have weird dreams all night long. Dreams of being stung by scorpions and chased by rattlers, and gored by javelina, and eaten by coyotes. She almost snickered at the ridiculous thoughts. The man would think her insane if he knew what went through her head. And to top it all off, she'd wake up tired. No, she couldn't eat that late.

The scent of cheese wafted under her nose, making her mouth water. If only onions didn't repulse her, didn't remind her of that creepy... She shuddered. Better to forget what happened than to think about that horrible night again. The only good that had come from it was meeting Sam. If he hadn't come to her rescue who knows what would have happened. But she knew for certain it wouldn't have been good.

Suddenly the room seemed eerily quiet. At least Baby had finally ceased her barking. Poor girl probably wore herself out.

The cramping of her stomach forced her to reconsider his offer to take the food. At least with the salad she could pick out the onions and discard them. The tangy aroma of vinegar greeted her nostrils, making her stomach growl once more.

"Oh, never mind. I'll just keep it and pick out the onions. Please, don't bother coming back."

She directed him to the door, trying her best to avoid looking into his sympathetic eyes. She didn't want to start sobbing like a hysterical woman. What more could possibly go wrong tonight? "Thanks, for being so nice..."

Intending to steal a quick glance, she paused, and then she couldn't look away.

His tender smile did funny things to her insides. His kind eyes held hers, making something warm flutter in her chest. Now even her body betrayed Sam's memory.

Was she truly so forlorn that she'd find a delivery guy -- someone she'd probably never see again -- that appealing? With a groan, she waited for him to step outside. The moment he cleared the frame, she shut the door and locked the deadbolt.

She cursed her loneliness and her intense longing for Sam. Pulling her cell phone from her pocket, she located Sam's picture and hit delete before she could change her mind. The question popped up, "Are you sure you want to delete this?"

With a frown, she confirmed her choice.

Sam disappeared.

Stuffing her cell phone back in her pocket, she debated what to do next as she approached the bay window. Peering between the slats of the blinds, she watched the man pull out of her driveway. A tremor -- like a tiny earthquake -- worked its way up her spine as the taillights of his car retreated, and coldness again settled over her heart.

Then it struck her. He'd also forgotten the cannoli. That figured.

Tears collected on her lashes, and she blinked them away. Part of her longed to follow Bob right out of her comfort zone, to insist he bring her the correct order so she could bask again in the heat of his presence. But that would mean risking her heart, and the notion of caring for a man again made her insides tremble.

She nearly laughed out loud when she thought about how the entire time Bob stood in her dining room, her Chihuahua had yipped and yelped to the point Laney wanted to scream. Yet he had remained calm. She longed for that kind of peace.

A shiver caught her by surprise, snapping her from her reverie. Why did she keep getting the feeling that someone watched her? She turned the handle on the blinds and closed the slats, but that did little to ease her anxiety.

Baby didn't remain silent for long, letting out more high-pitched yips.

Baby didn't usually bark unless someone approached. But she was alone. She had to tell herself that or she'd go nuts. The next time someone stopped by with a delivery, she'd place Baby's travel cage out in the garage. She didn't have a car parked there anyway. At least then she wouldn't hear the constant ear piercing barks coming from her needy pet.

With a sigh, she strolled toward the dog cage. Baby liked onions, though they gave her horrible gas. Tonight, Laney didn't care. Her special evening was already ruined.

She hoisted her pet from the cage, balancing the little dog on her hip as she plucked an onion from her salad.

"Want an onion, sweet girl?" Baby yipped and lunged for the morsel, snapping it from her hand. "Relax, sweetie. I'm not eating them. Believe me."

With a sigh, she lifted the pizza box, and then stepped on the trash can pedal until the lid popped up. The last time she'd shared her spinach pizza with Baby, her dog hacked all over the carpet. She'd learned her lesson after having to get the rug shampooed.

Twice.

Smiling sadly as she returned to her candlelit table for two, Laney reflected on the deliveryman's too-adorable accent. If she ever dated again, she could go for someone with his rugged good looks, his deep voice, and honey brown eyes.

His five o'clock shadow reminded her so much of Sam. She remembered the day she'd surprised him after his five-year absence from her life. He'd gone away to med school and they hadn't seen each other since the summer he left town.

In her mind's eye she saw his sleepy smile and the way he'd gazed at her -- as if with new eyes. Her heart throbbed as she remembered the first time he'd told her he loved her. Up to that point they'd been friends and neighbors, but nothing more.

Her thoughts shifted to the delivery guy's attractive smile and his heart-stopping personality. The tender way he caressed her with his honeyed gaze made her tremble with longing. Not to mention how hot he looked with his broad shoulders, narrow hips and...

What was she thinking? She covered her face with her hands, doubting they'd have much in common anyway. Even if they did get along, he'd never want someone with her issues. With so much pain held captive inside, she feared the day she'd burst wide open. She pitied the person who'd find her in such a state.

And someone as good-looking and friendly as Bob probably had a woman waiting for him at home. No way would he be available.

With a gentle squeeze, she hugged Baby and kissed her pet's tiny head. Turning toward the stereo, she ignored the doggy smell and snuggled close as she pushed *play*. With a sigh, she waited for her favorite song to begin.

"*I've got you, Babe,*" Cher belted out. Laney crooned along, then swallowed hard. Humming, she spun around the room in a waltz until she grew so dizzy she had to stop.

"You're all I need, right, my sweet baby?" she whispered in her pet's ear. With tears streaming down her face, she wished with her whole heart it were true.

Chapter Three

Bojan had trouble focusing on the drive down the mountain. His thoughts kept returning to the sad woman with the long dark hair and gorgeous, but woeful, blue eyes. He couldn't help feeling sorry for her. She reminded him so much of his beloved sister.

He'd known the sharp pain of grief since the day five years ago when his sister went missing. And though he'd never lost a fiancée, he couldn't imagine the piercing sense of emptiness that would follow such a tragedy.

His clumsiness with words had increased her heartache, filling him with shame. Though teachers had complimented him on his intelligence, he felt like a complete idiot. Not only had his thick accent made him sound stupid, his error had made him look like a bumbling *budala* -- a fool -- in front of a beautiful woman.

A woman he desired to impress.

With a frustrated sigh, he pulled into the restaurant's parking lot and killed the engine. Clutching the steering wheel with both hands, he refrained from banging his forehead on the wheel. How he wished he hadn't messed up her order. Next time he'd not only get it right, but he'd dazzle her with his brilliant comments. Maybe he'd even ask her to go to a movie with him some time.

Bojan rubbed the stubble on his chin. Maybe he could take an English class and improve his language skills. He could read and write well, but speaking proved to be a major challenge. Right now he'd do just about anything to be more fluent.

He jumped when Johnny Brigand pounded on the window.

"Outrageous orders, man," his employee yelled to be heard through the steamed glass. "Things are getting way backed up in there."

Bojan trusted Johnny to run the restaurant because his uncle had trusted Johnny for the past two years. With three prosperous franchises to oversee, Bojan needed people he could count on. *Tetko* had said Johnny was a good man, and he had no reason to doubt his *tetko*'s wisdom.

Yet.

Bojan opened the door and stepped from the car. "You go on next run. I cook for you. Take keys." He dropped them into Johnny's hand.

"But--" Johnny's mouth hung open.

"Just do for boss."

"But who's gonna--"

With a firm clap on the back, he reassured Johnny. "You go for next run. You know city good. You keep tips and I pay you more for trouble."

A broad grin covered his employee's face. "You got it, boss. Thanks.

Oh, and sorry about being so testy with you. Sometimes I get overwhelmed. I just wish we weren't so short staffed."

Bojan laughed. "Tom be back for work soon. And you no worry about tests. You do fine."

His employee scrunched his brow, then shrugged. "Yeah, sure, boss."

Warmth filled Bojan's heart as he observed delight in his employee's eyes. Johnny had two young children at home to feed and he really needed the money. Since God had blessed the restaurants Bojan owned, and he had plenty of money to spare, he didn't mind throwing in a little extra to reward such a hard-working and dedicated employee.

"And if it help, take one car home. Then you no need for call cab for ride after restaurant have closed."

"One of the company cars? Are you sure?"

"You help boss, so boss helps you. Is very good, yes?"

With a nod, Johnny grinned. "I've never had a boss like you. You keep this up, and I may just come to church with you one of these days." Johnny blinked rapidly and coughed into his hand. "Thanks a lot, man." He turned away and muttered loud enough for Bojan to hear, "Since my car got stolen, I wasn't sure what I'd do."

Warmth filled Bojan's soul. He loved blessing others. "I loan money for you if need credit for buy *kola*."

"Oh, no, boss. I can't let you do that for me, too. I'll be fine. Just give me a few months, okay?"

Bojan nodded and said a quick prayer for his employee, then added one for Laney. *Hold Laney close, Lord. She hurts very much. Please, give her a good friend.*

Johnny jingled the keys. "My wife ain't gonna believe this."

"Is no problem. Holiday come soon. You need *kola*, I mean, car. Yes? Boss need help." Bojan inhaled with a satisfied grin. As the acrid scent of fireplaces burning wood wafted in the frigid air and filled his nostrils, he sighed contentedly. "Help for you is good for both."

*****

Laney woke the next morning to Baby yipping near her ear. Demanding her breakfast in doggy language, of course. With a yawn, Laney stretched and nudged her pet away.

"Give me some space, girl. I don't want to step on you like I did the last time."

A sharp look appeared in Baby's eyes, then quickly disappeared. For a second she almost believed Baby had understood her comment.

Baby nudged Laney's bare ankle with her cold, wet nose and yipped once.

"Hold up, girl. I'm moving. Just give me a sec."

She pushed off the couch and fluffed her hair. From the corner of her eye, she spied the tapered candles on the table.

Barely flickering, the candlesticks had burned down to nubs, leaving wax deposited at the base of the holders, piled like clusters of thick white snow. She shuddered and blew out the flames, relieved she hadn't torched her house while she slept.

She lumbered to the kitchen and opened the pantry where she kept Baby's dog food. Grabbing a can, she stepped over to the electric opener, removed the lid, and then spooned a third of the contents into Baby's special bowl. The stuff smelled like beef gravy, but no doubt tasted like--

Ding-dong!

The sound made her suck in her breath. She hadn't expected a visitor. It had been a while since she'd ordered anything from a catalogue, and she'd just received her latest shipment of dictations for her medical record transcribing business.

Unless border patrol agents had come to check on her again. One officer in particular seemed to fancy visiting whenever she least expected it. It gave her the willies.

Hesitating for a moment, she decided to risk answering the door. At least during the daytime hours she could see who stood outside. If it were dark out... She shuddered and thanked the Lord that He watched over her even when she chose to ignore Him.

Another thing she felt terribly guilty about.

She peered through the peephole. A van from the local florist had parked on her driveway.

Who could possibly have remembered her grief? Maybe one of the doctors she did dictation for had realized the significance of the date. And why not? She worked hard for the doctors to eke out a living and she never complained about the lousy pay.

Several doctors at the regional health center had also been friends with Sam. That was how she'd found him again. One doctor she contracted with had asked her to deliver a set of dictated records to the hospital four years ago and Sam was one of the residents on staff.

And though the home Sam had left to her was probably worth a small fortune, her only actual earnings came from her transcribing business. She rarely brought in enough to pay the bills, especially during the winter months when she needed additional propane to heat the enormous house.

She really needed to purchase a smaller home. But Sam had left her the dog, the house, and an outrageously huge engagement ring, which she now had stored in her jewelry box. She couldn't bring herself to give up any of them.

So she struggled to pay the bills. And even if she'd wanted a car at this point, she couldn't afford one. Not after Sam had totaled their Lexus the week after she'd blown the engine of her Nissan.

A twinge in her chest made her pause.

The money from the settlement had just run out. The insurance company had claimed the accident was partly Sam's fault. Not only had he hydroplaned on the slick road, but he'd also reportedly fallen asleep at the wheel according to their investigation. So the company had covered very little beyond the cost of replacing the vehicle.

Tears formed on her lashes. She turned the knob, pasted on a smile, and then whipped the door open, forcing a cheerful tone. "Can I help you?"

The heavyset woman standing on her front landing peered around a large floral arrangement and offered a broad grin.

"I don't know who likes you, ma'am, but this is the most expensive bouquet I've ever delivered. Isn't it just gorgeous?"

Almost afraid to touch the burst of colorful flowers, Laney stared, her mouth agape. The most beautiful arrangement she'd ever seen graced an elegant crystal vase. She paused to admire the work of art.

Roses of every color, snapdragons, mums, tulips, birds of paradise, ferns, and other flowers she couldn't name filled the container. Each delicate flower was perfect, and abundantly fragrant.

Especially the roses.

She smiled. Who in the world...

"Please, take this... There's more." The delivery woman placed the bouquet in Laney's hands and returned to the van. She hopped inside and emerged with the most adorable stuffed Chihuahua Laney had ever seen.

"Oh, how sweet."

Laney covered her face with her hand and stifled a giggle. It had to be one of the old cronies Sam had worked with who had remembered the anniversary of his death. Who else would know she had a Chihuahua? Especially since she usually tucked Baby into her cage when a rare visitor stopped over.

The woman handed Laney the stuffed toy. "That's it. Can you please sign here?" She pointed to the line on the clipboard and handed Laney a pen.

Laney set the gifts down and applied her signature. "Thank you so much."

"My pleasure." With a nod, the woman hustled to her van, cranked the engine, and turned around in the circular driveway at the end of the road, before heading back down the mountain. A cloud of dust followed the pink vehicle as it picked up speed.

Laney grabbed the flowers and the toy, kicked the door shut with her heel, and strolled into the living room with her gifts.

How sweet of George to think of her this week. She would have to let him know how much she appreciated his kind gesture before she ate breakfast.

Setting the stuffed dog on the couch next to Baby, she turned her attention to the vase of flowers and found the tiny envelope buried between the leaves. Pulling the card free, she read the neatly written lines.

For comfort during this difficult time.

No one had signed the bottom, but that didn't matter. George wouldn't forget her grief. For years she'd worked transcribing records for his practice.

Then Sam had died.

The horror came rushing back... the scent of formaldehyde, the funeral, and the crushed dreams. She forced the images from her thoughts. She had to stop thinking about Sam. He was gone, and he was never coming home.

Forcing a smile, she flipped open her cell phone and dialed.

"Hello. You have reached Dr. George Donahue. I will be in Africa with the Peace Corps from November first until January thirtieth. If this is an emergency--"

Laney hung up. George wasn't in town. She doubted he'd think of her while serving overseas. Maybe he was better at remembering things than he used to be.

So then who could it be? She didn't have Dr. Rodgers's number anymore, so she couldn't ask him about it.

Maybe Jerry, Sam's former college roommate, had sent them. She dug through the junk drawer where she kept her address books, and stabbed herself with the letter opener.

"Ouch."

Sucking the tip of her finger, the metallic taste of blood touched her tongue as she continued to dig around with her other hand. She finally found Jerry's number.

"Yes?"

"Hey, Jer? This is Laney. Hey, I need to ask, um... Did you send me something?"

"No, I didn't send you anything. Why?"

"Oh. I thought maybe... well, thanks anyway. I'll talk to you soon, okay?" Her voice cracked with disappointment. She winced.

"Sure. Hey, are you okay?"

"Tough day. Maybe I'll tell you about it sometime." As if he'd want to hear her sob story. Nobody wanted to hear about her troubles. Well, except for Bob. He'd listened to her with empathy, and she felt at ease telling him about her grief, more than when other people had asked how she was doing.

"Great. Well, then take care, Lane." Jerry's tone suggested he really didn't want to know about her problems. Just like she'd figured.

A tangerine-sized lump clogged her throat. She'd been away from some of Sam's friends for so long that she'd lost touch. For many months it had been too hard to associate with his former doctor friends. In fact, if she were honest, it still bothered her. That was one of the reasons she'd stayed away from offices and contracted work for her home business instead.

Her fear of dying in an accident only added to her stress. While it might seem excessive, it made perfect sense to her. If she never drove, she couldn't get in a wreck.

Turning toward her Chihuahua, Laney grinned at what she saw. Baby had poked her nose into the ribcage of the stuffed animal and wrapped her paws around its middle. Her pet slept with a serene expression on her tiny black face. Her best -- and only -- friend. She'd die if anything ever happened to Baby.

Biting her lip, the sting of tears pricked at her eyes. Even Baby had found contentment this weekend. So when would her turn finally come?

*****

Two days later Bojan rubbed his hands together and snickered to himself. He wondered if she'd even have a clue that he'd sent her such a lovely gift. Then he imagined the smile creeping over her sad lips and lighting her face.

Bringing joy to hurting people gave him tremendous satisfaction, which was why he sought God's will on his knees every morning and asked, "Who do You want me to bless today?"

God never failed to answer his prayer. The desire to send Laney flowers was so strong he knew it had to be God prompting him to do it.

With a sigh, he lifted his bomber jacket from its hook and shrugged into it. While the air was nippy out this morning, the afternoon forecast sounded promising. Maybe he'd go for a hike during the early evening if things were slow at the restaurant.

Though it had been dark when he'd searched for the lonely woman's house a few nights before, he recalled taking a wrong turn and heading up a dirt road. The same one he'd explored early this morning. Set behind the woman's house, the wide path traced the mountain. The whole area would be great terrain for four-wheeling.

He'd thought it strange when he saw a man had parked on the road, sitting in the bed of his truck with a pair of binoculars around his neck. When asked, the man mumbled something about bird watching as he cracked open a can of beer. The man wore sunglasses and a baseball cap low on his forehead, concealing most of his face.

Bojan had heard Sierra Vista was the hummingbird capital of the state, so who was he to argue? He did think it strange, however, that the birdwatcher faced the back of Laney's house and there were no birds in sight.

He shrugged off the thought.

With his Hummer H2, Bojan had no trouble that morning scaling the steep terrain. A gift from Uncle Alek at his college graduation, the lavish vehicle drew attention from people, probably because of its sunflower yellow color. Not to mention its mammoth size.

Normally he'd choose a simple truck for himself, but after taking a spin in the Hummer, he couldn't imagine driving anything else. The salesman had told him yellow vehicles were easy to spot in a storm and thus safer to drive. How could he argue with that kind of logic?

As he pulled up in front of Little Italy, his newest acquisition, something seemed amiss. Johnny paced out front, his hands pushed deep into his pockets. Hopefully Johnny hadn't hired another ex-con. His employee was good at many things, but he had lousy discernment.

Bojan rolled down the window. "Something wrong?" he asked as Johnny approached, raking his hair with his fingers.

"I'll pay you back as soon as I can. I promise."

He groaned as he exited the Hummer, wondering if the new guy had stolen from the till. He followed Johnny to the company car. "Is problem with staff?"

"No." Johnny cringed and pointed to the side of the body. The word Little had partially caved in, and some paint had been scraped off. "It's awful, isn't it?"

Bojan inspected the door with his fingers. It looked like someone had kicked the door in with a steel boot, but he wouldn't doubt his employee's word. He had to trust Johnny if he were to leave him in charge.

"Is no problem for you. Restaurant have insurance. Is for to cover accidents."

"So you're not mad?" Johnny's mouth gaped.

A chuckle escaped Bojan's lips. Why did Americans worry about material things so much? Back home people were happy to have a working vehicle. "Is only dent. Not so big deal. Did accident hurt you?"

"Huh?" Johnny scratched his head.

"Is you hurt?" Bojan repeated.

"Oh, no..." Johnny laughed nervously. "I was picking up baby food on my way home last night. Must have happened while I was in the store shopping." Johnny cast his gaze down. Not a good sign. "After I drove home, I found the dent." He pointed and cringed again. "I still can't believe my luck."

Bojan failed to see the logic. "You think is lucky?"

"No, I meant bad luck. Bad stuff always seems to happen to me. I'm really sorry about the dent. You can take money out of my pay to fix it."

"No problem. No worry for cost for fix car. You work hard. I take care for everything, yes?"

Bojan wasn't sure he believed Johnny's story, but he needed him too much to make an issue of it.

With a heavy sigh, Johnny ran a shaky hand over his face. "My old lady was sure you'd fire me for that."

"Tell old lady she worry too much. Little Italy needs you." A broad grin tugged at his mouth as he wondered why Johnny's grandmother would care about the damage. "Tell her the boss not fire you for stupid dent."

"That's it, dude. I'm going to church with you now. I'm convinced you're a saint."

A laugh burst from Bojan's lips before he could contain it. "I'm just no-good sinner like you. Everyone is sinner."

"Hey." Johnny chuckled and punched Bojan's biceps.

After playfully rubbing his sleeve, Bojan draped his arm over Johnny's shoulder. "Bring wife and kids over for house after church. I tell you family about life before God had saved my soul. Yes?"

Rubbing his chin thoughtfully, and with his brow furrowed, Johnny replied, "All right, boss. I think I can make it for something like that."

"Oh, and don't forget for bring grandmother, okay?" Bojan added.

"My grandmother? She lives in Michigan." Johnny played with the bill of his cap.

"Then why you say old lady?"

Johnny furrowed his brow. "Huh? You're not making sense."

"Forget what I say. Just come bring wife and is okay for tell grandmother in Michigan. Is very good for you for come visit." Bojan slapped his employee's back. "And no bring food. I care for details, yes?"

Johnny avoided eye contact again as he shrugged. "Sure."

He'd only known Johnny for a month, but he liked the guy despite the fact that he didn't always seem up-front about things. He remembered his uncle saying Johnny seemed a bit sneaky at times. He'd have to keep a close eye on him. Johnny seemed to know more criminal-types than people with clean backgrounds. He just prayed Johnny would listen and stick to doing his job, and leave the hiring up to him.

Chapter Four

Bojan hummed as he sprinkled seasoning into the sauce. He stirred the mixture and inhaled deeply. Rather than his mouth watering at the pleasing aroma as expected, his nostrils flared and he stifled a sneeze.

Johnny approached, peered into the pot, and groaned. "No, no! That's not oregano! That's pepper. Read the label, boss. Why aren't you paying attention to what you're doing?"

Normally, having an employee correct him would raise his ire, but Johnny was right. Bojan couldn't stop thinking about Laney, the lovely brunette, and wondering about her reaction to his special delivery the other day.

Having botched yet another pot of sauce, he passed his apron to his number-one cook. "You take. I do delivery today."

"Are you sure, boss? It's getting dark out and I know how easily you can get lost."

Bojan chuckled. "Is very true. First, I check orders." He stepped over to the round metal tree and examined the individual orders. No Laney listed anywhere. His shoulders sagged... until he got an idea.

"Johnny, I need you for make one antipasto salad, no onions, and small spinach pizza, no onions. I deliver when you finish. Yes?"

His lead employee offered a knowing grin. "You're sweet on her, aren't you?"

Feigning innocence, Bojan shrugged. "What you mean, sweet?"

"I mean, you like her, don't you? The lady at 1437 Willow Lane."

Bojan's neck heated. "Yes. Is very beautiful woman, but very sad. Tonight I bring dinner. Is surprise."

Johnny snorted. "Don't bother. She's cold as ice, that one. A real..." He coughed into his hand, then smirked.

He stared. Sometimes Johnny made no sense at all.

"Anyway, I don't get it. She won't let any of us in her house even if it's freezing outside. I've never met a stranger lady. She's whacked. Catch my drift? And she never goes out. She even has her food delivered by Schwann's. Something's not right with that chick, even if she is a hottie, you know?"

Bojan rubbed his forehead. "Swan's deliver food? I think was babies."

Slapping Bojan on the back, Johnny snickered. "Not swans, Schwann's. You crack me up, boss."

Frowning, Bojan mused. American English made no sense. All the talk about hot chicks, cold ice, catching drifts, and cracking up made him more confused than ever. And what had the weather to do with going to see Laney?

Johnny gestured toward his head. He pointed and moved his finger in a circle while rolling his eyes. "She's pretty certifiable."

He had no idea what Johnny meant by that either, but it didn't matter, because unlike the other delivery guys, she'd invited him inside her house. That had to mean something. And she did have nice waves in her hair. Everything about her was pretty. "Ah, she is beautiful, is she not? But so very sad. It hurts my heart."

"Yes, boss. Certifiable and beautiful. Great combination." He winked.

Glad his employee agreed with his choice, Bojan smiled and decided that tonight he'd bring her dinner at his expense. Then he could find out what she thought of the flowers. The suspense was killing him. "Is okay. I deliver for you. You *svaren* -- I mean, you cook. Yes?"

"All right. You're the boss." Johnny tied the apron and tossed Bojan the keys.

He caught them and grinned. "Thank you very much. You make good food. I give you big raise."

Tipping his head back in a hearty laugh, Johnny scoffed. "On second thought, maybe you're just as certifiable as she is. But I like it. Makes for a good match. Have fun."

Bojan nodded and grabbed his coat, pondering why Johnny would call him good-looking, too. He collected his first stack of boxes to deliver. With a bounce in his step, he opened the door and sucked in his breath. The chilly air startled him back to reality. He hated making deliveries.

Yet the pleasing aroma of good Italian cooking filled his senses, and heat from the boxes warmed his hands, making the job bearable, at least. The anticipation of seeing Laney again warmed him to his toes. He smiled and imagined her peering at him from under lowered lids. How he wished she'd see him the way he saw her.

With deep longing and the desire to know him more.

Tonight he planned to make an impression on Laney with his quick wit. His surprise would be so wonderful, she'd completely forget about his bumbling comments last week. Then if all went well, maybe he'd ask her on a date.

He purposely saved her delivery for his last stop. His hands shook when he finally approached her mansion of a house an hour later. He wondered why his nerves were shot at the idea of being in her company for a few minutes. Maybe because though he'd fooled around in college, he'd had only one serious girlfriend and she'd dumped him once he told her he'd found Christ.

Bojan hadn't met a woman he wanted to spend time with since then, not until last weekend when he first met Laney. Something about her deep blue eyes and sad smile made him long to hold her. Not sure why his heart insisted on pounding, he parked the car and exhaled, and then gave himself a pep talk. "Must do this. Is lonely woman who needs friend. Not so hard. Just smile and say nice words."

Before exiting the car he noticed the Chihuahua standing on the sofa, nose pressed against the window. The curtains and blinds shook as the animal paced on the windowsill and barked. He could hear the ruckus outside.

The frenzied yelps intensified as he approached the front door and rang the bell. After waiting what seemed like forever, he rang the bell again. Still no answer. When he turned to leave, the front porch light flicked on.

Bojan spun around.

Laney stood with a towel in her hand, dabbing the sweat from her glistening forehead. Her heavy breathing made him shudder.

In a breathless voice she asked, "Bob? What are you doing here?"

Words escaped him as he admired her, taking in the thin sheen of perspiration that made her skin glow. Apparently he'd interrupted her workout, and she wasn't happy to see him. This was not at all like he'd imagined.

He swallowed hard and shoved the meal forward as an offering. "I bring special dinner. No onions."

The dog yipped and yapped in the background, but he couldn't see Baby. Laney must have locked up her pet.

Staring into her smoky blue eyes, which reminded him of *borovinkas,* blueberries, he offered a warm smile, hoping she'd see his appreciation for her company and know that he cared about her pain, her loss.

She averted her gaze, pursing her lips. "I didn't order anything." She started to close the door.

He slid his foot between the door and frame to keep it from closing. "Is treat for you. Boss is sorry for mistakes to order. You very good customer. Please, take." He held the food out with both hands.

An icy gust of wind made him suck in a sharp breath. He slapped one hand atop his head to keep his hat from blowing off.

Nibbling on her lip, she stared at him. A questioning look filled her gaze, as if she couldn't fathom his kindness. "All right. Come in a sec. I was just finishing my workout."

"You go to gym?" He stepped forward and set the boxes on the dining room table.

"No. I work out at home. I prefer exercising at night. It helps me sleep better."

"Ah, sleep is good, yes?" He cringed at how stupid that sounded.

She nodded. A slight frown formed on her face as her neck flushed. Somehow he'd offended her again.

She still looked beautiful. He drank in her curves like a parched man and inhaled her scent, which reminded him of succulent *jagodas,* strawberries. His mouth watered as he eyed her full lips and wondered what it would be like to taste them.

They stared at each other for several more seconds until she flipped the towel around her neck. "I'll get my checkbook."

"No. I say is treat. No pay. Little Italy pays."

With a wave of her hand, she dismissed his comment. "I can afford it." She opened her purse and dug inside. After finding a crisp bill, she held out a twenty.

He pressed his hand forward. "No. Is treat for you. Keep *pari*, I mean, keep money."

Shaking her head, she sighed and shoved the money back into her purse.

A grin tugged at his lips. He'd gotten her to relent. One point in his favor. Now to ask her out on a date. Glancing around the room, he finally spotted the vase of flowers on the mantle above the fireplace, and his smile grew wider. "Nice flowers. How you keep flowers fresh?"

Her brows scrunched, and she glanced at him from the corner of her eye. She peered at the bouquet with apparent fondness. "I put that powder stuff in the vase to preserve them. They last longer that way."

A shiver caught him by surprise.

She peered at him, concern clouding her eyes.

"Is cold." He wrapped his arms around his chest and shrugged his shoulders to his earlobes to make his point.

A flush darkened her cheeks. "I ran out of propane." He must have looked confused, because she added, "You know, gas to heat my house."

"Ah." He nodded and then peered into the other room. "Must use fireplace."

She shook her head, and her flush deepened. "I need to gather wood. I have plenty behind the house but I'd have to collect it, and I'm afraid of the scorpions and snakes."

"How about I help you. Yes?"

With a wary look in her eyes, she stepped back. "No, that's okay." She averted her gaze. "I suppose I could order some firewood and have it stacked in my garage."

They stood in silence. Bojan fought the urge to step close enough to slide his fingers into her silky hair. It looked so soft and provided far too much temptation.

He cleared his throat and finally blurted, "You have boyfriend?"

Her mouth curved into a deeper frown. "I think you need to leave."

Uh-oh. Wrong thing to say. "But I think you certifiable woman...and so very beautiful. I like you very much. Maybe--"

She gasped and flapped her arm toward the door. "I knew I never should have let you in. Go back to your boss and tell him I don't like his employees. They're rude and boorish and--" She turned away and dismissed him with her hand. "Just go."

He heard her sniffle and felt a heaviness settle on his chest. He wasn't sure how, but he'd made her upset. Balling his fists at his sides, he fought the urge to hit himself for saying something stupid again. "I am so sorry. You pretty whacked, yes, but I like you."

Refusing to even face him, she continued to wave. Her voice sounded scratchy. "And don't come back. Ever."

With defeat weighing on his shoulders, he slouched and stepped into the cold evening air, shutting the door behind him. He inhaled deeply. The acrid odor of burning logs in the neighborhood filled his nostrils, and he winced. The familiar scent had greeted him the night he'd made that first delivery, but this time the scent brought with it a sense of overwhelming shame.

She hated him.

Just when he'd given up hope, he spied her dog running down the road, chasing a rabbit. Before the *zhivotno,* the animal, scampered farther away, he took off running, hoping to catch Baby and return her to Laney as a peace offering.

*****

Her throat clogged, and she had trouble breathing. It wasn't until she shut the door with a firm click that she allowed herself to cry. He'd called her certifiable. Whacked. What a jerk!

That charming smile and adorable accent now set her teeth on edge. Who did he think he was barging in on her peaceful evening and invading her privacy? And then insulting her with a smile...*Oooh!* Balling her fists, she wanted to spit or kick or scream.

With indignation she pulled her cell phone from her purse and dialed the restaurant.

"Little Italy. May I take your order?"

"No, you may *not.* But I would like to speak to the owner."

"He's not here right now. Can I take a message?"

Clearing her throat, she closed her eyes and spoke slowly and clearly. "Tell him that I think he needs to take a closer look at the people he hires. Tell him I never want to see that Bob driver again. He needs to get rid of that guy. Got it?"

The man on the phone chuckled.

The nerve... "Something funny?"

"No, ma'am. I'll make sure I pass on the message just like you said."

"Good." She snapped the phone shut and rested her forehead on her palm. Refusing to care whether the man lost his job, she convinced herself she was doing him a favor. He needed to get a different career. One that didn't require manners or communication.

So what if she happened to be the one propelling him in that direction?

With tears in her eyes, she bent over to pull Baby from her cage. Her stomach burned. The cage had somehow opened.

"Baby!" She ran through the house, clicking her tongue and called her pet. "Baby, come here."

27

Plunging her fingers into her bangs, she stopped and exhaled. "Think. Where would she go?"

A knock on her door made her heart pound. She peered through the peephole. Bob had returned, with her dog perched on his hip.

"Baby, oh my sweet Baby!" She whipped the door open and snatched her dog from his arms. Kissing her pet's silky head, she scolded her. "You had Momma scared to death." Never before had Baby's doggy scent smelled so wonderful.

Sucking in her pride, she glanced up, her cheek against Baby's head, and she locked onto the handsome rescuer's gaze. "Thank you, Bob. I can't thank you enough. If you hadn't found her--"

"Is no problem. I'm sorry I made so angry. My English is not so good. I not understand what I say. Forgive, please?"

A slow smile tugged at her mouth. "Sure. Next time, make sure when you compliment a woman that it's truly a compliment."

His head tilted. "What I said hurt feelings?"

With a giggle, she realized that he probably hadn't a clue he'd insulted her. "You said I was crazy, you know, whacked, certifiable... they all mean the same thing."

His eyes widened. "Oh, no. I say *losho*, bad words. I am so very sorry. I must get teacher for English. Forgive?" He reached out his hand and this time she accepted it.

A tingle shot up her arm and made her pause. Big mistake. Touching him had done strange things to her insides, just like she'd suspected it would. Things she hadn't felt since Sam... She jerked away as if burned.

"Yeah, well, I'll see you later." Nodding toward the door, she closed her eyes and held her breath.

The sounds of retreating footsteps and the door clicking shut told her he'd gone. After opening her eyes, she exhaled with a whoosh, praying aloud for the first time in nearly a year.

"Oh, God, please keep me safe. I'm so afraid my heart will break again."

Peace, be still.

She stiffened. Had God spoken to her heart again? Even after all these months of setting Him aside, He still cared. Remorse sucked the air from her lungs, and she held her dog tightly against her chest, and wept. "I'm sorry, Lord. I'm so sorry..."

Chapter Five

Several times that evening Laney considered calling the restaurant and telling the owner she had made a mistake. She realized now that Bob hadn't meant to be mean. The intense look in his eyes spoke of compassion, not sarcasm or animosity.

He'd said he hadn't understood. And he'd looked so incredibly handsome, his eyes widened with innocence. He probably had no idea the effect he had on her.

The only way to fix it would be to contact the restaurant, but she couldn't bring herself to pick up the phone and call. Especially if he'd been fired because of her complaint. Better to not know and have him stay away.

Besides, the tenderness in those golden brown eyes threatened to undo her. The control over her emotions slipped a little more each time she allowed herself the slightest response to his attentions.

Better to turn off her feelings altogether than fall for someone. Especially someone as kindhearted as Bob, whose expressive gaze made her want to laugh and cry at the same time. Yes, the man held power. Too much.

"No one can measure up to Sam," she told herself. Her shoulders slumped. No one except maybe the tall, dark and handsome Slavic man she couldn't seem to get out of her mind. And she refused to let that happen.

*****

Bojan stormed into his restaurant and slammed the front door behind him. The skin on his forehead pulled tight as he scowled. He couldn't help feeling bitter. His employee had misled him, making him believe that whacked and certifiable were nice things to say to a woman. Knowing full well, of course, they weren't. *The jerk!*

Without looking in Johnny's direction, he marched through the kitchen and hurled his coat at the hook. His neck tightened and he clenched his hands at his sides. Clamping his lips together, he decided he should avoid Johnny until he had better control over his emotions.

Taking slow breaths didn't help, so he entered the supply room and shut the door. Rubbing his temples with his fingers, he prayed quietly. "Lord Jesus, give me words to say. I not want for be bad witness." He sighed. "And I punch him if You not help me control anger."

A rap on the door grabbed his attention. "Who is there?"

"It's me, boss. I gotta tell you something funny."

Bojan grunted, not trusting himself to speak to Johnny without showing animosity.

"That whacked-out chick called, and guess what she said? She said not to send that rude guy Bob over ever again. Said the owner should get rid of him." He opened the door and entered the room, rubbing the sauce coating his fingers onto his apron. Johnny chuckled. "Isn't that a hoot?"

Swallowing the bile rising in his throat, Bojan forced a grin despite his confusion about the term his employee used. "Is really big hoot. So big I no talk to you so I not hurt you with bare hands. I not *se zasmee,* not laughing."

The young man sobered. "It was a joke, boss. Supposed to be funny. I didn't think you liked her enough to get ticked off over it."

"Is not funny for tease." Bojan stared hard into Johnny's eyes. "How you say... hmmm... is mocking? No respect *za mene,* for me."

"I do respect you, boss. Really, I do. It's a guy thing to tease. Cultural, you know?" Johnny offered his hand and shrugged. "Forgive me, please?"

With reluctance, Bojan received his employee's hand and muttered, "Forgive because Jesus said I must forgive. Is hard for me to do. Is not right for you be mocking boss."

"You're right. I'm really sorry." Johnny shook his hand and held on tight. "Maybe you should get an English tutor so you can learn the language better."

"Is very possible." He looked away from Johnny's contrite face. Never before had he confronted a more daunting task than to keep from firing his employee in anger.

"Want me to call Laney and apologize?"

Bojan raised his hand. "I not need you for help. I talk with her for things said. Laney know my English is *losho,* is bad, and I make many mistake."

"Good. Then everything should be okay, right?"

With tight shoulders, Bojan conceded he must let go of his resentment and get a fresh perspective on things. "Is hard for me to trust, but thanks for God, He help."

A loud buzzer sounded.

"Yes, He sure does, boss." Johnny spun around and grabbed an oven mitt. "Talk at ya later. Gotta take the Parmesan chicken out of the oven."

A gust of fragrant heat from the oven warmed Bojan's face as he passed by the stove. An idea popped into his head. He shivered with exhilaration as he thought about how God could still use him to touch Laney's heart. She may not like him, but that wouldn't stop God from using him.

*****

A week later, after a night encumbered with dreams of cars spinning off the freeway and wrapping around utility poles, Laney awoke crying and drenched in sweat. The most vivid dream had her especially flipped out because Bob's face had replaced Sam's. It was almost as if her psyche warned her that getting emotionally involved with him would hurt her just as much as losing Sam, and maybe even more.

She sat up and fought a wave of dizziness. Great. Her head throbbed and now she had to walk across the house for medication to ease her pain. With a sigh, she slid her legs over the side of the bed and eased her feet onto the ice-cold Mexican tile floor.

A shiver zinged up her spine. Why did she keep getting the sense that someone watched her house? She lived out in the middle of nowhere, for Pete's sake. Then again, maybe that was part of the problem. She was too isolated.

No sooner had she reached for the headache medicine and downed a couple of pills than someone knocked at the door. She nearly dropped the bottle.

Sucking in a deep breath, she peered through the blinds. An older, balding man she didn't recognize stood on her porch, wearing a shirt with a logo from a local propane company. He didn't seem very dangerous, wearing a disarming smile.

Opening the door, she greeted him with a stiff, apologetic tone. "I'll pay the bill as soon as I can."

His grin widened. "Don't know what you're talking about, lady. Your bill is paid up just fine. This is my scheduled time to come out. I just pumped your fuel tank to seventy percent."

Surprise stole her breath. "But there must be some mistake. I'm sure I still owe your company money."

"Nope. Your account is paid in full, and so is this delivery. You must've made a simple mistake. Happens all the time."

"But..." Doubtful she'd miss something so huge, she grabbed the crinkled paper and inspected the ticket. Sure enough, it said she owed nothing. Could she really have paid ahead and not realized it? Anything was possible, given her scatterbrained thinking over the past months.

But still...

After offering a tentative smile and a warm thank you, Laney shut the door. She leaned on the frame and marveled at her own stupidity. And to think she worried about the gas bill when all along it had been paid. But how could she forget something so major? It made no sense.

Rather than look the proverbial gift horse in the mouth, she turned up the heat to take the chill from the room. Within minutes the area had warmed enough so she could remove the thick, wool-lined sweater she'd draped over her shoulders.

Within half an hour, her home returned to a comfortable temperature, and she thanked the Lord for little mistakes that had turned into big blessings. For the first time in days she entered the shower without feeling the urge to jump up and down and rub the chill from her arms.

After styling her hair and getting dressed, she decided to pass on a traditional breakfast and scooped up a bowl of her favorite ice cream in celebration of once more having a heated home. She then sat at her computer and indulged, letting the cool silk chocolate texture melt on her tongue.

Several minutes passed as she waited until everything had loaded. Deciding to check the local online want ads for supplemental income opportunities, Laney skimmed over various job descriptions. Her gaze captured an ad that described the perfect job for her.

Wanted... English tutor. Excellent pay. Must be available to work weekday mornings.

With a grin, she dialed the number and listened to an electronic voice that prompted her to leave a message.

"Yes. Hi. My name is Elaine Cooper and I'm interested in applying for the tutor position. I majored in English in college and am very good with grammar. Please let me know if you want to discuss this further. My e-mail is yobaby@gmail.com or just call me back at 803-1121. Thanks."

She cleared her throat. Her scratchy voice didn't sound right. She'd just had a little ice cream. But still, ice cream usually made her throat thicken with mucus. Hopefully her message hadn't sounded stupid.

Minutes later, in the middle of transcribing a batch of medical records, she received an e-mail from someone named lovethistown@iglide.com.

Let's meet at the Sierra Vista library tomorrow morning at ten.

~Eager Student.

With a groan, Laney realized she couldn't do the job after all. Not if it meant leaving the safety of her house. She typed an answer.

Sorry, but I can't travel into town due to health problems. I'm assuming you're not an axe murderer, since you offered to meet in a public place. I'd rather meet at my home. Please respond if you still want to interview me.

With a smirk, she hit send, wondering what the person will think when they see that invitation.

*****

The next morning when Bojan arrived at work, Johnny greeted him with a sneaky gleam in his eyes and two takeout containers. "Boss, check this out. I already have a delivery for you."

Bojan paused and stared at the boxes, then double-checked the time. "But not time for open."

"Ha, well, you know that chick you like -- Laney? She asked for her salad and cannoli to be delivered early. Said she had a craving. Anyway, don't ask me why, but she insisted you bring it and no one else." Johnny waggled his eyebrows.

"But is much too early for lunch." Bojan jiggled his keys in his hands, still stunned by Johnny's announcement. Somehow she'd changed her mind about him. And he really liked that. A grin tugged at his mouth, and he chuckled. "But I take for you. Is no problem."

"Great." Johnny slapped him on the back. "You just go there and charm her socks off. Got it, Bob -- I mean, boss?"

"What you mean, charm socks off?"

"Just play the lover boy like she wants, smile, and show her those pearly whites of yours. She'll totally fall for you, and then everything will be right in the world again."

"Okay." Confused by the slang, Bojan decided to go ahead and take the food to Laney, grateful she now saw him as a lover boy and not a jerk. He wasn't too sure of the actual meaning of the phrase, but it still sounded good to him.

"Much thanks, Johnny. I think is good plan."

"Great." Johnny rubbed his hands together and muttered with a broad grin, "Good luck, man."

Ignoring Johnny's weird attitude, Bojan turned and strode out of the building. Instead of taking the Hummer, he climbed into one of the company cars. He wanted to look official when he rode up to her house so she wouldn't think he was going there to bug her.

And this time he would say things correctly and stick to words he understood.

A shiver of anticipation coursed through him when he pictured her blue eyes, long hair, and curves. And those full lips, ah... What a great way to start the day. "Much thanks, God. Is very good."

Peace settled over him as he started the engine and headed for the familiar dirt road. An old folk song spun though his mind, and he hummed as he drove. If she agreed to go out with him to dinner or a movie, he would call his parents right away. They'd been nagging him for years to find a wife.

He'd fallen in love with an American after moving to the United States, much to the horror of his traditional parents. They wanted him to marry an Orthodox or Macedonian woman, but they finally accepted his decision to date Erika. Everything was fine, until he became a Christian and realized his behavior didn't please God. Then Erika had dumped him when he wouldn't compromise.

In the end, he knew he'd done the right thing, but breaking up with her had torn his heart from his chest. Obeying the Lord's commands had been the hardest thing he'd ever done. A few years had passed since, and now God had healed his spirit enough to consider a new relationship. This time he would honor God.

Tears pooled in his eyes. Gratitude for God's forgiveness filled his chest with warmth. He would never understand God's mercy, but he sure appreciated it.

Laney's gorgeous home loomed ahead. Even before he parked, his upper lip beaded with sweat until it itched. He wiped his face with the back of his trembling hand and released a shaky breath. "Lord, give me much strength."

Pasting on what he hoped was a confident grin, he grabbed the food and approached the front door. Raucous barking emanated from the front room.

Bojan balanced the boxes on one hand and rang the bell with the other, shifting on his feet like a man anticipating his first date. He thanked the Lord for restoring some of his innocence when he accepted Christ as his Savior and gave his life over to Him.

Soon the barking faded, and she opened the door.

"Bob?" Her cheeks flushed and her brows knit together. She looked surprised to see him. Odd, considering she specifically requested he deliver the food.

But he didn't dare question her. He worried he'd say the wrong thing again. Instead, he extended his hand. "I brought you good food. Is free for beautiful lady."

"Um, thanks. I suppose we could have lunch in an hour or so." Grabbing the boxes, she eyed him closely and smirked. "I assume you're here for your first English lesson, Mr. *Eager* Student?"

Not sure why she'd called him that, he decided to take her up on the offer. "Yes, of course. I like lessons for English very much. Thank you."

"How much do you plan to pay me?" Setting the food down, she cleared her throat. "I mean, that's not the only thing that's important, but I do have to pay my bills."

He frowned. It had never occurred to him that he'd need to pay her. He had no idea what the going rate for tutoring was. "Um, is two twenties good for pay?"

"For an hour?" Her eyes rounded and her soft mouth gaped, looking extremely *vkusno,* delicious -- like ripe fruit. How he longed to taste her sweetness.

He realized he was staring at her mouth and glanced away, then returned to gaze into her lovely eyes. "Yes. Is good pay?" His heart pounded as he slid his hands into his back pockets and tried to look unflustered.

A wry grin curled the corner of her mouth. "Oh, yes. Very, very good pay. But I can't accept that much. Twenty is a more reasonable wage. I won't let you pay me more than that." Reaching for his arm, she grabbed him by the elbow and ushered him into her living room, then sat him down. Plopping next to him on the couch, she tucked several loose strands of silky hair behind her ear and said, "Ready to begin?"

Not sure what he'd done to deserve such a blessing, he thanked God that not only had she forgiven him, but she sat so close to him that his skin tingled. He felt like Jesus being tempted in the wilderness, only his flesh cried, "Yes! Go for it!" and he had no scriptures coming to mind to help counter his actions.

Swallowing hard to relax his tight throat, he nodded. "I do whatever beautiful woman wishes for."

"Anything?" Her eyes lit up as her full lips curved in an inviting smile. She leaned closer. "You sure about that, mister?"

Sucking in his breath, he slowly nodded as he closed his eyes and leaned forward to meet her lips halfway. His heart pounded mercilessly. Try as he might, he couldn't resist the temptation. Not with Laney sitting so close that he could hear her breathing.

Bojan forced himself to relax -- released the air he held in his lungs -- so he could thoroughly enjoy the moment. He hadn't kissed a woman in nearly two years.

Chapter Six

Laney tried not to giggle when Bob closed his dreamy, lover-boy eyes. The notion that he obviously found her appealing sent a surge of adrenaline rushing through her veins. These English lessons might be more enjoyable than she'd ever imagined. If only she could refrain from getting emotionally entangled with her student.

She touched his hand to get his attention.

Bob shuddered.

"You cold? It *is* a bit chilly in here."

His eyes opened, and confusion filled his tender gaze. The flicker of disappointment she glimpsed made her stomach do a little flip.

"Is cold. Very cold." He glanced around. "Is big house."

"It's not so big." She suppressed a smile. He looked so cute staring at her with rounded eyes, a look of innocence on his handsome face.

Maybe she shouldn't be such a tightwad with the heat. She was just trying to make sure the propane lasted.

His brow furrowed, and he glanced around, as if suddenly worried.

"Something wrong? I'm just trying to conserve my propane."

"Is very big house for to keep warm. I help you make fire." He nodded toward her fireplace.

She shrugged. "If you want to." Peering at him a moment, she asked, "Do you have a big house, too?"

He burst out laughing. "No. Is very, very small."

"Like an apartment?"

Rubbing his chin, he looked up as if searching for the right words. "Is like trailer, no, is called RV. Yes. Very small. I must pull house on wheels."

She never pictured him as a trailer kind of guy. That would explain why he came in the company car. Poor guy probably didn't have his own vehicle. For some crazy reason, the thought made him more appealing.

If he drove only for work and locally for errands, the chances of his getting killed were much lower. Oh, why did she keep thinking about him that way? He was at her house to improve his English, not to hook up with her.

Bob stood, and she tugged at his hand.

"That's all right. Sit down. I'll just turn up the heat to take the chill--"

"No. Is okay. I wear my coat." He slid his brown leather bomber jacket over his shoulders and shrugged it back on.

"There's no need. I have propane now. I'm not sure how it

happened, but somehow I'd paid ahead on my bill and didn't realize it."

A broad grin covered his face, and he winked. "Is okay then." He rubbed his hands together and blew on them, before adding, "Be quick, please."

She nodded and sashayed over to the thermostat. Though she couldn't see him with her face turned away, she felt his eyes following her. A warm surge overtook the chill. Suddenly opening the window sounded like a great plan.

Turning to face him again, she noticed his neck had reddened. Maybe turning up the heat wasn't such a good idea, for her attraction to Bob felt like it had kicked her temperature up by several degrees already.

"I'm feeling a bit warm all of a sudden." She swallowed hard. "Maybe I should leave it alone."

"Is no big deal. Do what you think best choice."

A faint yipping sound greeted her ears. She'd forgotten all about Baby.

"Can you excuse me a minute?" After sliding the thermostat up a few degrees, she slipped from the room and retrieved her pet.

Baby leapt from her arms. Her dog took a liking to Bob instantly. Must be because the handsome man on her couch had brought sweet Baby back to her Momma, and she recognized him as a friend.

Laney's eyes welled with tears at the memory of how she thought she'd lost Baby. Thankfully Bob had seen her dog outside and chased her down.

"Baby so cute." He rubbed the top of her pet's head and crooned. "I think Dude find Baby much pretty."

"Dude? Who's that?"

"Is Chihuahua. Uncle Alek had give me for gift. Dude is part for business. Dog come for home, but we live okay."

Not sure what he'd said, she asked, "You have a male Chihuahua?" Pressing her hands over her mouth, she tried to not burst out laughing. The image of him with a little brown dog just didn't fit. A Doberman, a pit bull, a German shepherd maybe, but a little doggy? No way.

She couldn't hold her amusement in another minute, and snorted in an unladylike manner.

"Is funny for me for own *kuche* -- I mean, for have dog?" He scrunched his face.

"It's just...Chihuahuas are so little, and you're big and strong and..." Oops, that shouldn't have slipped out. She sounded like a star-struck silly groupie.

He beamed at her and held her dog against his chest, alternately stroking and kissing her ears. "Many things about me are surprise then?" He winked and kissed Baby on the top of her head again before setting her on his lap.

A tingle shot up Laney's spine, and for a moment she was jealous of her dog. What would it be like to have the attractive man on her couch kissing her head, and holding her possessively on his lap? She closed her eyes and imagined for a moment, then pushed the thought aside.

He probably had a flock of female admirers. No man with Antonio Banderas's good looks and such a hot accent would be single for long. For all she knew he might already have a girlfriend, or even a wife. The thought made her shudder. She did *not* want to date a man who was already taken.

The last thing she needed was to join a harem of girls panting after him. Why did she always find herself attracted to the super-good-looking guys? Why not date an average man? She didn't need the headache of wondering who might be hitting on her man whenever he left the house when she had to deal with everything else.

"We'd better get started. I'd hate to have you waste your money. It's been ten minutes already. Oh, and I was wondering. How did you pass your college classes if you had so much trouble with your English?"

His eyes lost their sparkle. "I had tutor. No big deal. No need for to hurry and finish." He pinched his lips together and furrowed his brow.

"Everything all right?" The expression on his face made her hesitate. Something she said had bothered him. But what?

"I have question. I ask for you to... must please go for... with... me out for movie and dinner. Yes?"

Her heart pounded. Though he stumbled over the words, it sounded like he'd said he wanted to take her on a date. Though tempted to accept, she couldn't imagine going all the way to town for any reason. Not after so many months of hiding out at home. Not even for someone as good looking and nice as Bojan.

"I'm sorry. I don't go to dinner and movies with people I barely know."

"Then you must know me more, my *prijatelka*, my sweet friend." He stood and reached for her hand, pulling her up from the sofa.

Once she faced him, she couldn't move. The warmth of his strong, thick fingers covering hers felt so good. No one had touched her in a very long time. Not since she stopped attending church and she no longer received sympathetic hugs from the little old ladies who understood her pain. When leaving her house became too frightening.

His light brown eyes bored into hers, and she couldn't breathe or move or think.

"I..." She licked her lips.

He gazed back at her, his eyes suddenly serious.

"Um... maybe we should... uh..." She hesitated. How was she going to get out of this one? The temptation was too great.

"Is okay. I not bite. I promise."

The fresh gleam in his eye suggested otherwise. Though he said he wouldn't bite, he'd already taken a chunk out of her heart. The problem would be taking it back. Maybe if she came up with something offensive to say, then he wouldn't like her anymore.

Instead of accepting his invitation, she blurted, "Do you have a girlfriend?"

He let go of her hand and stepped an inch closer, watching her intently. "Why for you ask me this?"

Her hands trembled, and she resisted the urge to step back. "I'm sorry. That was a stupid question. Of course you--"

"No. Have no *devojka,* no girlfriend for long time. But sound good for me." His intense gaze rendered her speechless. Then, as if he suddenly realized how close he stood, he stepped away from her.

Resisting the urge to pull him back in her direction, she nodded at the couch.

"We really do need to get started. Why don't you just say something, and I'll tell you how to say it in correct English. Agreed?"

"Is agreed." He closed his eyes and then said, "I want for *bakni* very much."

"What is *bakni?*" The tightness in her voice made him open his eyes. He winked. "*Bakni* is kiss."

*****

The look on her face after he winked told him that was the worst thing he could have said. She looked like a frightened rabbit, staring at him with her pretty mouth gaping.

"Uh, okay." She licked her lips, and with a shy grin bit the corner of her mouth. He'd never seen a cuter expression than when her cheeks blushed and she smiled at him like she did right now. Like she wanted him. It was a heady feeling.

"I would very much like to kiss you." She winced. "But that sounds too formal, so even though it's wrong some people would say 'I want to kiss you really bad'."

His blood ran cold. "Is *losho* for want to kiss you?"

"No," she laughed. "In American English when we say really bad, or really badly, it means very much "

"Oh." His shoulders relaxed. "Then is very good."

"Now, can we stick to a subject that's less embarrassing?" Her hands clasped together on her lap and she shrugged. "Please?"

"I like lesson very much. Want many lessons from you." He couldn't help but smile at that one.

"I like these lessons very much. I want more lessons from you."

"Why say *povekje,* more?"

"It's hard to explain. Just keep coming up with things to say and I'll help you say them the right way, okay?"

"I think Dude have liked Baby very much. Want for playing together soon."

Her neck reddened before she answered, "I think Dude will like

39

Baby. I want them to play together very soon."

"Yes. Very soon."

His heart pounded with excitement. She actually understood him. The lesson was already helping them to communicate better.

"But that would mean you'd have to come over with your dog on your day off." She shifted on the couch. "And that--"

"Is okay?" He held his breath in anticipation.

"I think it could be arranged." She smiled and averted her gaze, covering the side of her face with her palm.

He loved shy women. They were so *zhenski*, so feminine. So delicate and wonderful. He closed his eyes and imagined taking her to dinner and gazing across the table at her in a candlelit room.

"Am I boring you?" She touched his hand, and he opened his eyes.

"No. I thinking how I want for brought you for dinner. Is correct to say?" He held her gaze and pleaded with her the best he could through the look he gave. Surely, she must see his interest in her.

"I would like to take you to dinner. Say that, okay?"

"I would like to take you to dinner, please?" He raised his brows.

"No," she laughed, "but you can eat here with me if you insist. Maybe our next lesson can be at night."

"Is great idea! I make special *gjuvech* for dinner."

She grinned. "Sounds interesting. What is it?"

"*Gjuvech* is chicken stew from Macedonia. Is very good."

"I'll bet. When would you like to have this dinner?"

"Tomorrow? Is too soon?" His hands trembled. *She said yes.* He wanted to dance right there, but decided she'd change her mind if she saw him acting foolishly.

"Um, tomorrow is Thanksgiving. Don't you want to spend it with your family?"

He shrugged. "My family in Macedonia on holiday. I have no one for spend time with tomorrow."

"Me, either." Her eyes glistened and she offered a shaky grin. "Well, it's settled then. For Thanksgiving dinner we'll have chicken stew at my house."

"Yes." He stood and squeezed her hand, his voice husky, "Now I must give goodbye *bakni*. Is tradition." Without giving her a chance to protest, he cradled her face and slowly kissed her three times on the cheek. "Much thanks for good lesson. I come again tomorrow. I bring much food and *svaren*. Yes?"

Her body stiffened under his touch. She didn't answer but merely nodded. She looked flustered as she walked him to the door. Pulling it open, she smiled that same shy grin and glanced away. "See you tomorrow."

He nodded. "Yes. Tomorrow. Cannot wait for to see you again."

After heading down the mountain, he realized that he'd forgotten to ask her how she knew he'd wanted English lessons, but decided to save that question. For now, he'd savor his small victory.

Maybe next time she'd let him kiss her on the lips.

*****

He scowled and lowered his binoculars. It had taken him a few months, but he'd finally found Sam's girl. So who was the guy visiting her? And where was Sam? Was she having an affair? She didn't seem the type. So what was going on? He thought for sure she'd be married to his rich cousin by now.

The wuss wouldn't have dumped Laney. That much he knew for certain.

Maybe if he could find someone who knew Sam... But they had no friends in common. Sam always thought he was too good for his poor cousin. Well, he showed Sam, didn't he? When he'd slammed into his car had he somehow paralyzed his cousin? He grinned at the thought. That would be poetic justice, wouldn't it?

Rubbing his face, he tried to decide what to do. So far Laney hadn't left her house to go anywhere. He'd scouted out the place every chance he got, but her home was locked up tighter than the jailhouse. He couldn't even get into the garage. Last night he almost set off the house alarm just trying to see inside. He had to be more careful.

At least he'd found the right house this time. He thought he'd found Laney last year, but ended up in some other woman's house. She'd fought him off, but he won. He always won. Thankfully she hadn't told the police a thing. Nope. She was too scared.

He liked that.

If only he hadn't been busted for drinking and driving the night he'd followed Sam home from work and tapped his car with his bumper. His stupid cousin sped to get away, and took a turn a bit too fast. Sam must have wrecked his car. That much was obvious.

What if Sam hadn't survived?

The thought made him smile. Without Sam in the picture there'd be no one to get in his way this time. Maybe Laney would finally want him. Without Sam interfering, she'd get to know him as a man instead of just Sam's poor orphaned cousin.

It wasn't his fault he'd wished his Momma dead. Nobody hurt him without consequences.

Nobody.

Chapter Seven

Minutes after swapping the delivery car for his own, Bojan's excitement deflated faster than his tires. The lump-bump-lump sound told him he had a flat. Even his Hummer would have difficulty safely navigating to a mechanic in that condition.

Hopping out of the cab, Bojan surveyed the damage. Two tires out on the right-hand side. With a groan, he pulled out his cell phone and called a tow truck.

He checked his watch. If he didn't get his vehicle to a shop before sunset, he wouldn't be able to get it back before close of business. That meant he wouldn't have a way to get to Laney's. If worse came to worst, he'd take a company car, but he hated to use it for personal matters, even if he did own the business.

An hour later, a tow truck finally appeared. He requested that his Hummer H2 be taken to the only dealership in town that provided maintenance services for specialty vehicles. He rode in the front seat of the tow truck with the driver, and noted the time. Hopping out, he prayed he wasn't too late already.

With a shove, he opened the door to the office and saw the sign. Closing early due to the Thanksgiving holiday. He groaned and waited at the front desk for someone to appear. After several minutes, he pushed the bell on the counter.

A hefty, older gentleman approached with a greasy rag clutched in his hand. "Can I help you, sir?"

"My Hummer have two flat tires from nails. I need fixed today, please."

The man nodded toward the clock on the wall. "We close in ten minutes. No way can we change out the tires today. Especially not tires that large. I don't think we even have any that size in stock."

"When can you fix?"

"We're open again on Friday. That's the earliest. You need a ride somewhere?" The man examined Bojan's tires, running his finger along the tread. "This doesn't look like an accident to me."

With a frustrated sigh, he conceded that he wouldn't be getting his Hummer back today. "I need ride for go to Little Italy on Route 92." He suddenly realized what the man had said. "What you mean is no accident?"

"Look here." The man pointed to a cut in the rubber. "Someone sliced your tires with a knife. Didn't you think it a bit strange that you had two flats and both on the same side?"

He frowned. "Why would people cut tires?"

"Not sure. The neighborhood ain't what it used to be."

Bojan thought about that for a moment. The restaurant's location was in a nice area. Oh well. Must be whoever did it had him confused with someone else. He had no enemies.

But Johnny did.

His employee had his tires cut before. He should warn him when he got back. *Double check references before hiring any new help.*

"Tell you what. Here's my number. Page me tomorrow for an update. Just fill out this form and attach your keys. I'll log you in and give you a ride to the restaurant."

"Is very good for me. Thank you." Despite his disappointment over not getting his vehicle back, he appreciated the offer for a ride. People in Sierra Vista were so kind. He could see himself staying there and being perfectly content.

Maybe rather than moving to Phoenix in January like he'd originally planned, he'd just hire a manager for his Greek restaurant there and check in on the business on a quarterly basis, or when needed.

Then again, if Laney showed no interest in him, it might be better if he moved out of town. His heart would not hurt as much if he never saw her again.

But he prayed she'd return his affection. And hopefully very soon.

*****

Laney pondered Bob's surprised expression when she'd first asked him about the English lessons. It hadn't occurred to her that he might not be the student she'd scheduled to come to her house for an interview. Since no one else had shown up at that time, what else could she conclude? Now she wondered.

She decided to e-mail lovethistown@iglide.com to find out if she had the right man.

Within minutes of sending the inquiry, she received a response. "Sorry I didn't make it to your house today. But I see my friend made it. I wanted the lessons for him as a surprise, anyway. I'm sure you saw how much he needs help. I assume it was a pleasurable experience for you both?"

She reread the last line several times. What was that supposed to mean? Was he trying to set her up with Bob? Why, the nerve...

With a smirk, she decided to send him a vague response. "Haven't a clue what you mean by that. I tolerated the lesson well enough. He seems to pick up things, and the pay is great. I really appreciate the referral."

Her mystery friend replied, "Ah, so lover boy failed miserably. I need to talk to him about that."

Though she hated to stereotype people, the comment struck a nerve. Maybe she'd been right about Bob -- Bojan -- oh, whatever his name was.... Maybe he *did* have a harem of admirers. Why else would his friend imply the man should have scored? But with a name like Bob... Well, it just didn't suit him.

And what kind of woman did he think she was, anyway? She'd always planned to wait for her wedding day to become physically intimate with a man. Unfortunately she'd lost Sam before she'd had the chance to love him the way they'd both waited so very long to experience.

Sometimes she wished they hadn't waited. At least then she'd have something special to treasure that only Sam could've given her. But then again, it would have gone against everything she'd believed in, and that would've hurt them both. No, better that she'd waited.

Not that it would matter now.

She still hadn't gotten back on track with her faith, because doing so would mean she'd have to admit God knew best. And losing Sam had been devastating. What if she loved again and God felt the need to take that man, too? A flash of Bob's kind eyes and endearing smile flitted through her mind. She stiffened.

His charm had wormed its way into her heart. She couldn't help wondering if he was so intense with every woman he met, or if she really did mean something to him. After all, he'd be spending Thanksgiving at *her* home. He'd said he didn't have a girlfriend.

She wanted so much to believe him.

*****

Laney spent the entire morning cleaning her house. She'd forgotten how much of a chore it could be until she rolled up her sleeves and dug in with a scrub brush. Baby followed her around, sniffing out everything Laney did and getting underfoot. With a laugh, she washed her now-aching hands and scooped up her dog.

"My silly baby girl. You hate it when you don't have Momma's full attention, don't you? One last chore, and then I'm getting in the shower."

She carried Baby to the garage and set her down. Grabbing the papers lying in the corner, she held her breath and folded her dog's potty messes before stuffing them into a black garbage bag. After tying it in a knot and setting the bag aside, she replaced the old papers with a fresh new batch and smoothed them out. Cleaning up after Baby seemed a small sacrifice in exchange for having such a sweet pet for a companion.

Baby used the papers consistently and rarely had an accident in the house. Laney refused to let her potty outside because then she'd have to clean up the mess. That would mean a possible run-in with snakes, spiders, and scorpions -- something she wanted to avoid. Disposing of soiled papers was much safer.

After hauling the garbage bag to the barrel out front, she peeled off her latex gloves and tossed them in after it. Returning to the safety of her home, she shut the garage door and headed for the shower. All of that hard work had made her back ache. A hot shower sounded like the perfect solution for her sore muscles.

An hour after she'd dressed in her finest black slacks and matching silk blouse, she applied a trace amount of makeup to highlight her large eyes and full lips. Wearing a smile, she chuckled at her reflection in the mirror. She looked ready for a hot night on the town, not a quiet meal at home.

With a sigh, she set the table and poured them each a glass of sparkling cranberry cider. Pressing her cold fingers against her cheeks, she shivered and rubbed her hands together. The chill in the house would be gone once Bob started cooking, so she refused to worry about it.

As she lit tapered candles, she paused. The familiar action caused a lump of guilt to knot in her throat. She'd been doing the same thing the night she met Bob. A shudder snaked up her spine at the similarity, and she prayed God would forgive her for keeping so spiritually distant after Sam died.

"Please, Lord, be with us today. In Jesus name I pray--"

Ding-dong!

Her pulse kicked up a notch, and she rubbed her hands together. "I'm coming."

Baby yipped and danced around her legs as if she couldn't wait for Laney to open the door. It pleased her that Baby had taken a liking to Bob. That certainly made getting together easier, because once her dog liked someone, she could be controlled.

"Shh... No need to go crazy, Baby. Calm down."

She peered through the peephole and smiled. Bob had his hands full.

Whipping open the door with a greeting on her lips, she blurted, "Happy Thanksgiving," and opened her arms to take one of the paper sacks from him. "Mmmm... this smells heavenly."

"Happy Thanksgiving. Food is cooked. You like?" Before she could answer, he held up his hand.

"Wait! I have more." He jogged to the Little Italy car and retrieved more items.

Wondering why he drove the delivery car on a holiday, she asked, "Where's your own car?"

"In shop. Have two flat tires."

"Oh. How'd you get to borrow that one?"

He shrugged, then bent to reach for another sack before kicking the door closed. "Not need for holiday. Restaurant is closed. Is no problem."

"Oh, that's good." It made sense, sort of. The restaurant was closed. Maybe the boss really liked him. If nothing else, the fact that Bob was still driving the company car told her he hadn't been fired because of her complaint.

45

He strode toward her, his muscles bulging as he carried the bag. His turtleneck clung to his form like it had been sprayed on. She hadn't seen a man in a turtleneck in years. How did he make it look so good?

And his designer jeans matched perfectly. His dark brown hair ruffled in the slight breeze. She had to turn away before she embarrassed herself by staring like a star-struck teenager.

Turning to shoo Baby away, she shuffled over to the kitchen and set the bag down. The succulent aroma of chicken floated up. Must be the stew. Heat radiated from the bag.

Looked like they wouldn't be working together in her kitchen. Disappointment constricted her throat.

She'd wanted to help, but it seemed everything had already been prepared, right down to the rolls. And she couldn't help noticing them sitting on the stew container because they smelled delicious, like fresh buttermilk biscuits.

Her stomach grumbled in complaint, the sound preceeded by footsteps following her down the hall. She glanced over her shoulder. "Go to the kitchen and set your bag down."

Bob grinned over the top of the bag he held and said, "Food smell good. Yes?"

"It sure does." This time her stomach did a little flip in response to his cheerful smile. All of those gut gymnastics were taking a toll on her otherwise good mood.

"I have bring baklava. Is good for dessert."

"Ooh, did you make the baklava, too?" She raised her eyebrows, impressed by his culinary abilities.

"So sorry. Store make dessert. I just buy for you."

Oh, well, he can't be good at everything. In fact, she liked knowing that about him, because then he seemed more human and less perfect. Not that she needed reasons to like him more; she was just involved with him to help him learn to speak correctly.

"You need to say it like this... 'The store made the dessert. I bought it'. That's past tense. Buy is present tense. Since you already did it, it would be past tense."

"Ah, I bought it, yes? I make cabbage and stew."

"And it smells wonderful. Especially the biscuits."

He grinned and said slowly, enunciating each word, "I made the biscuits. Is correct to say?"

"Yes, that's the right way to say it."

"Is very good." He inched closer and smiled, his eyes never leaving hers. "Is okay to give traditional greeting?"

Her cheeks heated at his nearness. "Um, sure."

Reaching for her hands, he clasped them with his own and kissed her three times on the cheek. She shuddered as his warm breath tickled her face.

His neck had reddened, and the notion that he might be shy

appealed to her and made her want to draw him close, to kiss him senseless, to toss her head back and giggle like a schoolgirl. Instead, she merely stepped back.

Swallowing to help regain her focus, she whispered, "Want to help me set the table?"

"Okay." He seemed to relax at her redirection. Like he appreciated her backing away. That was a bit unnerving.

Maybe she'd read him wrong, and he just wanted to be friends. But she couldn't imagine that. Not when he looked at her with such intensity in his eyes, unless his behavior was typical of someone from his country. If she could only muster the courage, she'd ask.

Yeah, right. That'd be the day.

On the other hand, if he were Sam... She groaned inwardly, refusing to think about Sam today. That would only make her sad, and no fun to be with.

Sorry, Sam...

Once they finished setting the table, she returned to the kitchen and lifted the various containers from the bags. Bob reached for a bowl, and she tapped his hand. That simple touch made electric sparks shoot up her arm. He must have felt it, too, because he stared for a moment as if in awe of the connection between them.

Then again, it could have been static electricity. It was certainly dry enough inside her house, and she *had* dragged her shoes a bit on the tile. But the jolt had been pleasant and not painful like static tended to be.

"Uh-uh, you did all the cooking. I'm setting up the food." She scanned the kitchen with her gaze. "Why don't you go find something else to do?"

"Is okay." He stuffed his hands into his back pockets and watched her, shifting on his feet as he scanned her from head to toe.

The heat of his stare made her stomach flutter.

She glanced at his bulging muscles and tensed. The overwhelming urge to get close and feel his biceps made her heart melt like butter, and her pulse jumped like popcorn in the microwave. Maybe if she struck up a conversation it would ease her anxiety. She had to pick a neutral subject. One that didn't make her all warm and tingly.

"Where's your dog?"

"*Zhivotno* is home. I no bring him today. Too much for carry food and Dude." He winked.

That sounded so funny, she couldn't help smiling. Bob had a way of making her want to giggle, and that eased her stress every time. "Makes sense. Maybe next time."

A gleam appeared in his eyes. "Yes. Next time." He nodded and glanced around, then stepped into the other room. "Want fire in fireplace after eat food?"

She shrugged, but then realized he couldn't see her from where he stood.

47

"If you want one. But you'll have to collect wood. I have kindling outside and a pile of logs stacked against the back wall. You can bring some inside if you want."

He stepped into the kitchen and rubbed his hands together. "You have gloves?"

Tipping her head toward the closet by the back door, she said with a smile, "They're in there."

"There?" He pointed. When she nodded, he opened the door and grabbed the gloves, and then slid them on. "Is very big gloves." His grin broadened as he held up his hands.

Her vision blurred as she blinked back tears. "They were... Sam's," she rasped.

"So sorry." His eyes widened. "Is stupid for me to say. Is sad for you today with no Sam, yes?"

Before she could contain her grief she bit her lip and choked on tears. He laid the gloves on the counter and pulled her into his arms, stroking her hair and back. "So sorry I hurt you feelings."

Of course, that made her cry harder. His warm touch felt so good, she didn't want him to let go. And the scent of his woodsy cologne combined with his powerful arms surrounding her body made her stomach tremble. She could easily get lost in the heat of him if she had no moral convictions. But she did have convictions. She had to remember that or she'd get into a compromising situation she didn't want or need.

After several deep breaths, she collected herself. She nudged him away. "Thanks for the hug. I needed one."

"Is no problem. You want hug, you ask me for hug, okay?" With a friendly wink, he smiled and touched her cheek for a whisper of a moment. Turning, Bob suddenly snatched up the gloves and put them back on. He opened the door, and backed away from her. Baby ran out after him.

She panicked and grabbed the door before it closed. "Baby, come back inside!"

Baby danced around Bob's legs just like she did with Laney every morning. A twinge of jealousy mixed with compassion made her hesitate. If her dog wanted to play, she shouldn't deny her the pleasure. Poor thing probably missed going out back. It had been so long since she let her dog run freely outside.

"Is okay. I keep Baby safe." He laughed and grabbed several logs from the woodpile. "No worry. Trust is good for you."

With a sigh, she conceded. While she might have fear about going outside, there was no reason to deprive her dog of a good romp out back. Especially on a sunny day like today. She swallowed hard and shut the door, praying everything would be fine, but still worried sick that something would go wrong.

*****

He lowered his binoculars. Why did that guy keep coming back? He thought for sure that slashing the man's tires would have slowed him down. He'd obviously underestimated the pizza man with the fancy-schmancy Hummer.

Tomorrow he'd wait for another chance to pounce. Pizza man had to go to work sooner or later. At lease now he knew that she lived alone. He'd found out from a local that his hoity-toity cousin had died in the accident. The thought made him smile.

Tonight he would go back to his broad. While not much to look at in the daytime, she met his needs every night and cooked him a hot meal daily. Better than jail food, too. And to his surprise, she liked it when he got rough with her. Who'd a thought dropping a UA for a drug test at the mental health clinic would've helped hook him up with a willing woman? He chuckled under his breath. Maybe finding a crazy chick on meds *was* the way to go.

For now, anyway.

Chapter Eight

Bojan's arms were filled with a second load of wood when he heard pitiful sounding high-pitched yipping, as though he'd stepped on Baby's foot. The hair-curling howls lasted several seconds. He tried to peer over the stack, but couldn't, so he stumbled to the back door, his arms full. He intended to check on Baby after dropping the load.

When he stepped back outside, Baby appeared fine. He dusted himself off and held the door open to let the dog back inside. "Come, Baby." He clicked his tongue.

"Dinner's ready." Laney smiled at him, and he imagined for a moment that they were married, and she'd prepared a meal for them. How wonderful that would be.

But he hadn't consulted God on the matter yet. Maybe because he feared the answer would be no. Better not to ask than to hear a 'no' or 'wait'.

Surely God understood a man's loneliness. The Bible said Jesus suffered in every way, right? "Much thanks, Laney."

Her flush deepened, and she gestured toward the table.

The soft glow of the candles at dusk made for an extremely romantic setting. Longing filled every fiber of his being, but he held back. Now would be a good time to bring up his faith and see how Laney responded to it.

"We pray first, yes?"

Her eyes widened, but she nodded.

Grabbing her hand, he closed his eyes, took a deep breath, and prayed from his heart.

"Lord Jesus, I come ask for blessing over food with Laney. Ask for much love for fill hearts and thank for grace and mercy. Also much thanks for salvation. In name for Jesus Christ, Amen."

He glanced up and examined her closely.

"Wow. You're... a Christian?" she asked, breathless.

The smile in her eyes made hummingbirds swarm in his gut. "I love Jesus very much. He saved soul for me. I live for Jesus now."

"I can't believe it. I thought maybe--"

"Bojan Muslim?"

She nodded, her eyes never leaving his.

"Most people in Macedonia Orthodox Christian. But many still not understand Jesus and Bible. Many people lost." His voice wobbled, so he cleared his throat. "My mother and father are very much religious on holidays. Go for church in Peoria for Holy days when in America. Is no more for Macedonian Orthodox churches in Arizona."

"That's really great." She blinked, her eyes blank as if trying to comprehend. "I—I'm a Christian, too. Though not a very good one lately." Her shoulders slumped and she tipped her face down.

He nodded and grabbed his fork as he considered how he should respond to what she'd said. "Eat."

She complied and chewed thoroughly. "This is very good."

Pausing, he took a deep breath and asked, "Why you say you not very good Christian?"

"I dunno." She tucked her hair behind her ear and shrugged. "I guess because I haven't prayed or read my Bible or gone to church in a very long time."

"You love Jesus? You believe He is Christ?" His brows furrowed as he studied her.

"Yes, I do." She licked her lips and averted her gaze.

"Then is enough." He resumed eating.

"But I don't do anything with my faith. I--"

He set his fork down. "You must listen. Jesus want all for you. If ready, Jesus have you whole heart. He live in you. Is very good."

"I did give him my heart once. I've just been ignoring Him because I've been angry. At first I blamed God--"

Bojan pushed his plate off to the side and gave Laney his full attention. "God is not for to kill. Satan hurt and destroy heart. God is for heal and for love."

"I know. It sounds pretty dumb to be mad at God, huh?" Her eyes shone with tears and she blinked them away.

He touched her hand. "Not dumb for saying truth. You talk about feelings. Jesus listen. I listen, too."

Lifting her glass of sparkling cider, she grinned. "Okay, then. Let's make a toast to our new friendship."

"Yes, for friend -- I mean, to our friendship. Is correct to say?" He smiled wide, pleased with himself.

She took a long drink of her cider. Apparently the fizz had entered her nose because she coughed and put the glass down. When she opened her mouth to respond, she glanced past him. A hair-raising scream erupted from her lips, and she leaped from her chair.

*****

"Baby!" Laney scrambled over to her dog. Her Chihuahua lay on the gray Berber carpeting, her jaw slackened. Saliva dripped from her mouth and her eyes appeared glassy. A pool of vomit lay within inches of her head.

"Is Baby sick?" She heard Bob's voice through the fog of terror surrounding her like a swarm of bees.

With shaky hands, she placed her knuckles in front of Baby's mouth. A faint puff of air touched her fingers.

"She's breathing, but she looks like she's in a coma. What's happened to my Baby?" She moaned and scooped her dog into her arms.

"Must call vet. Who gave shots for dog?"

"Coronado Animal Hospital. I'll call them."

Moments later, she reached the veterinarian who was on call.

"This is Doctor Brown. What's your emergency?"

"My dog. She's limp and looks like she's gone into a coma. I don't know what happened."

"Has she been outside?" The calm voice of the doctor helped her relax enough to think and not hyperventilate.

"Yes, for a few minutes. Why?"

"Was it around dusk?"

Laney paced, Baby tight against her chest.

"Yes." She peered at Bob, who seemed genuinely concerned as he tossed his hands in the air in frustration.

"Check your dog's gums. What do they look like?"

"Hold on a sec." She handed Bob the phone and moved Baby's lips so she could see her gums, then grabbed the phone again. "They're white. She looks bad, but she's still breathing. What should I do?"

"Sounds like something bit or stung your dog and she went into shock. Meet me at the hospital in five minutes. She'll need to be stabilized before it gets any worse."

Her heart clenched. "Is she gonna be all right?"

"Let's hope so. It can't hurt to pray."

Laney hung up the phone. Anger scorched through her like fire when she rehashed the doctor's statement in her mind. "Something bit her outside."

She snapped her head up and pointed at Bob's chest. "None of this would have happened if you hadn't insisted she'd be safe with you. I knew it was a bad idea. I knew it. But I trusted you." Her voice broke and she sobbed into her free hand, clinging to her dog with the other.

"I so sorry." He frowned, looking contrite.

Pulling her hand away from her mouth, she bit back a sarcastic comment and scowled.

His eyes glistened as he blinked rapidly.

Obviously she'd upset him. Good! At that moment she was too ticked off to care.

"That's what you always say. 'So sorry'. Well, it isn't going to help Baby to be sorry. I need to get her to the animal hospital and I don't have any way to get there."

The realization that she'd have to leave her house made her suck in her breath. But to keep Baby alive she had to do it. A sob crept up her throat.

"I take Baby for hospital." Bob grabbed his keys, pulled on his jacket and ran out the front door.

She hesitated, then followed, her breath coming in choked gasps as she approached the car. Now was not the time to have a panic attack.

God, help me.

Bob's hand touched her arm and he guided her to the car. He uttered a prayer, and at once her animosity toward him evaporated. It wasn't his fault, and she knew it.

"I'm sorry I snapped at you. I was scared..." *I still am. Oh, Lord, help me not to lose my lunch here.*

"Is okay. I understand fear." He opened her door and got her settled inside.

Turning the ignition, he backed out of her driveway. Dust kicked up behind them as he peeled down the road above the speed limit. A few times they hit potholes deep enough to make her lift off the seat.

"Sorry," he repeated.

Fear squeezed her throat. She nodded and clutched her dog even tighter, amazed she hadn't squished Baby to death during the drive down the mountain. Within minutes they arrived at the veterinary hospital and met the doctor standing outside. Apparently, he'd just arrived.

"Thank you for coming out on Thanksgiving," she said in a rush as she held out her precious dog, still limp and glassy-eyed, but breathing.

"Ah, I recognize Baby. Haven't seen her since she got her shots last year." He opened the doors and ushered them inside. The vet received Baby into his arms and left the room

Minutes later another staff person arrived. "Excuse me." He cut past them and entered the back room.

The worried look on the man's face as he brushed past was her undoing. The dam burst, and Laney reached for Bob and grabbed his arms.

"What am I gonna do if my sweet Baby dies? She can't die. I can't lose her. I can't..." Sobs burst from deep within, exploding like mini-geysers as she clung to Bob, who held her tight.

He tried to soothe her with gentle taps to her back.

Emotionally drained from crying, she sagged against him.

Easing toward a couch in the waiting area, he pulled her down with him. The sounds of unfamiliar words greeted her ears as he mumbled in another language and stroked her hair. She relaxed into his arms and let her mind wander until she nearly dozed off.

"Laney, the doctor need for speak with you."

She blinked and fixed her gaze on the vet. Unable to discern the outcome from his expression, she straightened in her seat and asked, "Is Baby gonna be all right?"

"I believe so. She's sleeping, but you can see her now."

*****

Bojan waited patiently for Laney to return from her meeting with the doctor. His arms felt so cold with her gone. He'd enjoyed soothing her and feeling her close to him as she'd nearly cried herself to sleep.

Her grief touched him deeply, and he'd shed a few tears himself as he watched her rest. He'd wanted to kiss her tears away, but worried she'd take offense, so he spoke loving words to her in his native tongue.

Words of promise -- of hope.

Words she didn't understand, but he prayed would someday come true.

The moment she appeared from the other room with red-rimmed eyes, he feared that something had gone wrong.

"I'll give you all the time you need," the doctor said as he nodded. "Let me know what you want to do."

A sudden cacophony of several barking dogs erupted from the back of the hospital. The ruckus ended when the vet closed the door and retreated.

Laney peered at the floor, then up at Bojan. While the doctor had said Baby would be okay, Laney's eyes held such intense sadness that he couldn't imagine what had brought on such grief.

Standing to meet her, he held his arms open. "Come and tell what have made you look so sad."

Several tears rolled down her cheeks and she swiped them away. "I can't afford to keep Baby here, but if I bring her home she could die." Her face crumpled, and she cried, "What am I going to do? I can't give them a deposit. I don't have any money. Even if I were to sell my house I won't get the money in time." Tears streamed down. "I can't lose her. She's all I have left. She's my family."

He sighed with relief. "Is no problem. I pay for deposit." Bojan reached for his wallet.

"You can't. It's too much." She sobbed and bit her lip.

"How much is deposit cost?" Withdrawing his wallet, he peered inside.

"Five hundred," she squeaked.

A smile tugged at his mouth. Not nearly as bad as she'd made it sound. "Is no problem."

Pulling out a credit card, he stepped toward the front desk. He had more than ten times that amount just sitting in his checking account and more stashed in his savings.

"No. I can't let you do that. Put the card away." She touched his hand, sending shivers rippling through him. He could easily fall in love with Laney. Their chemistry was amazing, among other things. He raised her hand to his lips and kissed her knuckles.

"I want for help with Baby."

She wrenched her hand from his. "I'll figure something out. Just give me a minute."

"No. I pay. I want for Baby back with you so happy and smile again. Yes?" A lump knotted his throat.

"It's not that simple. Then I'll owe you, and I don't know if I can handle that." The pain in her eyes made him pause. What did she mean by that?

He furrowed his brow. "You owe nothing. I pay for Baby."

The doctor emerged from the back room. "Were you able to figure something out?"

"Yes," he answered at the same time she said, "No."

Pushing the bankcard on the counter toward the doctor, he nudged Laney's hand away when she tried to intercept it. "Let me pay for Baby. Is my fault."

She finally sighed, and then walked over to the couch, and plopped down. He hoped he hadn't made her angry again, but what else could he do? Her dog would die without his help, and he couldn't let Baby's death ruin Laney's newfound peace. Not when she had finally smiled and was starting to enjoy life a little.

She deserved to be happy. And for some reason he wanted to make her smile every day for the rest of her life.

If only she would let him.

Chapter Nine

Laney groaned inwardly as Bob forked over the deposit. How would she ever pay him back? He'd said she wouldn't owe him, but she knew better.

Even if she never had to give him back the money, she would still feel obligated to him, and that made her stomach cramp. The last thing she wanted was to owe a man anything, especially one as attractive and nice as the man standing beside the counter and covering her bill.

Still, tremendous relief washed over her when she thought about how Baby would now get the treatment she needed, and would soon be back home where she belonged. Gratitude made her throat constrict.

Her cheeks heated as she scanned Bob's strong physique. Such a fine looking man must have female admirers. How could she compete with women more attractive and confident than she would ever be?

A shy half-grin tugged at the corner of his mouth when he reached for her hand to help her from the couch. "Is done. Now go for my house."

Her pulse skipped a beat. Had he already anticipated extracting payment from her in another form? Maybe she shouldn't trust him after all. Maybe he played kind and innocent but manipulated women for his own pleasure. The thought of being alone with him in his RV made her uneasy.

"Do w-we have to stop there?" Her voice shook.

"Yes. I need for get cell phone for trip back for your house." He winked. "I promise no bite. Trust, please."

With a skeptical glance, she considered his request. He looked so good. Like an Italian model. While *he* might be trustworthy, she suddenly worried she couldn't trust herself. Every time he drew near she felt her insides turn to mush. And she'd been lonely for a long time.

Hopefully, he wouldn't have a clue about her attraction to him and would help her stick to friendship. She feared if he sensed her interest in him then he'd have a reason to push physical contact, and she worried about sharing more than friendship with any man. With her heart still guarded, she received his offered hand.

"Okay, I'll trust you."

Bob shrugged as he pulled her up. "Then why you have scared frown on face?"

She swallowed hard. How truthful should she be?

"It's... um... more like I don't trust... me." Her neck heated, and she glanced at her free hand.

When she peered up she recognized the moment he caught on to her meaning, because a broad grin covered his face, and he sighed.

"Is big -- how you say -- compliment. Yes. Much thanks." He gave her fingers a gentle squeeze and slowly stroked her knuckles with his thumb.

They walked to the car hand in hand. The gentle stroking made her knees weak, and though she loved the feel of his strong fingers twined with hers, she feared her heart's response. When they arrived beside the car, she extracted her hand and averted her gaze so he wouldn't see her desire.

Regardless, she felt his eyes on her.

When he guided her to her seat, his hand lingered on her arm. His voice low and husky, he asked, "Is okay for me help you visit Baby tomorrow?"

"Don't you have to work?" She stared at her hands. Looking into his eyes was too dangerous, especially when she felt so vulnerable. He'd just seen her emoting in raw form. Other than her family, no one had ever seen her sob like that. Not even Sam -- except for the time he'd rescued her from 'onion boy' when they were teens.

She shuddered at the memory -- the reason she hated onions.

"Restaurant closed for holiday. Open again for Saturday. So day free for me."

"I'd like to see her tomorrow." Clearing her throat, she held his gaze and whispered, "Thank you so much for helping me pay for Baby's care. I can never thank you en--"

"Is my pleasure for help. Is no big deal." He stepped around the car and climbed into the driver's seat.

Though she had noticed the woodsy scent of his cologne before, it seemed even more intoxicating as they shared the close quarters of the front seat.

Bob pulled into an RV resort and parked the car. "My home. Be back soon." He nodded toward a very expensive-looking fifth wheel with a satellite dish on top and exited the vehicle. By no means the trailer or trailer park she'd envisioned.

She watched him enter the abode and wondered how she'd drawn such a lame conclusion about him. The man had to have some money to afford such a nice place.

Her thoughts drifted to when Sam had taken her to check out several models when they were engaged. They'd talked about taking a fifth wheel on mission trips to Mexico and occasional vacations once he was settled at the hospital in town. But none of that mattered anymore. Sam would never be coming back. Tears collected on her lashes.

Staring out the window, she blinked to clear her vision. A line of quail marched across the dirt path. Five babies stood between their parents, with dad at the lead and mom flanking the group. The way the birds peered with caution, then stopped to check before crossing, made her smile.

The sudden urge to use a bathroom broke her reverie. Stepping out of the car, she debated on whether to use the public restroom on the far end of the park, or just ask Bojan to use the facilities in his home. She chose the latter and tapped on the door.

The yipping of his Chihuahua made her eyes moisten. *My poor Baby.*

"Is okay, come in." Bojan clutched his dog in one hand and his cell phone in the other as she opened the door. He smiled warmly as she entered the narrow passage and inched closer. From the look on his face, he had a serious conversation going with the person who had him on the phone. "Is ready for morning?" He peered at his watch. "Can get for nine tomorrow morning, yes?"

"Where's your bathroom?" she whispered.

He'd positioned himself in the center of the room, his stance broad as he stood at ease. He nodded toward a door on the far end of the RV. "Help self."

With her breath sucked in, she inched past him to get to the restroom on the other side. Her body tingled where she brushed against his legs as she slipped by him. He paused a moment and examined her with interest, then glanced away.

Minutes later, she returned to the main room and found him sitting on the tan couch, smiling and petting his shorthaired Chihuahua. He cooed to the dog in another language, and the sound comforted her.

He grinned. "I talking for Dude about Baby and tell Dude he need for meet Baby very much."

She couldn't resist teasing him. "What does Dude think?"

Bob rolled his eyes. "Dude ask when he must meet Baby. I say Baby must first feel good for visit."

That gave her an idea on how she could repay him. She could breed their dogs and sell their puppies.

"Can Dude make babies? I mean -- was he neutered?"

Bob paused before answering her with a smirk. "Dude is healthy boy dog. Is no problem."

"They would make cute puppies, don't you think? Assuming Baby gets better, of course." Her voice hitched at the end of her sentence, and she swallowed hard. "Thanks again, Bob. If you hadn't helped me--"

"I say is no big deal." Bob set his dog down and tilted his head. "Can I ask for favor?"

"Sure. I'll see what I can do." She had no clue what he wanted, but figured if it didn't require anything too embarrassing or strenuous, she should be able to help.

"I need you for drive Hummer. Is ready in morning."

The room started spinning. "I--I don't drive."

He stood and touched her arm. "Is feeling sick?"

"No, I just can't... I'm sorry. Anything else, but not driving." She bit the inside of her cheek and willed herself not to cry.

"Is no problem. I teach. You help with English. I help you drive car.

Is good for you?"

"It's not that. I know how to drive. I just can't get behind a wheel without getting dizzy and throwing up. Even thinking about it gives me the sweats."

Reaching for her other arm, he held them both and looked at her until she couldn't resist his gaze.

"I'm sorry. I don't know how to fix it. Ever since Sam..." The rest of her sentence stuck in her throat.

"Is okay. No need for drive if make you sick." He pulled her into his arms and slowly rubbed her back as she nestled against his chest. She could get very used to the proximity of his body and the fresh scent of soap on his skin.

They lingered with their arms around each other for several minutes until he nudged her. Glancing up into his eyes, she stood transfixed as they turned a smoky shade of brown, the color of rich coffee. She rubbed her lips together, unable to move as he slowly lowered his mouth toward hers. All the air sucked from her lungs.

Her body hummed in anticipation until his cell phone started chirping an electronic version of the *Mission Impossible* theme song.

Taking a step back, he answered the phone. "*Zdravo*?"

Disappointed that the moment had passed, she watched his eyes widen. When he broke into a string of foreign words and phrases, she sat down and waited, sneaking a glance over at him every few seconds. To her surprise, his eyes welled with tears, and he wiped them away.

With a sigh, he flipped his cell phone shut and rubbed his forehead. "I must leave."

Panic assaulted her chest, and her lungs constricted. Not when she'd finally accepted the idea that she could care for him. He couldn't leave. She wouldn't let him.

Like I can stop him.

"When?" She clenched her hands.

"Over weekend. I must get ready for trip. Parents bought ticket for Macedonia. For ten days." He frowned. "Sorry, I must leave so soon."

"Ten whole days? Why?"

He blinked rapidly and rubbed his face. "Jovana is found. Parents make great celebration. I must be home for show her much love and support."

Wondering about the woman whose name evoked such passion in his voice, she wanted to know more but dared not ask. He could volunteer the information if he so chose.

"I don't mean to be nosy, but why were you crying?"

"I miss my Jovana. Family very sad when she no more home, and my *baba*, she cried for long time. Now Jovana has come back to me, and I must celebrate with family."

Several more tears slipped from his eyes and she held her breath. Whoever Jovana was, he obviously loved her. She felt a twinge of jealousy, wondering if he'd ever care for her with like passion.

Dare she hope Bob could feel such intense affection for her? Moments earlier he'd looked like he wanted to kiss her. But that was before the phone call. "Sounds like you really love her." She nibbled on her lip. "Tell me. Is Jovana your old--"

"Yes. Is true. Jovanichka is my heart, but is not for old. She much young care for people. Has beautiful smile." He wiped his eyes with his palm and turned his face away.

"Oh. That's so... sweet." *But the timing stinks!*

"Sorry, if hurt you for me to go for home country, but my Jovanichka, she need me very much. I take for you to visit Baby before I leave?"

"Yes." She swallowed hard. So he had an old girlfriend. That should come as no surprise, but it still made her chest ache. She unclenched her fists, willing her pulse to slow. Oh, why did the old girlfriend have to come back now? *And why do I care so much?*

Her attention darted to a photo on the desk showing a much younger Bob with his arms around a very attractive woman with dark hair and a gorgeous smile. "Who's the woman in the picture?"

"Ah, is picture for me with Jovana in high school in Macedonia." He pointed. "Our... hmmm... how you say... bond, is not easy for break. She's beautiful, yes?"

"Yes, too beautiful," she muttered as she tore her gaze from the photo. They looked like high school sweethearts. "I think I'm ready to go now."

"Thank you for nice day. Sorry bad happened for Baby, but God made for good, yes?" His broad grin warmed her insides, despite her attempt to resist his charm.

Maybe someday he would smile at her the way he smiled when he spoke of Jovana. Of course, that was wishful thinking, but who could blame a girl for dreaming? He'd had a girlfriend. So they'd been separated for years, but his love for her had obviously not diminished with the passage of time.

What she wouldn't do to trade places with Jovana... in Bob's heart.

Chapter Ten

Bob arrived the next morning to pick her up before she'd finished getting ready. His annoying punctuality made her smile. So opposite from her usual tardiness, which was one of the main reasons she enjoyed working from her home. She opened the door. "Morning."

He scanned her from head to toe and grinned. "You look good, my *prijatelka*."

She rolled her eyes. "I don't have a bit of makeup on and I'm in nightclothes."

"Like I say, very beautiful. No need for change clothes. You have cute *papuchis*." He winked, and his gaze lingered on her mouth before straying back to her eyes.

A laugh burst from her lips. She tapped his arm. "I'm not going out in my pajamas and slippers no matter how nice you think I look in them."

Stepping inside, he clutched a package in his hand. "Is no big deal. I wait for you to change *pidjami* and *papuchis*."

Her gaze darted toward the parcel he held, and she raised her brows.

A deep flush spread from his neck to his ears. "Is small present for Baby. For to cheer up."

With a smirk, she eyed him. "So you brought a gift for my dog but not for me, eh?" She cringed inwardly at her boldness. She hadn't a clue what had happened to change her into such a competitive woman, but she enjoyed the feeling of power surging through her veins every time he looked at her with adoration.

Just like Sam used to.

"Oh, I have special gift for Laney after visit for see Baby. Is surprise." He touched her chin and smiled.

The heat in his eyes warmed her stomach until it twitched and fluttered. She glanced away. Every time their skin made contact, something amazing and wonderful happened inside her heart, something she couldn't begin to describe, something even more wonderful than she'd felt with Sam.

Casting further thoughts of Sam aside, she determined to treat Bob as an individual, and not just a man who reminded her of her feelings for her former fiancé. Bob could stand on his own merit, for he had many attractive qualities that went beyond skin deep.

Glancing up, she caught him scanning her face. His gaze lingered on her lips again. It was enough to make her insides quiver like Jell-O on a dessert tray. Before she could stop herself, she stepped on her tiptoes and quickly kissed his cheek three times, then giggled, her hand covering her mouth. "Greeted you first."

As he opened his mouth to comment, she took off running upstairs. "Be back in a few. Make yourself comfortable."

*****

Bojan's pulse hummed from the sensation of Laney's soft lips on his cheek. After rubbing his skin, he covered his mouth and yawned. He'd hardly slept the night before, and though his brain was tired, his body felt alive.

The previous night he'd dreamt of his sister, picturing his reunion with her and wondering how she'd respond to him. For years the family hadn't known if she was dead or alive. With all of the civil unrest in the country's recent past there was no way to know if violence had touched her in some way.

He still couldn't believe she'd just shown up at their parents' vacation home in Macedonia after being gone over five years without any contact. If their parents hadn't been there on holiday she might not have known where to look for them.

Laney slowly descended the stairs with her hand resting on the oak railing, and looking like a contestant in a beauty pageant. The dark green shade of her blouse brought out the creamy tone of her skin, which resembled the tan paint on the walls behind her. Her eyes fixed on him as her feet alternately descended onto each step. The sound of her feet tapping rivaled the staccato rhythm of his heart, which thumped mercilessly. He shifted feet as he drank her in with his gaze.

It took every ounce of self-control he possessed not to devour her on sight. But he must show her respect. She was obviously nervous around him, and he didn't want that.

He wanted to enjoy every moment he had with Laney. Once he arrived at the airport in New York, he wouldn't see her for at least ten days. Though he could try and call her often, it wouldn't be the same as seeing her in person. Not by a long shot.

Before he realized it, she stood in front of him toe to toe. Her forehead placed mere inches from his lips, it begged to be kissed. He obliged, and pressed his lips to her smooth skin before pulling her into his arms and mumbled into her silky hair -- which smelled rich, like vanilla beans. "Ready for to go see Baby now?"

She nodded, nudging away from him as she poked him in the chest. "Are you almost ready to leave town to see... uh, what's her name again?"

He closed his eyes and smiled. "Ah, yes, Jovana."

When he opened his eyes, he noted a worried look on her face. Deciding to help Laney so she'd understand that he did not care for his sister the same way he felt about her, he tipped her chin toward him with the end of his finger and lowered his voice. "My sister is beautiful woman, but I want Laney for *devojka*."

Her eyes rounded with apparent surprise. "Me? But why?"

A broad smile covered his face, and he sighed. "I think is for God's will for me."

"Is Jovana not a Christian?" She bit her lip. "I mean, is that a problem for you?"

Sadness filled his chest, and he frowned. "She is not Christian. Is very lost."

"Oh, that's sad." They stared at each other for a moment, until she broke away with a sigh. "I'll be praying for you. I hope it goes well when you go home."

She peered back at him. He touched her cheek before tucking several wayward locks behind her ear. "I will be much sad with you far away. Will miss you very much. Want to..." He coughed into his hand before turning his face away for a moment. Somehow he had to get a grip on his emotions.

He sensed her watching him closely. She seemed to wait for him to finish. But he couldn't. Not yet.

Stuffing his hands into his back pockets, he sucked in a breath as he forced himself to look deeply into her eyes, assessing her reaction to him. "Ready for to go now?"

Without breaking her gaze, she nodded and adjusted her purse on her shoulder. What he wouldn't do to assure her of his feelings for her. But it was too soon. They'd barely met. Better to take it slowly.

He stepped down from the landing and headed straight for his Hummer. When he noticed she hadn't followed him, he turned to find out what was wrong.

Laney stared at his vehicle, with eyes wide and her lower lip trembling. She reminded him of someone in shock as she remained rigid, yet mildly quaking. He thought of the victims he'd seen in Kosovo, and returned to her side. "Something wrong?"

"I can't go with you. I can't..." She trembled and clutched her purse, her eyes glazed and unfocused.

"You must see Baby. I help you. Hold on." He offered his arm to her, but she didn't flinch or even acknowledge his presence. Like a bunny staring at headlights, she froze.

Now worried about her mental status, he waved his hand in front of her eyes and whispered. "Laney, we must go."

She finally blinked and peered at him with her brow furrowed. "I can't. Please, just bring Baby home to me. I'll be here waiting for you." Turning, she inserted the key to her front door into the lock.

"No. Wait. Is not good. Baby needs for you, not me."

"I know, but I'm feeling really sick to my stomach. I don't want to get in an accident. I know I went with you yesterday, but that was an emergency. Please, just go without me."

"Is not okay." He put his arm around her shoulder, locked the door, and guided her to the side of the Hummer. "Is safe car. Air bags protect. Is good?"

She shook her head. "No. I told you. I can't do it."

With a sigh, he decided not to argue and scooped her up in his arms. "You must go. I help you feel safe. Is not good for to stay home afraid."

Her face burrowed in his jacket, and he could swear she trembled, but she didn't fight him. A heady sensation, her warm skin burned through his clothing as he imagined her as his bride. The notion made his muscles tighten in anticipation. Maybe someday, if God willed it.

Would his parents approve? She was not Greek or Macedonian, but American. It would be difficult for them. They had never liked Erika, either, though they'd eventually accepted her as part of his life. Not that it mattered now.

He'd have to pray and hope that God would give him clear direction. Maybe God would give him an answer that he could not only live with, but also embrace.

*****

Terrified, Laney pressed against Bob. She appreciated his effort to help her break through her fear, but was unable to respond in a calm way. She held her breath as she allowed him to settle her on the front seat.

After he safely buckled her in, she relaxed enough to take in her surroundings. The vehicle wasn't a delivery car but a very expensive-looking SUV. Had he suddenly grown rich, or were her eyes playing tricks on her?

"What kind of vehicle is this?" she asked, her voice shaky as she ran her hand over the leather upholstery.

"Is Hummer H-2 model. Mid-size. Very safe. You okay now?" He touched her arm.

"I...I don't feel the world spinning anymore. I think I'll be okay." She swallowed hard and closed her eyes, mentally challenging herself. *Get a grip, Laney.*

"Is very good. I must pray for you." He mumbled foreign words.

Her mind wandered. What man delivered pizzas for a living, yet could afford a Hummer? Then she remembered him saying his Uncle Alek had given it to him. "Must be nice to have rich relatives," she muttered.

He stopped jabbering and his voice softened. "I hate for see you afraid. What happened for make you have so much *strav*, so much fear for drive in car?"

Her throat tightened as she debated on whether to tell him the full extent of her anxiety. Deciding it couldn't hurt to be honest, she exhaled and closed her eyes.

"Everyone I've ever loved died in a car accident." There. She got that much out. Exhaling, she opened her eyes. "I know it sounds bizarre, but first my best friend from high school died, then my parents, and last year my fiancé. I feel like if I never drive, then I can't get killed in a wreck. That's kept me home most of the year. I don't go anywhere. Not even to the bank."

She couldn't tell him about Onion Boy... not yet.

"Oh, sweet Laney." He turned to face her and whispered, "Let me pray for you come over fear."

She nodded. "Yes, please pray. But can you do it in English this time? I need help. I don't know what to do."

He squeezed her hands and closed his eyes.

In the short time she'd known him, she'd grown to care for him quite a bit. His offer to pray had stirred her interest in him even more.

"Is good for you for see need for help." In a husky voice Bob brought her before the Lord. "Jesus, hold Laney close and comfort, please. Help with *stravs,* with coming over fears. Make her have peace. Fill Laney's heart and give much strength. In name of Jesus Christ, Amen."

"Amen." She opened her eyes and blinked back tears. "Thank you for praying. I feel a bit better already."

"Is good." He winked and turned the key in the ignition.

The engine roared to life. Worship music floated through the cab of the vehicle, and Laney's spirit felt at peace for the first time in months. With a smile, she reached for his hand. "Thanks for being my friend."

"Is no problem." He winked and stroked her fingers with his thumb. "I will always be friend for you."

Her heart fluttered, and she thanked the Lord for giving her a guardian angel. As her thought turned into a prayer, she wondered if something so wonderful could last.

She peeked at his profile from the corner of her eye and shook her head sadly. No, nothing so wonderful could last. Hadn't she learned as much before?

Chapter Eleven

Poor Laney looked as white as a sheet when Bojan hit a pothole as he drove down the mountain. He offered silent prayers, convinced she needed every one of them.

The moment they pulled onto Route 92, Laney grabbed his hand so tightly his fingers tingled.

"Is okay, Laney. No need for *strav*." He winced and gently squeezed back. "What happened for you peace?"

Her hand relaxed for a moment. "I don't know... I'm sorry. Did I hurt you?"

"You have strong grip for woman." He winked, then returned his eyes to the road. With animals crossing at any time, one could not be too careful. His first week in town he'd nearly hit a javelina head-on, which taught him never to let his attention stray. And given Laney's level of fear, he needed to be all the more conscientious.

He stroked her knuckles with his thumb to help calm her, round and round until he felt her shudder. "Is problem?" He glanced from the corner of his eye.

"No. It's, um, nice, actually." A nervous-sounding giggle erupted from her lips. "I'm just not used to so much touching, you know?"

He withdrew his hand. "You no like touch?"

"No. It isn't that." She reached for his fingers and held them. "I love your hands... your touch. Don't stop being sweet to me just because I'm a little skittish around you." She bit her lip and her face turned a rosy shade of red.

"What you mean by skittish?" His gaze darted between her face and the road. This was not a good time to have a serious discussion, but he had to know if the word meant something good.

She sighed. "It means I'm nervous around you. Kind of like... scared."

He raised his brows. "I scare you? Is problem?"

"Not scared in a bad way, silly." She chuckled lightly. "It's good. It makes me feel all goofy inside when you treat me so nicely. I suppose I'll have to get used to it if we're going to be friends."

"I no understand word goofy. Is like Disney?"

She giggled. "How do I explain it? Hmmmm... It's more like the sensation of butterflies fluttering around in my stomach. That nervous feeling."

"Ah, I think I understand." He grinned. "You like for me to treat you nicely. Very much."

"Yes. I like everything you do. Sometimes I think you're too good to be true." Her tone sounded wistful.

He couldn't believe she thought that about him, given his past. Then again, she didn't know anything about it. And if she did, would she still feel that way toward him? He doubted that. "I am not so good."

"Yes, you are. You're a real sweetheart compared to most American guys."

He laughed. "American guys not all so bad."

"Yeah, well, you've never dated a guy here, so you wouldn't know."

"Gross. That make me sick." He shivered. "I never date man. Is not okay for Bible. Is not okay for me."

She chuckled even though what he'd said wasn't funny. Strange.

He pulled into the parking lot of the animal hospital and turned off the car. Hopefully Baby would be ready to go home soon. Then he'd ask Laney to take care of Dude while he was out of town. Maybe their dogs would want to mate and they'd have puppies. The image of them connecting made his neck heat.

"Oh, I'm sorry. Did I embarrass you? I didn't mean it that way. I never thought you would like guys or anything."

"Is okay. I not think you embarrass for me." He turned and touched her cheek. "When I think of you, it makes for butterflies in stomach."

She closed her eyes and smiled. "You do understand."

He sighed.

Opening her eyes wide, she held onto his gaze and tilted her head thoughtfully. "I think I'm really going to like being your friend, Bob. Or should I call you Bo-john? You don't look like a Bob, and Bo-john sounds kind of fancy."

The way she said his name gave him goose bumps. The delicious kind that made him want to hear more. "Um hmm...I wish for you say name, Bojan. Say like bullion, yes?"

"Sorry, Bojan. Did I say it right that time?"

"Yes, is very good. I call you Elaine? Is such beautiful name for you. Sound much fancy, too."

She poked him in the chest and laughed. "Sounds like an old lady's name to me."

He frowned.

"I'll think about it. Maybe if you introduce me to your family someday. Until then, maybe you should stick to Laney. I promise I won't call you Bob if you prefer Bojan. Just forgive me if sometimes I say it wrong."

He couldn't believe she just implied she wanted to meet his family. Did she really feel so strongly for him that she'd consider getting acquainted with his parents? Too bad they were in Macedonia on holiday for a month.

His mind conjured up images of scowls on their faces. Looks of disapproval like they'd given him when they'd found out about Erika. But Laney was different. He hoped they would like her. "Is very good."

Before she had a chance to comment, he opened her door and

helped her out. She stepped right into his arms. When she tipped her face to whisper in his ear, the end of her nose rubbed against his hair. She inhaled deeply and chuckled low in her throat.

The sensation made him shudder and he longed to nuzzle her in return, but resisted despite the heady scent of vanilla wafting around him from her hair. He grinned. "Why you blow in my ear?" Her eyes widened, and for a moment he wished he had kept his thought to himself. So he winked. "But I think is no problem."

Placing her hand over her lips, she glanced at her feet. "Sorry. I didn't mean to. I meant to tell you something, but when we got close I couldn't remember what it was."

After several awkward moments, he said, "Is no big deal." Smiling, he opened the door to the veterinary hospital before following her inside.

Laney approached the front desk and clutched her hands together. She addressed the receptionist. "I... is Baby doing better today?"

"And you are?" The woman peered over reading glasses.

"Laney. Laney Cooper. Baby is my black longhaired Chihuahua. She was admitted last night."

"Chihuahua's yours?" The woman raised her brows. "She's not doing well enough to go home yet. Doc said she'll need at least another day for observation, probably two, and then she'll be safe to go home."

Laney turned and stared into his eyes, her skin paling. "You'll be gone by then, won't you?"

He nodded. "You need to find way for get Baby home."

"Maybe I can take a cab." She nibbled on her cuticle.

"Or you drive Hummer." He smiled and dangled the keys in front of her nose.

She rubbed her forehead. "I'm sure it's very safe, but I'll call a cab." Laney turned to the receptionist. "Can I visit Baby?"

"Sure. Follow me." The elder woman pushed up from her chair and waddled toward an exam room. "Wait right here."

While the woman went to look for Baby, Bojan decided to ask Laney about taking care of Dude during his absence.

"Is okay for you for care for Dude when I go back for my home country?"

Her eyes glazed over as if she had her mind focused elsewhere. "Huh? I didn't hear what you said."

"Can you care for Dude?"

A broad grin broke out on her face and she squeezed his hands. "Sure. That'll be fun. Baby would love the company."

"And what you wish for?"

A shy grin formed on her lips. "I love dogs. It'll be great. And besides, that means I'll get to see you again, right? If I have your dog, you'll have to come get him."

"Is true." He released her hand.

"Okay, then. Sounds like a plan, as long as you bring me a souvenir from your hometown."

He tapped his forehead. "I have perfect gift for you in mind." His voice grew husky. "For show much love... and friendship."

Her smile faltered for a second. "Sure, um, thanks."

Suddenly she looked sad, and he wondered what he'd said that had stolen her joy. If only he knew her thoughts, then he could be more careful about what he said.

Maybe he just needed to brush up on his English. Of course, she would have to help him with that. But not until he returned from his visit. It would be pointless to learn more before then, as he'd forget everything he'd learned once he left the U.S.

He suddenly remembered his earlier question. "How you know I want for English lessons?"

Her forehead wrinkled. "You placed an ad on the Internet. Then you showed up at my house at the exact time you said you wanted to meet." She shrugged and raised her hands. "I figured it had to be you because I hadn't ordered anything to eat. Then I found out later it was just a friend of yours."

"Is big mistake. I no place ad for English lessons." He rubbed his forehead as a queasy sensation rippled through his gut. "So if I no place ad, and no friend place ad, then who send you message for answer?"

She blinked. "You didn't know about the ad?"

He shook his head. "No use Internet for post ad."

Nibbling on the edge of her nail, she paused, her eyes widening. "Oh my goodness, do you think some pervert answered my e-mail?"

He mulled over various scenarios. Then his thoughts hovered around someone whose recent behavior made perfect sense. Of course...

He'd been set up.

The question was... Should he fire the man for interfering, or thank him?

Bojan would have to pray hard on that one.

*****

He groaned as he grabbed the plastic garbage bag and gloves and went to work. Cleaning trash off the streets of Old Town Bisbee was not what he considered a respectable job, but it *was* work... for now. Unfortunately, Sam's girl lived twenty-five miles away. Keeping an eye on her from that distance was no easy task. Not when he'd just started a new job. He had to come up with a better plan. A way to get closer to her.

Lugging his tools across the street, he paused to read a sign.

A paper note taped to the inside of an antique shop door on Main Street captured his attention. *Help Wanted. Must be available to work weekends. Apply within.*

Smiling, he pondered his options. Delivering furniture might be fun. Especially if it gave him a chance to scope out rich people's homes. One never knew when that knowledge might come in handy. Yeah, one never knew...

Chapter Twelve

Watching Baby with a heavy heart, Laney swallowed the lump in her throat. Her dog seemed so weak. Anyone who knew Baby would swear the Chihuahua in the bed wasn't even distantly related to her pet. She had no spunk at all.

Laney had all she could do to hold back tears as Bojan placed the bone he'd brought Baby next to her head. Baby didn't lift her chin or even attempt to sniff it.

Bojan must have sensed her distress because he put his arm over her shoulder and offered a gentle squeeze. "Baby need rest, then be okay."

"I know. She just looks so... pitiful."

They left the room after she kissed the top of her Chihuahua's head.

"Dude cheer up Baby when play together. You still care for Dude for me?"

"Sure. I said I would." Laney glanced into his warm, golden-brown eyes. She touched the side of his face. "Thank you for bringing me here and not letting me run back into my house."

His face broke out into a wide grin. "You welcome for help. We start up English lessons when I return from Macedonia?"

"Sure. We'll do that," she whispered, then bit her lip.

"Why you look sad?" He tipped her chin up.

Her pulse throbbed at his touch. She swallowed hard and stared back at him. "I... I'm not sure. Maybe because I'll miss you. Next to Baby, you're the only friend I have."

"Is not good for stay home and have no friends."

While true, it didn't make facing her fears any easier. She just prayed he wouldn't push her.

"Laney, you must look here." He tipped her chin up and pointed his fingers at his eyes. "Is important for understand."

Her pulse kicked up a notch as she returned the gaze, and she wanted to run away before she did something that she'd regret. All of his tender touches and deep, intense stares were scaring her out of her wits.

If she didn't know better, she'd swear she was falling in love with him. But she couldn't be. It must be loneliness making her so easily enthralled with him. It had to be, or that would mean she'd have to take a chance on love again.

And love had let her down...

"I would care very much for you. When I return from home country I introduce for parents." His gaze grew more intense until she thought she'd melt.

She glanced away before she started sobbing. No one had cared for her in a very long time. Not the way he expressed his feelings, anyway. What she didn't understand was what he found so appealing about her. Especially with all of her hang-ups getting in the way of their friendship at times.

"No, please look." His voice softened.

Her knees grew weak as she stared into his eyes, and at that moment she could swear she saw straight into his soul. He was a good man who loved God. What more could a girl want? "I...I'm looking."

Her cheeks heated as he caressed her face with his gaze. For a few seconds, time and space stood still. They lingered in the parking lot, with no sense of urgency to move, and no concern about their surroundings. Just warmth emanating between two people.

And sparks flying.

"I pray for you. I would call much if okay with you. First, I want for take you special place."

That was all it took to snap her back to reality. The less driving the better. "I'd rather just go on home, if that's okay with you."

"Is not good for stay home so much." He stroked her cheek with his thumb. "Let me give special day before I leave."

Thinking about his offer, her eyes drifting shut from the soft caress of his hand on her face. Maybe she'd taken leave of her senses, but for a moment she considered saying yes. Something deep within her heart wanted to please Bojan, and she knew saying yes would do just that.

With some hesitation, she opened her eyes and sucked in a deep breath. "I'm nervous about driving any more than necessary. How far would we be going?"

"Is secret." He tipped his head down and whispered. "Wait for surprise, please. Is good, I promise."

The warmth of his breath against her neck and the light scent of his spicy aftershave made her long to do whatever he wanted, and that frightened her even more. She could easily lose herself.

As he watched her with a soft look in his eyes, she didn't have the courage to deny him anything.

"Okay, but just this once. Don't be surprised if I close my eyes for the whole drive. Sometimes it's the only way I can keep from throwing up."

Okay, now that was just about the most unattractive thing she could have said to him at that moment.

He hesitated and stepped back. "We go now?"

Opening her door, he waited as she climbed into the Hummer and buckled herself in. This time her hands shook violently, but she still managed to clip the belt herself.

As Bojan stepped around the vehicle she prayed under her breath, "Lord, give me peace today. I can't do this without Your help."

*****

Bojan's heart danced in his chest. She'd agreed to go with him despite her ever-widening eyes. Though obviously scared, the fact that she set aside her issues to please him brought him indescribable satisfaction. He refrained from doing a victory punch before starting the engine.

Laney clutched her hands on her lap and tensed. The motor rumbled and she squealed. She gripped her seatbelt. Grabbing her trembling hand, he rubbed the top. The silky feeling of her skin under his thumb made him smile.

"Is okay. Is safe in Hummer. You stop thinking for crash. Think for fun today, yes?"

She offered a shaky grin. "I'll try."

He placed his arm behind her seat as he backed out of the parking space. "Is very good. I proud for courage."

A laugh burst from her lips. "You must be talking about someone else. I'm so scared my legs are trembling."

"Ah, but you go, so have much courage."

"If you say so..." Her eyes glazed over and she yawned, then lay her head against the window. She closed her eyes and seemed to force each breath, slowly in and out, until her breathing deepened.

They drove all the way to Bisbee in silence as Laney slept.

Pulling into a reserved space with a sigh, Bojan rubbed his hands together. He would find a very special gift for Laney today in Old Town Bisbee, and no matter the cost, he would buy something wonderful for her. Something that would make her think of him often, like a necklace or painting, or antique furniture for her massive, but sparsely furnished home.

She stirred, and the sound of her soft grunt when she stretched made his heart zing.

"Where are we?" Blinking several times, she turned and stared into his eyes. "Did I fall asleep? I can't believe I was so relaxed. That's so strange."

"I pray for peace for drive."

"Yeah, so did I." She licked her lips. "Have you ever prayed for something and wanted it really bad, but never thought you'd actually get it?"

The yearning in her eyes was unmistakable, and he struggled to find his voice. He wanted so much to make her happy. "Yes, is true," he whispered, his words laced with emotion.

"That's what happened. God answered our prayers." She nibbled on her lower lip. "Tell me. Why do we pray if we don't think God will answer?"

He rubbed his chin as he considered her question. "I think deep in heart believe. Head not always believe, but heart know truth."

"Yeah, I think you're right." She grinned. "You're so smart, you know that?"

"Thank you for nice words." The moment he took his first breath of Bisbee air he smelled incense burning. It made him pause.

Music from flutes and harps floated in the air. The atmosphere reminded him of places where the gypsies lived back home, with their carefree spirits and relaxed atmosphere. He started to smile, but remembered how his sister had spent time with the gypsies, and then she went missing. He squelched the thought before it ruined his mood.

Laney smirked. "So you're artsy, are you?"

"No understand artsy." He reached for her hand.

"It means... I don't know how to explain it. I guess it's people who like music and craft fairs and stuff like that."

"Then I much artsy." He nodded and led her to the historical building.

A Mexican man strummed his guitar and sang a ballad in Spanish. Laney stopped, and closed her eyes as she listened. Bojan opened his wallet and dropped a twenty into the man's hat. The singer paused to thank him before continuing his song.

The Mexican singer stared at Laney as he crooned to her in Spanish. He acted as if he sang for an audience of one. Bojan felt a twinge of jealousy. He wished he could serenade her like that. Maybe he'd try it later and see how she responded.

Once she'd gotten her fill of music, they headed toward the historic post office. A crowd of people encircled a man. Bojan and Laney approached, and he couldn't believe his eyes. He tugged Laney's hand and ushered her closer.

"Look, Laney. Cat on dog and mouse on cat."

"Yeah, and there's a flea on the mouse if you look really close." The owner of the menagerie grinned at the crowd, and then chuckled. "That may be a slight exaggeration."

"How do you get them to do that?" Laney asked, her voice full of wonder. "I've never seen anything like it."

Several people snapped pictures of the tower of animals. All very much alive, the fact that they lay on each other without getting off totally stumped him. The man said he'd trained them to stay in that position.

Bojan was so impressed he pulled out his wallet and dropped ten dollars in the man's basket. "Is good show. Reminds me for gypsy act I saw in Macedonia."

Laney pulled him toward an antique store on Main Street called *Finders Keepers*. "I just love antiques. Can we look for a few minutes?"

"No problem." The excitement in her eyes made his pulse trip. He'd made her happy, and it felt great.

She stopped in front of the store window and turned. "Wait. I don't have any money on me. If I look around I'll want to get something, and it'll make me depressed."

"Is no problem. I buy whatever you wished for."

Rolling her eyes, she clasped her mouth and spoke through her fingers. "Yeah, right. Gimme a break. Some of this stuff costs a fortune."

"What you mean, gimme break? I not break stuff."

She paused and stared at him. "I'm not worried about that. Gimme a break means I don't believe you. You can't buy me anything I want."

He assessed her comment, then winked, knowing she would never ask for much. She didn't seem like the type of woman to use a man for his money. "I have much money. Is no big deal for me to spend money on beautiful woman."

Opening her mouth as if she wanted to say more, instead she clamped it shut and shook her head. "Forget about it. Let's just window shop."

Wondering why she wanted to look for windows to buy, he followed close behind. Maybe she wanted to look at stained glass windows.

She whipped the door of the shop open. He caught it before it slammed shut. Pushing past a customer, he caught up with her. "Why angry? I said is no problem. I have much money. I no tease for you."

Stopping suddenly, she paused, her gaze avoiding his. "But I don't want your money, Bojan."

He touched her shoulder, and turned her to face him. "Tell me. What you want?"

Glancing up, she whispered, "I don't know what I want, but one thing I do know..." She cleared her throat and blinked several times, her eyes pooling with tears. "I don't want to hurt you."

Chapter Thirteen

The soft look in Laney's eyes made him long to kiss her right where they stood, but he refused to show affection in the middle of the store. No, when he kissed her the first time it would be very romantic. Every woman's dream setting.

Grinning, he entertained the idea in his mind. Good thing Laney couldn't read his thoughts, or she'd probably slap him.

"Why are you staring at me?" she whispered.

He blinked several times. "Not mean for stare. How you say... hmmm... admire you beautiful skin and face. Not stare."

"You're too much." She rolled her eyes and walked toward the back of the store, which housed stacks of old photographs.

Following close behind, he tried not to fixate on the sway of her hips and kept his gaze at eye level. It turned out to be harder than he thought it would be, especially when she dropped her lip balm and stooped to pick it up.

He averted his eyes, but his neck still heated. When he glanced up again, she faced him, applying the stuff to her lips with long strokes. The air sucked from his lungs, and he groaned inwardly.

It was going to be a very long ten days, and though he loved his sister very much, he wished with all his heart he could bring Laney with him so he wouldn't miss her so much. Especially when they were just getting to know each other.

But the likelihood of her agreeing to go with him was zero to none. If she could hardly stand to ride in a car, he could only imagine her stress if they flew across the ocean. He figured asking her would make her uncomfortable. Plus, they still didn't know each other well enough to travel overseas. Now if they were married...

She giggled and stuck her lip balm back into her purse. "I love it when you watch me, but it makes me kind of nervous, too. Why do you do that so much?"

"No understand what you ask." He tried not to look at her lips and kept his mouth closed tight.

Her grin faltered. "It's nothing. Hey, let's check this out. I haven't been here in years. It's so much fun."

Touching a large bureau in the back of the store, she turned and reached for his hand. "Check this out. Some of these people were so homely, you won't believe it." Reaching into a drawer, she pulled out a stack of old photographs and plopped them onto the table. "And look at their horrible dresses."

He had no clue what homes had to do with the pictures of people in horrible dresses, but he nodded. "Let me see."

Sifting through the photos one at a time, he had to admit most of the ladies were unattractive. Some of them even looked like men. If not for their clothing and their lack of facial hair, he would've sworn some were guys.

"I want for marry woman like her..." He held out the most unattractive woman's picture in the stack and winked at Laney.

"Liar." She laughed, snatched the photo from him, and returned the stack to the drawer. They flipped through some photos of children, and when they finally tired of the game, he headed to the counter.

Bojan searched through a bowl of antique spoons from around the world. He found one made of pure silver with the inscription, Yugoslavia. Staring at the spoon, he swallowed hard. It broke his heart that his country had split apart. Since it no longer existed as such, he decided to purchase the collectable.

Turning, he followed Laney with his gaze. She stared in awe at a piece of furniture, stroking the wood with such longing he had to look away.

"How much is cost?" he asked the woman behind the counter and pointed at Laney.

"What? The dresser? That's an antique from the 1880s. Shipped from England and owned by a wealthy family during the mining boom. It's gorgeous, isn't it?"

"Is very beautiful. How much?"

"I think it's a thousand, but let me check the books." She stepped into the back room.

Bojan slid over to Laney. "You like?"

"Oh, yes," she sighed and gazed at the wood with admiration. "I've always wanted something like this, ever since I was a little girl."

"Is beautiful." He looked at her and she blushed as if she realized his admiration was not limited to the antiques in the building.

She licked her lips and searched the area.

"Something wrong?" Bojan touched her arm.

"I need to use the bathroom. Wait a sec for me, okay?" She nodded at a room toward the back.

"I wait for you." He stepped back to the counter.

The saleswoman emerged and said with a broad grin, "I found the description right here." She pointed to the book. "It's a Victorian-era highboy dresser and made from solid maple. The white marble top, ornate carving, and original varnish makes this a very valuable piece of furniture. I'll even toss in free delivery. Will that work?"

Bojan glanced over his shoulder. "Yes, but must make quick pay. Is surprise." He handed her his credit card and scribbled Laney's name and address on a sheet of paper while the saleswoman swiped his card.

The machine made a crunching sound and spit out a piece of paper for him to sign. He applied his signature and slipped the pen and paper back to the saleswoman just as Laney emerged from the back. Stuffing

77

the receipt into his pocket, he smiled. She was in for a big surprise tomorrow.

He couldn't wait to hear her reaction. He decided he'd call her early tomorrow evening while at JFK International Airport during his hour layover. Then when he returned, he'd take her antique shopping for a sofa.

She stepped behind him and pressed her chin into his back in a brief hug. He turned to face her, and she grinned. "Flirting with the saleswoman, I see. Can't leave you alone even for a minute, can I?"

Bojan tipped his head toward the elderly woman, who now appeared very flustered, and he smiled. "Is very beautiful woman. Made me miss my mother."

"Ahem. Yeah, sure, guy." She snickered.

"Is something you want buy for store?"

She scrunched her brow. "What did you say?"

"Want for buy something?"

"No. I told you I don't have any money. I really *do* enjoy just looking. I'd forgotten how much fun it could be. It's been so long since I've done anything like this." She grabbed his hand and rested her head on his upper arm. "Thanks so much for bringing me here."

He rubbed the side of her head with his cheek. "Is no problem. I want bring you on many shoppings for Bisbee."

"Let's go to my favorite trinket store now. Okay?"

"Is very good." He winked, a song playing in his heart. She was going to be very surprised indeed.

As he followed Laney, Bojan noticed a man watching them from across the road, staring at Laney while picking up trash. When the man saw Bojan peering at him, he ducked his head down, but not before Bojan got a quick look. The guy seemed familiar, but Bojan couldn't place him. He thought about the bird-watcher. But he couldn't be the same guy. That would be too coincidental.

*****

Laney had to get away before she confessed and told him she really wanted the highboy dresser. Until she saw the price tag, she'd entertained the idea of allowing him to get it for her and paying him back. Then reality hit home, and she remembered her lack of cash. Things were tight, especially during the winter months with increased heating costs.

If she couldn't afford to get Baby the care she needed at the hospital, she had no right fantasizing about purchasing Victorian-era furniture for her bedroom. A sigh escaped her lips. It sure was fun to dream, though.

With a forced smile on her lips, she stepped into the sunshine. Heat from the sun's rays made her face tingle with warmth until a cool gust of wind got under her blouse. The temperature had dropped while they were shopping, and she hadn't come prepared.

Her shudder caught Bojan's attention.

"You cold?" He removed his bomber jacket and draped it over her shoulders, gently lifting her long hair out from the collar. She shivered at his proximity and the feel of the heat radiating from his skin. It made her want to move closer and lay her head on his chest.

"Not too much. But thanks for the jacket." She watched as he rammed his hands into his pants pockets and shrugged his shoulders in an effort to keep warm. "What are you going to do?"

"Is no problem." He shivered and winked. "You keep me warm from smile."

"Oh, puhleeze." She rolled her eyes and grinned. "Here, you take it back. I'll survive." Removing his coat, she offered it back to him.

"No, I am hot for blood man. Woman need coat, not man."

She understood what he meant, but it sounded so funny she just had to correct him. "This is the way you say it... I'm a hot-blooded man and don't need the coat."

"Is true. You say in very good English." He winked.

"You're hopeless." She smiled and put the coat back on, then followed Bojan down the hill toward the craft booths. One woman sold handmade clothing.

Bojan grabbed Laney's hand and brought her to the booth. "I want see you wear this." He selected a white fur coat and handed it to her. "Is very beautiful for you."

She shook her head. "Oh, no, I couldn't."

He took the coat off the hanger and held it out to her. "You must try for wear, please."

"Oh, all right." She removed his coat and set it on the table next to him, then slipped into the white fur. She'd never felt anything so luxurious in her life and rubbed her cheek against the sleeves. "Oh, it's so cozy and soft."

As she glanced up, she noticed a man with a baseball cap and sunglasses covering much of his face watching her. She frowned and he ducked around the corner. She considered mentioning it to Bojan, but then decided she'd sound paranoid, so she let it go. But the creepy feelings lingered, and try as she might, she couldn't shake them.

*****

Bojan's chest grew warm at the sight of her pleasure, and he reached over and stroked her arms. A strange look appeared in her eyes, then disappeared as quickly as it had come. He worried if he'd offended her somehow.

"Coat is very soft. I want buy for you. Let me, please."

"No. I told you. I don't want you buying me stuff." She removed the coat and handed it back to the Indian saleswoman. Bojan handed the woman several green bills. "Please, keep change." He took the coat back.

"Is gift for you. Please wear." He offered the fur.

She frowned. "Why'd you do that? It costs over a hundred bucks. You can't afford that."

Her comment made him pause. Why did she keep insisting he couldn't afford things? It was insulting. "I said is no problem for me. Is no big deal."

"But I know you don't make much money delivering pizza, and I don't want to see you spend all of your money on me."

After the shock of her statement wore off, he laughed so hard he clutched his side. "You think I bring pizzas for delivery for work? Is very funny. No, I own half of restaurants with Uncle. Have three restaurants."

She stared at him with her mouth hanging open. "You mean you didn't just inherit the Hummer and RV? They're actually... yours?"

"Is hard for you believe?" He stopped, suddenly hurt by her reaction. "I work hard. Is not all gift from uncle."

Fear appeared in her eyes, and she scanned his face as if searching for the truth. "Why are you spending money on me? Tell me the truth." She held her purse tight against her hip. "Friends don't buy stuff like this for each other. Not even rich ones."

He grabbed his coat and shrugged it back on. Not sure how to respond to her question, he chose silence. The last time he'd tried to explain things he messed up the words. He refused to upset her with his flawed English.

"Tell me." She followed him, touching his arm, and causing him to turn around. "Why, Bojan?"

Lost in the deep blue color of her eyes and the sultry sound of his name on her lips, he opened his mouth, but the words refused to come. He mumbled to himself, "Is not *zabranet* for show *ljubov*."

"Stop using words I don't understand."

She sure was demanding a lot from him, and he didn't know what to say. So he decided to tell her the truth about the other gift. "Is not forbidden for want you beautiful gift for bedroom. Much love for you show."

Laney sucked in her breath and choked out, "I knew you were too good to be true. Well, you're not getting that from me. I'm waiting for -- oh, never mind. Please, just take me home." She bit her lip as tears rolled down her cheeks.

Fearing the worst, he knew he shouldn't have spoken his thoughts. So why had he opened his big mouth? She'd misunderstood him, and he didn't know how to fix it. It would help if he knew how his words had come out wrong.

He'd wanted her to have a nice gift, not take her virtue. A stolen glance over his shoulder confirmed that he'd hurt and confused her...

again.

With a groan he prayed under his breath, "Help me, Lord. Is *losho*. Is very bad."

Chapter Fourteen

Laney tore her gaze away from Bojan and broke into a sprint. A car honked as she dodged it on her way across the main road.

"What's your problem, lady?" a man with long graying hair and a beard shouted from his open window.

She ignored his shaking fist. Her gaze roamed the parking lot, searching for the yellow Hummer, and then it occurred to her that she didn't have to ride back to town with Bojan, and in fact, preferred to hail a cab. She waved at a cabbie cruising up the street.

"Need a lift?" The man raked her with his gaze as he chewed a toothpick.

His rank breath made her step back. Maybe she didn't need a ride after all. Better the enemy you know than the one you don't. The sound of footsteps pounding on pavement told her Bojan had followed her.

"Go!" He waved the cabbie on.

"What'd you do that for?"

"You no need ride from stranger. I bring you home free for charge." His eyes searched hers. "I sorry you upset with me. Something I say hurt you again? Must be big, stupid mistake."

"Sure was. A *huge* mistake."

"I am so sorry." He closed his eyes, releasing a frustrated-sounding sigh.

She hesitated, suddenly realizing that she'd probably judged him too harshly, again. He'd probably not meant what she thought he'd said, just like when he called her crazy.

"Look... I know you're not stupid." Licking her lips, she contemplated what to say next. "What you say is sometimes stupid, but I know you're not."

"What I say wrong?" He reached for her cheek, and she stepped back. His arm dropped and he avoided her gaze, tipping his head as if studying the sidewalk.

"You said you wanted to take me to bed with you, that's what you said." She held her breath, then released it slowly. "Isn't that what you meant?"

His head snapped up, and his eyes widened. "I not meant for say..." A deep shade of red crept up his neck, and he glanced at her lips. "I mean, I like you very much, but I show respect. Not use like *igratcha*, like toy."

She eyed him skeptically. "So you're saying you don't think of me that way?"

A slow grin curled the corner of his mouth and he chuckled lightly. "I want you very much, but I not take something you no want for give. I must please God and He want marriage for me."

"How do you know I don't..." Was she really having this conversation? Groaning, she decided to change the topic before it deteriorated further. "Never mind."

Soon he'd be off to visit that Jovana woman he seemed to love so much, and she would dog-sit for him, but their relationship couldn't progress further. Except she agreed to give him English lessons, even if they were informal in nature. If only her finances would allow her to quit.

Bojan laid his hand on her arm, and she looked up. Tenderness radiated from his eyes, and she struggled to breathe.

Before she succumbed to the stirring deep within her, she shrugged him off. "Let's just head home. It's starting to get dark, and we still need to bring your dog to my house before I settle in for the night. I'm exhausted."

He nodded. Without a word, he led her by the hand to his vehicle. She tugged her hand free, and rubbed the fur on her sleeves.

Sometimes Bojan confused her. He bought her lavish gifts, yet he said he loved someone with an exotic name, who also lived in his home country and spoke his language. He delivered pizzas, yet also owned restaurants and a very expensive vehicle and RV. His generosity seemed to have no limit, and that terrified her more than anything.

What if he did have expectations of her if she accepted his extravagant gifts? She'd owe him, and that would be repeating history, just like when she'd dated Luke. Expectations increased with every gift. Thankfully he'd moved away after her freshman year of college, or she wouldn't make it to the altar someday as a pure bride, something she'd vowed her whole life she would do.

Her thoughts returned to the man before her as Bojan's muscular body moved closer. He reached around her to open the Hummer door. Always the gentleman, she mused, even after she'd chewed him out. She sighed and tilted her face toward his. Time suspended as she gazed into his warm, beautiful eyes.

His smile faltered, and a serious, smoky haze darkened his pupils. She could feel his warm breath caressing her forehead as he leaned toward her. Such gentleness stirred her heart.

All anger had fled, and nothing but warmth vibrated between them. She dipped her head. Warmth and tension, a disconcerting combination.

A little voice inside disrupted her romantic thoughts. *He wants to win you over so he can have his way with you.*

Though part of her refused to believe it, the more practical side acknowledged that every man had some form of self-centeredness worming into his heart. Scriptures called it the sin nature. What made Bojan any different?

No one gave expecting nothing in return. Right?

Her physical response to him evaporated. She stiffened and glanced up. The dreamy expression on his face made her smile. They had yet to get into the Hummer.

His mouth curved in a lopsided grin, and he lowered his voice. "You not remember traditional greeting. I must give three kisses."

"I did."

Smirking, he shook his head. "But I not kiss."

With a low chuckle, she nudged him and teased. "Cut it out, lover boy. Just take me home." But her legs refused to move.

"You must get in Hummer for me drive you."

Renewed fear turned her blood cold, and despite the warm rabbit fur jacket, she shivered. Not sure what scared her more, riding in his Hummer, or riding with him.

"I can't.... I'm sorry, but I can't ride home with you."

"You must. Not okay for spend night in parking lot."

Her hands fisted. "I... know, but I can't seem to shake this... terror I feel." Tears stung her eyes. "I'm so tired of this--" Choking on a sob, she covered her face.

His warm hands covered hers, and he tugged her fingers away from her eyes. "You must. I help you. I pray *strav* not make you sick."

That made her cry harder, and she struggled against him, but he wouldn't let go of her hands. She shook her head.

"Laney, listen for my words. You must give God *strav*. Is not okay for carry burden on shoulders. Jesus ask for heavy load, want you give *strav* for Him." With a gentle smile, he dipped his head down. "So I must cheer. One..." he whispered, "two..."

His proximity made her feel wild inside. She shrugged off her fear, basking in his nearness instead. When he reached three, she forced thoughts of Jovana from her mind, and turned her face until her mouth met his. Salt from her own tears had wet her lips.

The kiss started out tentative, soft, and gentle... When she relaxed her mouth to indulge further, he pulled away.

"We must go now." He ruffled his wavy hair with both hands and exhaled. "Is not good kiss..."

The words pierced her heart. No doubt he'd remembered his feelings for Jovana, and he didn't want to muddy the waters. While she'd lapped up his affection, he'd found the contact unfulfilling. The idea of never kissing him again made her chest ache, but she wouldn't force herself on him, either. Not when he loved someone else. She bit her lip and glanced up, her cheeks heating.

"You're right. No more kissing."

"Is not what--" Bojan closed his eyes, groaning low in his throat. He cradled her face, kissing her firmly. When he released her mouth, she drew in a shaky breath.

Wow.

Licking the salt from her lips, she stared. Had he changed his mind about her? Tossed his feelings for Jovana aside? Her throat tightened and she whispered, "Why'd you do that?"

A loud sigh escaped him. He spoke slowly as if to make sure she understood every word, "I say for many times. I *want bakni*, for kiss you." He cracked a broad grin and slid his hands into his back pockets. "Is also very nice. I must *bakni*. Is good for heart."

He paused and tapped his chest, swaggering like a rogue.

Strange fluttering gyrations moved her heart as she drank in the dusky hue in his eyes. Without commenting, she slid onto the leather seat of his Hummer. Pondering the depth of her response to his kiss, she wondered if it would be wise to do that again. Especially with his old flame in the picture...

*****

Bojan stepped into his Hummer on shaky legs and started the engine. He still couldn't believe she'd kissed him first. And then complicating things further, he'd kissed her right back with such intensity it had scared him senseless. The thrill rippling through him when their lips connected had surpassed his loftiest expectation. Now he really had to watch himself.

He could forget his faith if he lingered too long in her arms. Not because he didn't love Jesus with his whole heart, but because his flesh cried for more. His recent struggles with loneliness didn't help matters.

Glancing over at Laney, he acknowledged the hint of pleasure forming on her lips as she pinched her eyes closed and smiled, while clutching her purse against her chest. Poor thing, she must be trying to sleep through the terror again. With a sigh, he focused on the road.

The setting sun pierced his vision as he entered the circular on-ramp. Blinking against the glare, his eyes blinded for a moment. Tires screeched and he jerked the wheel to the right. Laney screamed as the impact jarred them both sideways. Everything seemed to go in slow motion as he felt the impact of metal crunching metal.

The airbags exploded with a loud pop -- like gunfire, making the air whoosh from his lungs.

Taking a shaky breath, he choked on the dust. His pulse hammered as he wiped powder from his now-stinging cheeks.

Laney!

Chapter Fifteen

Laney's muscles ached, and her face stung as if she'd been slapped. She gave herself a mental shake. Had she just been in her first car accident? Glancing to the side, she found Bojan releasing his seatbelt and searching her eyes. Terror rushed through her veins, setting her nerves on edge the moment she realized she was trapped...

"You okay?"

She trembled deep inside, the sensation growing more pronounced until she felt a scream burst from her lips. Everything blurred as the hair on her arms stood on end. She had to get out of there. *Run!*

Lunging for the door, she yanked the handle. Bojan grabbed her waist and pulled her back.

"You must calm down. Stay inside for police."

"No! I can't..." She pulled away from him, but his arms tightened around her.

"Must calm down. I pray for..." He spoke in a foreign language. As she fought him, the sound of his melodic words grew louder. Wrestling with all her strength, she reached for his face, but he blocked her hands, holding them down.

With one last grunt she moaned, and then screamed. "Help! Help me!"

"You must stop. Police may think I hurt for you. Is not good." His eyes widened, and his gaze darted around.

Ignoring his plea, she shouted even louder. "Let me outta here!"

With a groan, Bojan said aloud, "Help. Please God." Before she could take another breath, his lips covered hers, and her protests died in her throat.

At that moment every ounce of fear and pain she'd bottled up inside intensified. Yet, instead of clawing him and trying to hurt him, she pulled him against her and plunged her fingers into his hair. Her lips caressed his with fervor, and she kept deepening the kiss until the world started spinning.

Bojan pushed away first and panted, "Is... is enough."

"No," she frowned, then lunged for his mouth again.

He chuckled and shoved her gently away. "Must stop. Is very dangerous for kissing like..."

"It's not wrong."

"For me is wrong. Much wrong for thinking more for you than kiss. I must stop."

The worried look in his eyes made her pause. She blinked back tears and could feel her chin trembling. "What do you mean? You kissed me first."

"I kiss you for stop you from screaming. Scared is okay, but scream is not okay. You must calm down." He touched her cheek and gazed tenderly into her eyes. "Feeling okay now?"

Laney sucked air into her lungs and exhaled a shaky breath. "I...I think so." Willing herself not to cry, she closed her eyes and counted to ten.

When she opened them again, she saw that Bojan had focused his attention elsewhere, and he now peered through the windshield. She followed his gaze and spotted a truck overturned on the second concrete island. The front end of the vehicle had caved in. Dread sucked the air from her lungs. Had the other passengers survived the crash?

"What happened?" She stared, not really seeing the wreckage, remembering instead the accident that had taken Sam's life. Willing the bloody visions to cease, she blinked several times and tried to focus on Bojan's face.

"I not see truck. Sun shined in my eyes."

She rubbed her face and coughed, just now realizing the itchy powder from the air bags really irritated her skin, and she dusted off as much as she could.

Bojan reached into a compartment and pulled out a folded cloth. "Truck hit hard, so must had drive too fast." He watched her tenderly as she stared at him. "Here, is for to wipe beautiful face."

Rolling her eyes, she took the cloth and rubbed her face clean. "I'm not that beautiful, Bojan. You're just trying to make me feel better."

"I never lie about beauty." He winked. "Now for we kiss on lips, you must call me Boki. Is familiar -- how you say... nickname. Like Laney is beautiful nickname."

"Ha ha ha. I think you like to flatter me too much."

He watched her wipe her face and whispered, "You must learn for accept good -- hmmm... how say... is good compliment for me. I much sincere." He touched his chest and tapped the area over his heart.

When she finished, she handed him the rag, and he wiped his face and hands. His eyes stayed on hers.

She stared back, still reeling from the accident and the kiss. Her doubts about his old girlfriend returned, taunting her. "Sure. Whatever."

Sirens shrieked, growing louder as they approached. Her heartbeat sped up, and panic squeezed her throat. She fought the urge to try and make another break for it.

"Do you think we should get out?" Laney asked in a tight voice, praying the other people weren't seriously injured.

"I think stay for police, then ask for help."

"Okay. That's a... good idea." She frowned and rubbed her stomach where her purse had smashed her gut when the air bag went off. Nothing felt broken, just bruised.

Bojan hadn't been exaggerating when he said the Hummer would keep them safe. Of course, their vehicle looked like a tank compared to the mangled pickup on the curb.

They watched as men hopped from emergency vehicles to check on the passengers. Police cordoned off the road and redirected traffic. One officer approached their window.

"Is everyone okay in here?"

"We... we think so, Officer," Laney replied, swallowing hard. "Are those people going to be okay?"

The officer shook his head. "Don't know, but it doesn't look good. Couple of kids drinking. The usual. The inside of the cab smells like a brewery. It's sad."

Bojan asked, "Officer, you think Hummer need tow?"

The policeman stepped back and surveyed the damage. "If you take it slow you may be able to drive it into town. But first we need to get photos of the damage to the back end on the driver's side. It shouldn't take long. Why don't you call your garage and let them know you're coming?"

Laney's hands shook as she listened. She still couldn't believe she'd been in a wreck, just like she'd always feared. Yet she was unharmed except for bruising from the seatbelt and irritating powder from the air bags. Not sure if her shaking limbs were due more to relief for her safety, or her reaction to the trauma, she reached for Bojan's hand and squeezed it.

He glanced at her with sad eyes. "Sorry for accident. But now you see Hummer is safe for drive, yes?"

She nodded. "My heart feels like it's going to explode, but my body isn't hurt."

"Is good." His warm smile helped her to relax. "Now we pray for people hurt in truck."

Agreeing with him in prayer, she whispered, "Amen."

They sat in silence as they waited for the emergency crew to deal with the other vehicle and its passengers. She could swear Bojan had tears in his eyes as he watched the drama unfold. She had to suppress the rising emotion in her throat in response. Just because the accident had shaken her up, didn't mean she had to lean on him for support again, though she wanted to.

In fact, she hoped he understood she didn't normally act that way in a crisis. Rubbing the fur on her sleeves, she shivered. The heater had kicked off when the engine stopped running.

"You cold?"

She couldn't help smiling at the innocent little boy expression in his eyes. Emotionally spent, she nodded and scooted closer, leaning over the console until he surrounded her with his well-muscled arms. She could feel his warm breath on her cheek as she cuddled against him.

"Hmmmm... nice." Nuzzling him, she closed her eyes and waited it out.

Minutes later, Bojan kissed her cheek. "I think officer is ready for you and me."

The officer took Bojan's statement first, and then took hers. When they finished, Bojan started the engine. "Must do seatbelt first."

Reaching over, she put on her seatbelt. Bojan already had his clipped together. "Where are we going now?"

He grabbed her hand and gave it a gentle squeeze before driving. "Hummer need fixed so I must bring for auto shop."

She rubbed her forehead. "Man, that sure was a scary accident."

"Is head hurt? You need go for hospital?"

"I'm just sore. We might as well go home."

*****

Bojan prayed as he drove to the mechanic. The damage to his vehicle was minimal compared to the totaled truck. He felt sorry for those kids. He honestly hadn't seen them coming. They must have been speeding and lost control around the bend.

He glanced over at Laney, who had her head resting against the window. Thankfully, she wasn't seriously injured.

He noticed her limbs weren't shaking as much as they had been earlier. Reaching for her hand, he stroked her knuckles with his thumbs -- the gesture quickly becoming a habit for him. She smiled and closed her eyes.

When they reached the shop, he touched her arm. "Wait for me inside?" He nodded at the room where he had to go fill out paperwork to have his Hummer checked.

Once Laney was safely inside, he allowed himself to inspect the vehicle more closely. The place where the truck hit his vehicle had caused less damage than he'd anticipated, but he'd need some bodywork done, and an alignment for sure. After arranging for a cab, Bojan entered the waiting area.

"Need a ride back, sir?" The attendant looked at him, then smiled with obvious appreciation at Laney.

Bojan didn't like the gleam in the man's eyes when he stared at her, so he shot him a hardened look. "I call cab for ride. No need from you, but thanks for offer."

"Anytime." The man frowned and slinked from the room.

Bojan reached for Laney's hand and led her outside. Neither spoke as a cab pulled up. He stepped toward the cab, still holding her hand, and felt her stiffen.

"I thought I could do it... but I'm not sure I can get in the car. Your Hummer was safe, but that cab..." She stared at her shoes, as if trying to get a grip on her anxiety.

"I promise I keep you safe if I must throw body down for protect you from accident." He touched her chin.

Her head snapped up. "What did you just say? You'd throw your

89

body in front of me?" A broad smile covered her face, and the tension in her shoulders eased. "That's funny, but it wouldn't do any good."

"You know what I mean. Prays first, then ride in car, yes?" He waved at the cab, then dipped his head, "I pray for God keep us safe for drive to homes. Amen."

Squeezing both of her hands, he waited until she looked up, and then nodded. "Is okay. You go first."

She stood still, tensing as she glanced at the vehicle, then at him. Her eyes widened. "I'm feeling... faint."

"Then I must carry." He scooped her into his arms and crouched over to place her in the cab. Once he'd settled her in, he slipped in beside her.

The cabbie pulled out of the parking lot, and Laney paled. She wrenched one hand from his and placed it over her mouth. "I feel sick," she whispered, her hand shaking.

"Then I must pray more." Bojan spoke in his native tongue this time and urged God to cover Laney with His peace and cover her with protecting angels. The next thing he knew, they'd pulled up in front of his RV. "Please, wait. I come right back."

"I'm coming with you." Laney reached for him, and he helped her from the car. She was unsteady on her feet, swaying slightly. He touched her hands and kissed her knuckles. "Wait on front step. Be right back."

Minutes later he emerged with Dude and his traveling cage filled with dog food, toys, and treats. "Is what you need for Dude." He nodded at the carrying case.

Smiling, Laney held out her arms. "Give me Dude. I'll hold onto him."

Dude watched Laney and barked several times. Bojan whispered, "*Mallchi,* Dude, shush..." in his dog's ear. As he rubbed his pet's head he added, "Laney will take good care of you."

Laney tipped her head and asked, "What did you say to him to get him to stop barking?"

"Is secret." Bojan winked.

*****

He couldn't believe his luck when he saw Laney leaving the antique shop. He'd been hired on that morning for weekend deliveries. If Laney had ordered furniture, he'd make sure he delivered it. And he'd bring the deaf kid.

He wouldn't hear her scream.

Chapter Sixteen

Laney tried to be brave, and this time didn't complain when she got back into the cab. Instead, she closed her eyes and held Dude against her chest and rubbed her cheek against his ears.

His doggy tongue lapped at her mouth several times, but she pulled back before he made contact. The pleading look in the Chihuahua's eyes made her giggle. Dude played the lover boy well, just like his owner. But was it a game for Bojan, or did he mean what he'd said?

Chancing a look at the confident Macedonian beside her, Laney offered a shy smile.

Bojan winked. "Dude is very smart. I am much jealous."

Smirking, she teased, "You're the one who stopped."

"Ah, but I no mean I am not smart in all things. Good with Bible, yes. Not so good with women."

"That's not true." She slapped his arm with her palm.

"Is very true. My English is bad and I say stupid words and get you so mad for me."

"I'm mad for you, all right." She averted her gaze when she felt her cheeks heat. Where had that bold thought come from?

Several seconds passed, and Laney glanced at him, wondering why he remained silent. The concern in his eyes made her pause. "What's wrong?"

He adjusted the items and placed the dog carrier on the cab floor. "What I say is wrong for make you mad?"

"I have no idea what you're talking about." She glanced down at the contented animal on her lap.

"You say you mad for me." He touched her chin, causing her to turn toward him. The woeful look in his eyes made her heart clench.

"I'm not mad *at* you, I'm mad *for* you. That means I'm nuts about you, silly." She flushed and bit her lip.

"I much stupid. I still not understand what mean nuts for me." The poor guy looked so confused, she had to do something significant to help him understand.

With a heavy sigh, she tipped her face toward him and gave him the warmest, wettest kiss she could manage. "That, my sweet man, was to show you what I mean when I say I'm nuts for you."

A wry grin tugged at his mouth, and he whispered huskily, "Then I much peanut butter and cashews for you."

She giggled nervously when he winked.

Maybe he was better at English than she'd thought. He obviously had her on that one.

"Well, I'm pecans and almonds for you, then." She batted her eyelashes. Okay, now she'd completely lost it.

She'd never flirted so much in her life, not even with Sam when they'd first met. But Bojan seemed to be enjoying her teasing. So why stop?

His lids lowered and he smiled. "You taste like *med*."

"What's med? Sounds gross."

"Is not gross. *Med* is honey. Tastes sweeter than *jagodas in shekjer*, than strawberries in sugar."

"You gonna start calling me honey now?" Ack, had she really said that?

He laughed. "Honey or sugar sounds more nice for say than pumpkin lovers."

The cab stopped in her driveway.

Having no clue what he'd meant, she grinned and said, "I'd better get out of here. Now you're confusing me." She reached for her purse. Dude stirred on her lap and craned his neck as if checking with Bojan to make sure it was okay to leave.

Bojan made a clicking sound with his tongue and rattled off a command in Macedonian. Dude yipped.

Reaching into his back pocket, Bojan pulled out his wallet. He handed the cab driver a twenty and said, "Wait until I ready for leave, yes?"

The cabbie glanced at the twenty. "You're the boss."

After Bojan helped her from the car, he leaned forward. "Is cab man think I boss because I give money for tip?"

She snorted. "No, silly. That's just an expression. It means yes, or sure thing. Something like that."

Shaking his head, he clucked his tongue. "I never understand you American slang phrases. Too many things make for no sense for me."

He walked her to her door with his arms loaded. He'd brought enough pet items to care for a pack of dogs.

Adjusting Dude and her purse on one side, she reached for her keys and opened the front door. She tipped her head toward the table in the foyer.

"Just set the stuff down there. I'll put it away later."

Bending down, she set Dude on the Berber carpet. He danced around Bojan's legs and scratched his jeans several times before Bojan picked him up.

"Yes, Dude, I will not forget you. Now you must listen. Is job for dog for protect woman alone in big house. Baby come home tomorrow, but will be much weak for days. Dude must be strong dog for me."

The little dog bared his teeth and offered the most ferocious snarl Laney had ever seen. Her heart lurched and she jumped back. "Does he bite?"

Bojan grinned. "Dude is showing best bark for protect you. Not hurt you, but if a person tries for hurt, then Dude tear up man's legs. Is very scarier when angry, yes?" He rubbed Dude's tummy and set him down.

*****

Laney's heart raced. While the explanation about Dude's posturing to protect her made sense, it had still scared her to see him snarling like that. But it was too late to back down now. She and Dude would have to find a way to get along for nearly two weeks.

"You worry?" He touched her arm, making every nerve hum in response. *Bad, bad idea.* Alone with Bojan, in the dark. In her house. And what about Jovana? Thankfully, the cabbie was waiting, or she'd be an even worse mess.

"I'll be fine." Glancing up, she noted the concern in his eyes, and it touched her deeply. "I will, I promise."

"Then I promise for call tomorrow and next day so you know I got for my country safe." His voice lowered, "Unless you not want me--"

"Don't be silly. Of course I want you to call." She scuffed the floor with her shoe. While she wanted to say good-bye, kissing in parting seemed too intimate after their last tangle. Her emotions in a tizzy, she worried how she should handle it if he did kiss her.

His hand touched the side of her face. Moments later his lips brushed her forehead. "Take care, my *prijatelka,* my friend. *S'agapo.*"

He stepped back and gazed at her. The warm look in his eyes made her toes tingle. Maybe she'd misread him. Maybe Jovana wasn't a threat after all.

"What does that mean, *s'agapo?*"

A low rumble came from deep within as he chuckled. "Is Greek word. I not tell you what *s'agapo* means. Is surprise for my *prijatelka.*"

Placing one hand on her hip, she playfully stomped her foot. "That's not fair. I don't know any other languages."

"Then I must teach." He winked and bent down to pat Dude on the head. "Be good, Dude. Care for Laney and protect."

Dude yipped, bouncing on his front feet.

His dog's answer sounded almost like a 'yes'. Her nerves tensed when she realized he would be leaving any minute. She didn't want to see him go. Glancing up, she captured his gaze and licked her lips.

His eyes traveled to her mouth. That stupid habit was going to get her in big trouble one of these days. But she couldn't help it. The tension in her body caused that automatic response.

"You want *bakni* before I go?" The soft sound of his voice made her knees weak.

What does a girl say to an offer like that? No? She'd be a fool to turn him down. So instead, she nodded, her eyes never leaving his.

Everything transpired in slow motion as he stepped closer. She could hear the sound of his erratic breathing and held her breath. His lips hovered and met hers in a tentative manner at first. Then he draped his arms around her as he angled his head to caress her lips more fully. He secured the back of her head with one hand as he suckled her, engaging one lip at a time, and exploring her mouth with abandon. The desperate, husky moans emitting from low in his throat made her body hum. His tongue slid against hers in an intimate dance and her body pulsed as she pressed against him. She wanted more, needed more. It didn't matter that they hadn't known each other very long. She yearned for intimacy. To experience things with him she had no business desiring. Not yet.

When he pulled away, an intense, bereft void filled that place, making her throat tighten. She couldn't say what she really felt. What she wanted to do was beg to go with him. Worse, to make love to him so he wouldn't forget her.

But that would be too needy, and she realized he wouldn't want her to come with him. His business was personal, and she had no part in it. The thought saddened her.

"Ah, Laney, your lips are sweet like *med*. Your eyes remind me of blue lake near hometown. So deep and wonderful." He touched her cheek. "But we must wait."

She swallowed hard and bit her lip. He was right, of course, but it didn't make the desire pulsing in her go away. Her body throbbed, and oh, it was a heady feeling.

"I call you soon. I must go now." His large fingers stroked the side of her head, tracing her cheek, her jaw, until his hand touched her chin and slowly slipped away.

She sensed his eyes on her and she nodded, refusing to look at him for fear she'd get tearful again. A sob crept up her throat, and she squelched the pain.

The door clicked shut. She leaned against the frame and sucked in a breath as she tried to keep her tears at bay. "God, help me. The way I feel... This can't be right."

Trust me. And wait.

She knew God did not exist directly above her head, and that His spirit lived within her heart, but she still glanced up and whispered, "I want to, Lord. Help my unbelief."

Chapter Seventeen

The next morning Bojan waited for his ride to the Tucson airport. Johnny had agreed to take him in the company car. As he sat on the couch missing his dog, he laughed to himself. In Macedonia dogs were not given the extravagant attention Americans gave their pets. His family would think he was too soft if they knew how much he loved on his feisty Chihuahua.

He admired the picture of his sister on the end table and imagined their reunion. What would he say to her? I'm sorry? Or, I missed you, Jovana, my long-lost sister. Welcome home.

He'd have to pray for the right words.

How Bojan wished Jovana had listened to him. Dating a gypsy was totally unacceptable to his parents, and they both knew it. He should never have agreed to keep her secret from them. If he hadn't, she might have gotten over Georg before things had gotten so out of hand.

He'd never expected her to run off with the man, especially given the gypsy's known history of criminal activity and abuse of women and children. Why hadn't she listened and stayed away from Georg? Well, he'd find out in about twenty-four hours.

Lord, help me to be a vessel of love, not condemnation.

If what his parents had said about her current appearance was true -- and he had no reason to doubt them -- then she probably already condemned herself. She needed love and acceptance, not judgment. He could give her what she needed. Christ had also loved him in his most unlovable state. He could offer her no less.

The insistent beep of a horn outside alerted him that Johnny had arrived.

Bojan locked up his RV, grabbed his suitcase and briefcase, and met Johnny outside. "Thank so much for drive for airport."

"Hey, it's the least I can do, boss."

"I must thank." Bojan set his bags in the backseat and climbed into the car next to his employee.

A package lay on the seat between them. "What is gift?"

"It's for you. Like I said, it's the least I could do..." Johnny pulled onto the road and headed north.

"Like I said before, I have no need for stuff. You need money for care for family." He nudged the present back.

"Come on. Open it first. I bought it with the extra tip money you gave me. It wasn't very expensive, and I can't return it. I lost the receipt." Johnny kept his eyes on the road, so Bojan couldn't tell if he was being straightforward or not. "Besides, you're always helping people. Are you too proud to receive it?"

"Okay. I accept gift." Bojan hadn't received a present from anyone in almost a year, so it was nice that his employee had bought him something to take on the trip. That was totally unexpected.

Tearing the paper from the package, he found a book and read the title aloud.

"*Idioms for Idiots.* Hey, thanks, Johnny. Is great gift." His sarcastic tone was meant to sound playful, because Johnny had said it was part of American male culture to tease others.

The title actually struck him as funny. Sometimes he truly felt like an idiot. "But I no understand what is idiom."

"Idioms are slang phrases. I know you struggle with them. Go ahead. Read the subtitle."

"*A pocket guide of common American phrases and slang for people who speak English as a second language.*" Bojan ran his fingers over the book and smiled. "Is very full of thoughts and is kind gift, Johnny. I read on plane when I... how you say... bored?"

"That's what I figured, boss." Johnny grinned, obviously pleased with himself.

Bojan's thoughts drifted to Laney. Now maybe he would understand some of those things that used to trip him up. Maybe when he returned home he could really dazzle her with his understanding of idioms. The notion made his heart flutter. He sorely missed her, and he hadn't even left yet.

Laney.

Everything about her was sweet and wonderful. A chuckle escaped his lips when he realized the antique dresser would arrive today. He could almost hear her squeal with delight. The thought of her bliss made his heart pound.

She would love his gift. Maybe now she would see that he really did care very much for her -- that he felt something beyond friendship. Hopefully she'd realize he didn't want to kiss her and run -- that she meant more to him.

As they drove in silence, he flipped through the pages. Some of the phrases sounded ridiculous. Like the apple of one's eye. The idiom referred to being the object of one's affection. He couldn't imagine saying with his voice full of emotion, "Laney, you is the apple of my eye."

Did people really talk like that? He chuckled and read further. Beating around the bush meant avoiding something. Who'd have thought it would mean that? He snickered.

"Some of that stuff is crazy, huh, boss?"

"Yes, is much nuts, but I like." He remembered the phrase from last night, and when Johnny snorted, he knew he'd said it correctly. He was finally getting the language expressions figured out. At least some of them, anyway.

"Why say think and thought, but not thunk and thank?"

"You got me there. I'm not an English expert."

"Hmmm... Listen for this one. Break the ice. It means to remove tension, help people relax. What is ice breaking have with people having much tension? It make no sense."

He flipped the book shut. Maybe later he'd read more. For now, he just wanted to reflect on his last meeting with Laney. Her lips had felt so soft, so warm and tender. His whole body heated at the memory. He couldn't wait to see her again.

No one had ever touched him as deeply as Laney had with her woeful blue eyes, the color of ripe *borovinkas*, of blueberries. So beautiful and expressive. He loved making her smile. A sigh escaped him, and he closed his eyes with the image of her face still fresh on his mind.

Before he knew it, they'd arrived at the airport. It was going to be a very long day, even longer than a twenty-four hour actual day. Macedonia's time zone would put him eight hours ahead. He'd have major jetlag. Hopefully, he could sleep on some of the flights.

He hated flying halfway around the world. There were two layovers, one in Texas and another in New York City. Then he'd be on his way to Athens via Olympic Airlines, then home to the airport in Skopje, Macedonia.

Though Slavic in ethnicity, his Middle Eastern appearance would probably make the guards pay closer attention to him than to the average passenger on his flight. Despite his last name being Trajkovski rather than Ali, airport security never took travelers with Mediterranean features lightly. He couldn't blame them, but that didn't make the security checks feel any less invasive.

Pulling out his Orthodox cross necklace, he displayed it over his dress shirt. Maybe the airport security would see the symbol of his faith and give him a break on at least a few flights. Optimistic, he knew, but a guy had to at least give it a try.

*****

Laney woke to the sound of her telephone ringing. Was Bojan calling to say good-bye? She rushed to the phone, but before she had a chance to answer it, the ringing ceased. With no caller ID and no answering machine, she had no way to know whom to call back. One of these days she'd catch up to the rest of the world when it came to technology. Once she could afford it.

She groaned and climbed back into bed, realizing she didn't even have his cell phone number. How would she call him back? In the midst of her tension last night she should have asked him for his number. But she'd been too focused on kissing him and wanting him in ways she had no business contemplating. Now she was paying for it.

If she worked on her transcribing assignments, the Internet would be on part of the day, which would tie up her line. But she had to work or she'd have no income.

Glancing over at Baby's bed in the corner, she took in the sight of Dude sleeping. He'd curled up against the toy Chihuahua the mystery person had given her. Laney felt a twinge of pain vibrating in her chest. She missed Baby so much.

Hopefully her dog wouldn't be seething that Dude had used her bed and left his scent all over it. She smiled. Dude didn't smell that badly, for a dog, anyway. Obviously, Bojan took good care of his beloved pet.

Bojan... She missed him already. His smile. His kind eyes. His deep, husky voice and thickly accented English. Her heart pounded as she pictured his face in her mind. Remembered his luscious kisses.

The way he'd looked at her with such desire in his eyes before he'd kissed her last night made her head all woozy. Even Sam, as wonderful as he had been, couldn't hold a candle to Bojan when it came to overall sex appeal.

Her heart seemed to thaw a little more each time she gazed into his intense golden brown eyes. The feelings bubbling within her chest scared her, yet intrigued her even more.

What if Bojan never came back? What if he decided after seeing Jovana that he wanted to be with her again? What if he changed his mind about wanting to be friends...who kiss? Could she handle that now that she'd experienced the kind of hunger a woman feels for a man? Insatiable hunger.

The list of things she could obsess over was longer than the dirt road that snaked down the mountain. She had no control over the what-ifs. But she could pray for strength.

Talk to me.

She pulled the covers up to her chin and blinked back tears. Did God really want to hear from her after all this time? She'd shot up a brief prayer or two since meeting Bojan and had felt God's presence and peace on several occasions, but could she bare her soul to Him now?

Deep inside, she knew He would listen and accept her no matter what she'd said, but it didn't make the raw vulnerability she felt in His presence any easier.

Dude must have sensed her emotion because he hopped up onto the end table, then catapulted onto the bed, plopping down on the pillow near her face. He started to lick the tears from her eyes. It brought to mind the scripture that said the Lord would wipe away every tear.

"Oh, Jesus, I'm sorry I've neglected You."

The feel of Dude's wet tongue and scent of his doggy breath made her smile. Giggling, she grabbed Dude around the tummy, and held him under her chin, rubbing her cheek against his soft fur. "Good morning, Dude. Maybe you'll meet Baby today. Would you like that?"

Dude sighed and snuggled closer. She had the funniest thought. What if Dude understood Greek and could tell her what *s'agapo* meant?

Holding him in front of her face, she whispered, "Dude, tell me what *s'agapo* means."

A little yip escaped his lips and he licked her nose. She sputtered. "What does *s'agapo* mean? Tell me."

Dude's tongue came out again, and he started licking her with tenacity. She pulled him away so he couldn't reach her with his tongue. "Does it mean lick? Is that it? I want to lick you? Or maybe it's a special kind of kiss?"

Though disconcerting, the thought made her smile. Dude really was smart, just like Bojan had said. Well, when Bojan called her she would show him how smart she was and she'd tell him *s'agapo* in her huskiest voice. Maybe he'd miss her even more. Then he'd want to come home sooner.

Maybe...

After lying curled under the quilt for several more minutes, she decided to get up and shower. The clock said it was already eleven o'clock. She'd never slept that late before, not even on weekends.

Thirty minutes later she emerged with a towel wrapped around her head and her thick terry cloth robe tied snugly against her waist. She wondered what airport Bojan was in right now. Maybe he was still in Tucson.

The cordless phone rang, and she nearly jumped out of her fuzzy pink slippers. This time she'd make it to the phone in time. Lunging, she grabbed it and answered with a breathless "Hello?"

Chapter Eighteen

Bojan shifted in his seat. His first-class accommodations were more than comfortable, but his legs still felt restless. The stewardess handed him a pair of headphones. "For the movie, if you wish to see it."

"What is movie playing?"

"I'm not sure. A love story, I think. I'll have to check."

"No, is okay. No need headphones for movie. Take." He handed them back to the young woman.

The last thing he needed was a movie that would make him yearn for Laney more. She already consumed his thoughts.

Closing his eyes, he drifted off to sleep. One more stop in New York and they'd cross the Atlantic. He'd be that much closer to home.

He opened his eyes when the stewardess tapped his arm. "Would you like turkey or roast beef?" She waited as he folded down his tray.

"Turkey, please."

"Would you like tomato juice with that?"

He lifted his hand. "No thanks. Water, please."

She set his food on his tray and opened a bottle of Perrier water. "Enjoy your meal."

Glancing up at the movie screen as he chewed his sandwich, he watched as a young couple embraced, then kissed deeply. He had to look away before he allowed his mind to wander where it shouldn't. Suddenly his meal looked ten times more appealing, and he focused on the bubbles in the green bottle.

Minutes later, he finished eating and chanced a look at the movie screen. That same couple now argued with passion until the man finally stormed out. Wasn't love just like that? Amazing, yet painful. Wonderful and rich, and yet confusing. But for Bojan, it was still worth it.

His mind drifted to Laney again. He couldn't believe he'd told her he loved her. Good thing she didn't know the language or he might've scared her off.

Sometimes the frightened look in her eyes after they kissed made strange things happen to his heart. She seemed afraid of her own feelings. A flashback flitted through his mind and made him shift uncomfortably in his seat. Never before had a simple kiss made him feel so crazy inside. So excited.

Forcing his mind to dwell on other things, he glanced at the movie screen. The young couple was going at it again. Watching them made him ache for Laney even more. He sighed and pulled out his book of Idioms.

*****

"What do you mean you tried to call me earlier?" Laney's throat tightened. She had to pick up Baby before the hospital closed at noon or she'd have to pay for more days in the hospital. She didn't have the money, and Bojan wasn't around to help.

"I'm sorry, ma'am, but this office is closing in thirty minutes. If you don't make it here in time you'll have to wait until Monday when the doctor returns from his trip."

"Can't someone else release my dog to me?"

"That's against policy. I'm sorry. Just call a cab and you'll be fine. I'll be waiting for you."

"Okay. I'll call a cab. Please, wait until the very last minute. Please." Her voice sounded desperate. Truthfully, she was. How would she get a cab that fast? She had to try.

Hanging up the phone, she dialed the number she had memorized for AAA Cab Company.

"Dispatch."

"Yes, I need a cab. Is one available? It's kind of an emergency." She swallowed hard and gave her address.

"All of our cabs are out right now. The soonest I can have one out to you is forty-five minutes. Will that work for you?" The woman's tone sounded sympathetic.

"No. I need to be somewhere in thirty."

"Can you ask a neighbor for a ride?"

She hadn't thought of that. "Maybe that's what I'll do. Thanks."

Racing to her closet, she stripped off her robe and pulled on her undergarments, jeans, and a sweatshirt. Running a comb through her hair, she grabbed a pair of sneakers with her free hand. Time was critical. Her pulse raced as she tried to calm her breathing.

The doorbell rang. Could God have sent help, or was it just another distraction? The only way to find out was to check. Hopefully, it was border patrol or someone safe. Otherwise, she didn't know what she'd do.

The comb had stuck in a tangle, and she stubbed her toes as she stepped quickly down the stairs and turned the corner. Hopping on one foot, she stopped long enough to peer through the peephole. A tall man and a shorter one, who looked more like a teenager, stood on her landing. They were both blondes. "Who is it?"

The man smiled and tipped his head toward the large moving truck behind him. "We have a delivery from *Finders Keepers.*"

She opened the door to get a better look, as she had no time to waste. Upon closer examination, she noted the older of the two wore a cap and glasses, and sported a neatly trimmed goatee, effectively hiding his face. A tattoo sprawled over the left side of his neck -- a mermaid with a naked torso.

Not a good sign.

A nervous-sounding laugh burst from her. "You must have the wrong house. I didn't order anything."

He pulled a piece of paper from his back pocket. "It says right here, Laney Cooper. Is that your name?"

"Yes, but--"

"Then it's yours. We're just here to deliver the thing."

She bit her lower lip. "Now is a really bad time. I need to get to the animal hospital. It's about a three-mile walk, and I have less than fifteen minutes to get there. Can you wait for me?"

"You ain't our only delivery." He offered a plastic smile. "But maybe we can give you a quick ride, then come back and set up. Would that work?" The intensity in his voice made her uneasy, but did she have a choice? At least the kid with him looked safe. Though muscular, he couldn't be more than seventeen.

"O-okay. Let's do that. Give me a sec, and I'll get my purse." She raced up the stairs, grabbed her purse, and paused to lock up Dude in the closet. "Come on. I don't want to be late."

She jogged to the delivery truck -- a medium-size Mercedes Benz -- and sucked in her breath, but not from the pain in her foot. At least the vehicle was large up front, like a tractor-trailer. She'd be safe, right?

The older man with the tattoo and bulging muscles opened her door. "After you, ma'am." Again, the plastic smile.

Why did he give her the creeps?

She had to grab the side of the door to climb in. Hands pushed on her backside, and squeezed. She flushed, her blood boiling with a mixture of fear and anger.

Not good at all.

Glaring with her eyes leveled at him, she spoke with conviction as she pointed in his face.

"Don't touch me like that again. I don't need a boost. I'm perfectly fine. Understood?"

The man smirked and raised his hands. "Sorry, I was just trying to help."

She didn't believe him, but desperate for a ride, she shoved the concern from her mind. Her hands refused to listen and trembled as she tightened the seatbelt. She had to get Baby, so she'd make herself tolerate him.

The only thing that kept her from getting sick was the size of the cab. When the teenager climbed in, and she was sandwiched between the men, she started sweating. Maybe it really was a bad idea.

"Ready, honey?" The driver chuckled and squeezed her knee, then rested his hand on her thigh.

She stiffened and removed his hand. "I just need a ride. That's all."

"Fine." The tension in his voice worried her, but she ignored her sense of discomfort.

They drove in silence, and she started to relax. The boy pulled out a pack of gum and shoved a few pieces in his mouth. He offered some to her. Without speaking, she dismissed him, and he put the gum away.

The kid started chewing and cracking his gum until it grated on her nerves. Right when she was ready to put her hands over her ears so she wouldn't scream, they pulled up in front of the hospital. The clock on the dash said 11:59.

One minute before closing.

The teen got out and she hopped down, ignoring the ache in her foot. "I'll be right back." Running to the door, she yanked it open. "I made it," she shouted.

"Good. This dog here misses you, huh, Baby?" The older woman picked up Baby and handed her to Laney.

Baby's vet nodded at Laney, then grabbed his keys. "Make sure she gets plenty of rest. She's still weak."

"Is there anything else I need to sign or do?" She blinked back tears and held the still weak-looking Chihuahua close. She kissed the top of Baby's head.

The woman pointed to the bottom of a form she set on the counter. "Sign here and you're free to go."

After scrawling her name, she left the building with Baby perched on her hip and her purse slung over her other shoulder. She did not want to ride back with that creepy man. But what choice did she have? Baby looked too weak to be carried the entire three-mile trek back to the house, and she already knew no cabs were available.

"Lord, help me."

She approached the moving truck and waited until the men finished their cigarettes.

"This is Baby. She's very thankful for the ride." With a weak grin, she allowed the teenager to open the door for her. She struggled to get into the large vehicle with her arms full. "Can you...?"

The youth pushed her up, but did so with tact, something his friend obviously knew nothing about. "Thank you," she whispered and struggled with her seatbelt. With Baby in her arms, she didn't feel scared at all. Well, not too much...

Was it possible she could be getting over her fear of riding in cars, or did it have more to do with the size of the vehicle she rode in? Whatever the reason, she rode back home without her stomach cramping for the first time in nearly a year, and it felt great.

The second they pulled up in front of her house, Tattoo Man turned and snapped, "Now, can we make this delivery so we can be on our way?"

A shock of his breath wafted by and she caught the faint scent of onions mixed with cigarettes. Her stomach cramped, but not because of the ride.

"Uh, sure.... Thank you for going out of your way for me. We appreciate it." She held up Baby's limp paw and had her wave at the man.

"No problem, honey." He paused for a moment, then turned his attention to the items in the back of his truck.

Curiosity overcame her, and she followed him and looked inside. The antique highboy dresser she'd longed for sat in the back of the truck. *No way!* Bojan had bought her the wardrobe of her dreams? Why would he do that?

Then it struck her. That's what he'd meant when he'd said he wanted something beautiful for her bedroom. He meant he wanted to buy her the dresser. And she'd gotten all over him.

The memory made her cheeks heat. Poor Bojan. She'd gotten mad at him three times now for no reason other than bad communication. When he called her later, she'd apologize right away.

Still stunned at the enormity of his gift, she watched as the men removed the furniture one item at a time and set it on her driveway. "Which way into the house, lady?"

Glancing at the garage, she decided to bring it in the back way. "Over here." She nodded at the garage and opened the door with the electronic key in her purse.

They grabbed the dresser and followed her as she led them to her bedroom. Her bed was unmade, and her robe and pajamas lay on the floor.

Self-conscious about the state of her room, she quickly removed the garments. "Um, can you guys set it over there?"

"Whatever you want, ma'am." His voice sounded sarcastic, confusing her about his meaning. She watched as he turned and pointed at the younger man and said something to him in sign language.

Why hadn't she noticed before that the boy hadn't spoken? She relaxed a little bit. Any man who spoke sign language couldn't be all that bad, could he? Praying her instincts about Tattoo Man were wrong, she turned to the door and paused.

She started to let Dude out of the room she'd locked him in, but he barked and yipped like a wild animal, reminding her of a rabid Tasmanian devil. No way would she chance him biting the delivery guys, even if the older one was creepy.

Setting Baby on her dog bed, she noticed that her Chihuahua's nose seemed to come alive and she sniffed around and whined. Uh-oh, Baby was unhappy that someone had slept in her bed, just as Laney had feared.

But after turning in circles three times, Baby plopped down and closed her eyes. Laney pulled the stuffed dog out from behind the bed and set it near Baby's nose. She sniffed the toy and sighed contentedly, then closed her eyes again.

Now if Laney could adjust so easily to changes in her life, that would be a miracle.

She still couldn't quite believe the present Bojan had given her. A broad smile covered her face. No man paid that much money for a gift if he wanted to be just friends.

When the guys finished, tattoo man signed something to the teenager and smiled. The young man grabbed the silver moving blanket, looked at her warily, then turned and left.

Chapter Nineteen

It took forever for the plane to park at JFK International. When Bojan looked at the clock he realized he had less than an hour before he was due to get on the next plane.

He entered a tram, lugging his carry-on bag and suitcase along. He sped as briskly as possible to the Olympic Airways boarding area. The heavenly aroma of cinnamon rolls and Starbucks coffee made his stomach grumble, but he couldn't stop without risking missing his flight.

By the time he arrived at the gate, the plane was already boarding passengers. He glanced at his Rolex. No time to call Laney. Hopefully, she would understand and not be angry with him. He would just have to explain that his flight had taken forever to taxi to the terminal.

And he wanted so much to hear her beautiful voice. All day the thought of talking to her -- the sultry way she said his name -- had kept him going. For an English-speaking woman, she pronounced his nickname, Boki, very well, and with affection evident in her pronunciation.

By the time he arrived in Athens, he'd worked himself into a frenzy, longing to speak with Laney. Or was it a sense of foreboding -- that something was wrong? Either way it would be too early in the morning to call. The time zone difference would make phoning any time a bit tricky.

Meanwhile, he closed his eyes and tried to rest. When sleep didn't come, he prayed for Laney. Within minutes he grew sleepy, and as he drifted off he hoped he'd dream of kissing her again.

*****

Laney wondered about the expression on the young man's face. A sudden sense of danger made her skin pebble in goose bumps.

The tattooed man approached her, bending down as he breathed in her ear. "How's about a tip, honey?"

The way he stood in front of her -- his sunglasses covering his eyes as he sneered behind his goatee -- made her skin crawl. She thought of the poor woman attacked in her home last year. A scream crept up her throat, but fear suppressed her voice, nearly paralyzing her.

Slowly backing up, she tried to think of a way to avoid trapping herself in her own bedroom. She gasped for breath as her pulse raced. Maybe someone would hear her if she screamed.

A sinking feeling, like concrete in her stomach, hit her full force. The deaf boy wouldn't hear her scream. Sweat beaded on her upper lip, and she swiped her face with her trembling hand.

"Let me get my purse. I'll be right--"

He grabbed her wrist, and twisted her arm. "You know what I mean, sugar."

She tried to wrest her arm from his, but he was too strong, and he twisted harder. Nausea made her stomach cramp as she sucked in the pain and tried to think. Jerking her head to the side, she noted that Baby slept soundly, unaware of the distress making Laney's pulse race.

Dude!

Bojan's dog was conspicuously quiet. Did he sense the danger? Would he be ready to pounce if she opened the door? She hoped her instincts were correct and as she fought the man, and steered her body toward the closet door.

The man's breath smelled of cinnamon, like freshly chewed gum, but still made her wince. There was something familiar -- and creepy about Tattoo Man, but she couldn't place him. He twisted her arm harder.

She cried out, the pain was so intense. "Please, don't hurt me. I'll give you anything. Please."

He hesitated as if considering her offer, and then loosened his grip. The smell of his perspiration made her stomach lurch, and she tried not to gag.

"I just want a little fun. Come on, sugar. Just give me one little kiss. You'll love it."

She screamed and turned her head away.

Now shaking, she prayed. "Please, God, help me!"

"Asking God to help won't do you no good, Laney. Neither will calling the cops. So don't even think about it," he hissed.

The way he said her name gave her the shivers. Something about his voice... She had to get away from him. But he was so strong.

Refusing to focus on her fear, she had to find a way to break free. With one last attempt to extract herself, she wrestled with him, then kneed him in the groin.

He hunched over and spewed foul threats.

Laney raced to the closet door, yanked the handle open, and then ran down the stairs screaming. She ripped the cordless phone from the wall and pushed the *ON* button.

Dude's barking echoed down the stairs. He snarled loud enough to make her hair curl. Still trembling, she ran outside, and with shaky hands dialed 911.

The man bellowed as he stumbled down the stairs and pushed past her, shoving her into the side of the house as he scrambled -- limping -- to the truck. Dude barked and chased behind him, hot on Tattoo Man's heels.

"9-1-1, what's your emergency?"

She placed a finger in her ear to block out the noise.

"There's a man in a yellow Mercedes moving van heading down Willow Lane toward Route 92. He just--" She clutched her stomach and sobbed. "He tried to assault me. He--"

"Is there a name on the side of the van?"

"No. It's just a plain yellow van. It doesn't say anything on the side."

"We're sending a squad car now. You said he's heading toward the highway?"

"Yes, but I live on a dirt road, so he can't drive very fast. If you hurry, you might catch him."

"We'll do our best."

The sound of pitiful yelping captured her attention as Dude stumbled toward her, swaying and limping.

She scooped him up into her arms, and he snarled at her.

"I have to go." Hanging up on the 911 operator, she tossed the phone on the sofa and tried to calm Dude.

"Did that man hurt you?" She carefully touched his rib area, and he snarled again. He looked so vicious when he bared his teeth that she almost dropped him. "It's okay. I won't touch you there again. I promise."

His ribs must be cracked or bruised. She could just about bet that sick man had kicked Dude in the ribs, and the brave dog had just now allowed himself to feel the pain. He was her hero.

All at once the realization of what had almost happened hit like a tsunami in the chest. She slammed the front door shut, clutching Dude against her as she set the alarm. A strangled moan tore from her throat.

Stumbling back over to the couch, she eased onto it and sobbed. "Oh, Jesus, thank You for helping me." She held Dude loosely and kissed his head. She swallowed hard and gazed down at the little brown dog. "And thank you for protecting me."

A chill zipped up her spine. Again, something about that man seemed so familiar, but she couldn't place it. She didn't know anyone with a goatee and tattoo on his neck, or anyone that knew sign language. She must be mistaken.

Still slightly hysterical, she wondered what she'd tell Bojan when he finally called to see how she fared. *By the way, Boki, the man who delivered the furniture you bought me assaulted me.*

No. That would freak him out. She didn't want him to feel guilty. Maybe she'd just tell him that Dude was worth his weight in gold, and then some...

*****

Bojan stretched to ease the stiffness in his neck and legs. The plane was finally preparing to land. Today he'd see his grandmother and aunts, uncles, and cousins, and his sister, for the first time in years. What a bittersweet reunion it would be.

He waited patiently as other people gathered their bags from the overhead bins, and then he exited the plane. The biting November wind penetrated his leather jacket. He'd lived in Arizona so long he'd forgotten how cold it could be in the Balkans.

Shrugging to keep his neck warm, and wishing he had a scarf, he held his briefcase against his hip and moved briskly toward the terminal. It would be the middle of the night in Arizona. He contemplated calling Laney as he patted the cell phone in his pocket and walked to the baggage claim area, but decided against it.

He could always wait until he got to his family's home, and then call her from there. Leaning against a post, he watched various pieces of luggage go by on a conveyor belt. When he spotted his black leather suitcase, he yanked it from the moving belt and dropped it at his side.

"*Kako si detto moya?*" How are you, my son? A familiar, deep voice approached from behind. His father often greeted him in Greek rather than Macedonian, though all members of his family spoke both languages fluently.

"*Dobro tatko moya, dobro.*" Papa, I'm well.

His father embraced him like they hadn't seen each other in years, when it had been only last month that they'd had dinner together at his father's home in Tempe. He kissed Bojan's cheek numerous times.

He waited, then kissed his father. Finally they broke apart. He allowed his father to carry his suitcase to the Fiat, while he carried his other bag. His *mayka* sat in the front seat and his *baba* sat in back.

A smile tugged at his mouth. His *baba* would smother him with more kisses than his father. Ah, but how he missed her. It had been four years since he last held her close.

"*Babo!*" He opened the door and slid into the back seat, only to be engulfed by her chubby arms. Those wonderful, strong arms that he missed so much. A lump knotted his throat as he inhaled her unique grandmotherly scent. It would be very hard for him to leave again. He'd forgotten how much he missed his family and culture.

On the drive to his family's home in Struga, near Lake Ohrid, he listened to his grandmother regale him with tales of things that had happened since he moved away. When he finally got a word in edgewise, he asked about his sister, Jovana. Everyone in the car grew quiet.

Chapter Twenty

Laney cried on her pillow as she tried to sleep. Bojan had never called like he'd said he would. Maybe he'd had second thoughts about their relationship. But then why would he buy her such a beautiful dresser?

She glanced at the polished maple wood. He must care a lot or why would he go to such extremes to show it? Unless he had millions. Then the cost of the highboy dresser would seem like a pittance.

But he didn't act like a rich man -- well, not really. He was very down-to-earth, though very generous. He'd said he had a lot of money and owned several restaurants, but she doubted he had millions from business. That would be an amazing accomplishment for anyone his age. He couldn't be more than thirty years old.

Awareness of her ignorance struck her, and her neck heated. She'd kissed him with such passion, and she didn't even know his age. What must he think of her? Maybe that was why he hadn't called. He'd thought about her boldness, and decided she wasn't right for him.

Tossing and turning, she finally groaned and sat up. She clicked on the light beside her bed. Peering over to the corner where Baby slept, she saw Dude snuggling up against Baby. He pressed against her, burying his nose in her side, like they'd known each other forever.

Dude licked Baby's ear. The sight made Laney's heart squeeze. Why couldn't people live simply, and love each other like God's creatures did innately? Why did life have to be so complicated?

With that thought on her mind, and worry over the incident with the movers, she grabbed her Bible, opening it to Psalm 23. "The Lord is my shepherd, I shall not want."

She'd read that verse many times, but tonight it struck her deeply. I shall not want. What did that mean? Shouldn't she want to be loved by a man? Wasn't that normal? Hadn't God created woman for man? Then why all the heartache?

Closing her eyes, she reflected on her relationship with God. Whenever she started making anything else in her life more important than her relationship with Him, her life would start falling to pieces. Guaranteed.

Maybe God wanted her to stop searching for anything else and just focus on her relationship with Him. Also, God would protect her. That must be what the psalmist meant.

If she truly believed the Lord was her shepherd, then she would be satisfied with Him alone. Anything above that would be additional. Her basic drive must be for God, not man. That much she knew.

The Lord continued to impress that upon her heart, but she feared if she let go of her desire to marry, God would choose to make her single. That would be hard since she'd longed to have a family to replace the one she'd lost.

But if she truly believed God was all she needed, then He should be enough, shouldn't He? So why did she have such an intense sense of longing and a deep need for male companionship?

Tears welled in her eyes, spilling onto her cheeks.

"Jesus, please help me to know You more, and love You so deeply, that I'll want nothing else. Fill my heart with Your presence..."

Laney couldn't finish her prayer as she choked on tears of repentance. She'd neglected her relationship with the Lord, and had allowed fear to grab her by the throat for too long. Now she must learn to overcome it, to depend on her Creator God and not her own strength.

Surely God didn't want her holed up in her house. She believed that much. But He would have to give her the strength to press on, because on her own, she felt as helpless as the lost sheep in the Psalms.

She set her Bible on the nightstand. Glancing over at the two Chihuahuas, she smiled. They looked so content as they nuzzled each other.

The sight made her miss Bojan afresh. She'd known him for only a few weeks, yet she felt as if they had grown just as attached as their pets had to each other, and in such a short time.

At least Bojan *seemed* fond of her. She had no reason to believe he would pretend to like her if he felt otherwise. Not if he loved the Lord like she believed he did. And that made him even more attractive.

Surely meeting Bojan had to be a sign of God's hand in her life, for the godly Slavic man had stepped into her world just when she'd needed a friend most.

Oh, Boki, why haven't you called?

*****

He stiffened as he reported in with his Probation Officer later that afternoon. "What do you mean I tested positive? I haven't used, I swear it."

"Yeah, yeah, that's what they all say. You're going to have to wear this bracelet for a while so we can track your every move. If you stay away from the drug dealers, we'll take it off in say, oh, two, maybe three weeks?"

He groaned. Now he'd have to steer clear of Laney's house for awhile. And after all the trouble he'd gone through to cover his tracks. When everything had gone down so lousy at Laney's, he'd bailed out of the truck before they hit the highway and told Charlie he'd kill him if he told... but he couldn't bet on the kid keeping his mouth shut.

Thankfully, he'd had a deaf cellmate in prison. His cellmate had taught him sign language, or he wouldn't have been able to

111

communicate with Charlie at all. That's why the old lady hired him. He was positive about that. He wouldn't get that lucky again, and he'd written off the delivery job as a lost cause. They could keep their lousy paycheck. Better to be out the money than get caught.

He rubbed his forehead. "So are you saying if I stay out of trouble I won't have to wear this thing more than a few weeks?"

"That's what I'm saying. Go to work, go home, and steer clear of the bars."

"That's going to be a problem, sir. I've lost both of my jobs." He'd lost the first for missing too many days, and his PO didn't need to know the real reasons for the second.

"So find another one. Just cover up that tattoo so maybe people will give you a chance. Got that?"

"Yeah, sure. I'll see what I can do." As he left the PO's office, he muttered under his breath, "I hope you die of brain rot, you stinkin' piece of garbage."

Now he had to find a way to keep Laney quiet if she hadn't already reported him. Didn't matter if she did, it wasn't like the antique place had his real name anyway. He'd just lie low until he had another opportunity. This time he'd wear a shirt with a collar, and he wouldn't get interrupted. He'd handled things wrong, been too rough with her. Next time he'd woo her a bit, make her interested before he tightened his hold. Yeah, that's what he'd do.

*****

"About your sister..."

"*Tate*? *Mayko*? What is wrong? Is she not well?"

"Your sister is not the same. She is...different." As his father spoke, his voice tensed. "What has happened has...changed her. There is no light in her eyes, no joy. You must understand that I am only telling you this so you won't be as shocked when you greet her at our home."

"She is staying with you?"

He rubbed his forehead. Before his sister ran off, she'd refused to speak to their parents. Now she lived with them? She must be a wreck to change so dramatically.

"Yes, Boki." His mother frowned. "You must understand. Your sister is very fragile right now."

His father added, "We are afraid for her mental state. She had so many bad things happen since she left home. But we will let her tell you about them herself."

"Yes, *Tate*. I think that is best."

They drove the rest of the way in silence. Other than the sound of *Baba's* snoring and the bumpy road under their tires, a sense of somber quietness filled the air.

He gazed out the window of the tiny car and absorbed the beauty of the countryside. Arizona was beautiful in many ways, but it paled in comparison to the fall colors blanketing the land before his eyes.

His chest fluttered with affection for his homeland. Laney would love his country. He felt it in his bones. It was much colder in the winter than Arizona, but Macedonia's beauty and culture made up for its frigid temperatures.

Maybe they could return someday for a honeymoon. The image of her in his arms made his chest ache. Closing his eyes to rest, he prayed God would comfort her in his absence.

A short while later his grandmother nudged him. "Your mother is talking to you."

"You have a girlfriend, Boki?" his *mayka* asked from the front seat. "You did not say you had a new love in your life. What is her name?"

His face heated. He must have mumbled something in his sleep. How else would his mother know? "Elaine Cooper. But she goes by her nickname, Laney."

"That is a beautiful name, *detto moya*. Tell us. What is this young woman like?"

"She is very beautiful. Her eyes are deep blue like Lake Ohrid, and so lovely and full of feeling. Her hair is like brown silk, and her skin is smooth and as soft as the flesh of a nectarine. She is so wonderful. I wish for you to meet her soon."

His father sighed. "Your mother and I won't be returning to the States until the middle of January, right after winter break. The introduction will have to wait."

His grandmother leaned closer and whispered, "Is this woman someone you are serious about?"

Closing his eyes, he nodded. "I care for her more each day. I think of her all the time." He opened his eyes and smiled at his *baba,* and then touched her prune-like cheek.

His grandmother's soft skin moved under his hands when he caressed her face. She was pushing eighty. How much longer would she be with them? His chest squeezed at the thought of losing someone so dear to him. He would miss her terribly when she was gone.

"Then she must be truly lovely."

"That she is." Bojan grinned, pleased that his *baba* understood.

His grandmother closed her eyes for a moment, as if thinking. "Tell me. Is she worthy of you, Grandson?" Her brows rose, and she watched him closely.

Reaching for his grandmother's hands, he held them in his own. "Yes, *Babo.* I worry that I am not worthy of her."

"Is she Christian?" his *mayka* asked without turning to look at him.

"Yes, *Mayko,* she is Christian, but she is not Orthodox."

"Is she Macedonian?" his *tate* implored, glancing at Bojan through the rearview mirror.

His *mayka* craned her neck to watch his face, and his *baba* stared into his eyes.

Clasping his hands on his lap, he tried not to wring them the way a woman would. He'd known that question was bound to come eventually. "No, *Tate*, she is not."

"First Jovana runs away with a gypsy, and now this?" His *mayka* threw her hands in the air.

Silence filled the vehicle, and for the rest of the trip, no one spoke.

Chapter Twenty-One

The next morning Laney stretched and glanced at the clock. She'd missed church again, not that she would have attended a service anyway. Sometimes she chose to watch her favorite preacher on television. He always had inspiring sermons. But even his show was over now.

She sighed. Maybe she'd surf the Internet for a while. It wasn't like she had anyplace to go... anything to do.

Laney turned on her computer, and while it booted up, she wondered what time it was in Macedonia. What was Bojan doing right now and why hadn't he called? Maybe he hadn't made it there yet. The thought made her shudder. What if he'd been in an accident?

Her world started spinning as she imagined all kinds of horrible things happening to him. She took one last look at the clock and went to her favorites on her web browser.

This morning she'd go to her poetry sites and find inspiration that way. She sure needed something to fill her soul in his absence. Since Sam had died, Laney had avoided the poetry sites, but this morning her heart ached for beautifully crafted prose.

Maybe she would visit Sam's grave while Bojan was out of town. Then she could say good-bye to Sam's memory and move forward with Bojan, but without the nagging guilt. That would feel so wonderful.

She scanned the pages of lovely verses until her eyes captured another poem, one that perfectly described her current state. So much so, it made her skin tingle. Was God trying to speak to her from the verse.

Fear

"Good morning, fear!"
I greeted the friendly ghost in my bed.
As if friendship would make
Her compassionate.
She smiled at me and spoke
Words of hypocrisy
I like her when she plays hide and seek.
I feel secure when she acts as dead.
Oh, I wish she were.
I wish I did find her dead in my bed.
I wish she was but a decomposed ghost
Looking at her own disappearance.
Oh, that she'd be afraid of loss and time.

*Fear, creature of my pride and dishonesty,
gift from my blind reality.*

If only Laney could grasp the full meaning of the scripture that said *Perfect love casts out all fear. He who fears does not have love.*

"Lord, please take my fears. I give them to You this morning. Help me to leave them in Your hands."

A sensation of warmth washed over her, unlike anything she'd felt before. A spiritual sense of wellbeing, a calmness, filled the air around her, and she smiled as she basked in the peace now filling her soul. God was with her even in the midst of her fear. She could sense His presence -- His gentle nudging -- for the first time in nearly a year.

*****

Bojan checked his cell phone again. No signal. Why hadn't he thought of that? How would he call Laney? She was certain to be worried sick by now.

"*Tetko*, Uncle Alek, may I please use your telephone? I will pay you for the call."

"Do not worry, Nephew. You may use the phone as you wish. God provides, yes?"

Bojan nodded. "Indeed He does."

He dialed Laney's number, and the phone was busy. "Is this the right way to dial the United States?"

His *tetko* glanced at the numbers Bojan had written down. "Yes, that is correct."

"Thank you. I must try again." The phone was still busy. Worried that he had a bad connection, he tried a third time. Maybe she was on the Internet. But why would she use it knowing he would try and call her?

He finally gave up. "*Tetko* Alek, when is *Vuyche* Boban coming back with my Jovanichka?"

"Soon. She had to go to the doctor because she was not feeling well."

"What is wrong?" Bojan touched his Uncle Alek's arm. "Please, tell me what is wrong."

His *Tetko* Alek sighed. "She is very big with child, yet very thin. After nearly beating her to death, the man she lived with left her on the streets to fend for herself."

"You are serious? She is that bad off?"

"Even worse. The light in her eyes is no more."

He couldn't imagine Jovana without a smile. She'd been a happy child and she'd had such a carefree spirit.

The sound of *Vuyche* Boban's Alpha Romeo's motor echoed as they drove toward the house. Jovanichka had returned. From what he

116

understood, she would be a shocking sight to behold. He prayed she'd be open to his companionship.

The front door shut with a firm click. He searched the front hall. She walked into the room with tiny steps, her face cast down. The shame she carried was apparently a heavy burden.

His throat knotted. "My Jovanichka. It's your *bratko*."

She looked up and their eyes met. The sadness he glimpsed in the depths of his sister's once beautiful brown eyes made his heart weep. Tears rolled down his cheeks. "Come, I must hold you."

With a trembling chin, she leapt into his arms and cried. He grabbed her tightly, kissing her cheek until he tasted the salt of her tears. Her ribs stuck out despite her swollen abdomen. She was truly fragile, as his parents had said.

His heart pounded as he held her against him. She sobbed into his shirt, and more tears streamed down his face. His parents and other relatives merely stared in silence. Compassion filled their faces, and he knew they were thrilled to have her home. She once was lost, but now she'd been found.

The prodigal daughter had returned. Like in the story, when his father had first called him, he'd said with great emotion, "You must return home, *detto moya*. Your sister was dead, but now she is alive. We must celebrate!"

He would never forget that day. Laney had watched him as he cried tears of joy. He'd never felt such strong emotion, and he could not hold back the tears.

Laney had stared at him with awe, almost reverence, and it humbled him. He would never understand why men suppressed emotion when it could provide such healing when used to bless others.

"*S'agapo poli, adelfouli mou*. I love you so much my brother." She squeezed him once more, then stepped back.

He drank in the sight of her and whispered, "*S'agapo*, too." With a groan he pulled her to his chest again, and said into her hair, "I am so very sorry if I hurt you, my sister. I never meant to. I swear I cared only about your wellbeing. I swear--"

The child in his sister's belly kicked him in the ribs, and he suppressed a delighted laugh.

Jovana nudged away from him. "I was so wrong to be angry with you, Boki. It was never you." She framed his face with her hands and stared deep into his eyes. "I do forgive you and pray that you will one day forgive me, too." Her chin trembled.

He kissed her cheek and pressed his hand against her jaw as he gazed intently into her eyes. "There is nothing to forgive."

Her face contorted, and she clutched her stomach and groaned. "Ayeeee!"

Chapter Twenty-Two

After praying and drawing closer to the Lord, Laney felt a strong conviction that she should call the police and do whatever she could to help apprehend the man who had assaulted her.

At first, ignoring the situation had seemed the best solution, because then Bojan wouldn't know that his gift had come with a risk to her safety. But that was before God had strengthened her spirit. He'd also shown her that He, God, was enough. That didn't lessen her feelings for Bojan, but just put them in perspective. God had to be enough, so she would trust Him.

Besides, she had no idea when Bojan would finally call her, and waiting by the phone made her crazy. Laney decided to take Dude to the mailbox with her that morning. She left Baby at home, because she was not quite strong enough to go for such a long walk.

On the way, she absorbed the heat from the November sun and enjoyed the way it made her skin tingle. In a few short days December would begin. She would turn twenty-six on December twelfth.

Then came Christmas.

If Bojan returned as planned, he would be there for her birthday. Her heart fluttered at the thought of celebrating with him. What would they do? Whatever he planned, he was sure to make it fun. He brought a spark of life with him wherever he went. Just being with him would be wonderful enough.

Dude stopped walking to sniff a lizard that had frozen on a rock when the curious dog approached him. She smirked at the way Dude examined the creature and walked around it while sizing up his opponent. So much like a person.

How often had she done just that? Tiptoed around people while watching them to see if they could be trusted, or if they would try to exploit her weaknesses.

But God had spoken to her heart through the poem she'd read. She couldn't keep living in fear. It was not of God, and according to the scriptures, perfect love casts out fear and God is love.

So she gave the Lord her fears. The question was whether she could leave them in His hands.

Dude soon tired of staring down the lizard, so they proceeded to the mailbox. She opened her mail slot with her key and pulled out numerous envelopes.

Most of what she'd extracted was either junk mail or bills, but a card from the county assessor's office captured her attention. She'd never seen a property assessment notification before -- Sam had always taken care of monetary issues -- but she knew it had something to do with the value of the property and taxes owed.

The bottom line made her tremble. Her house had an estimated value of over half a million dollars. She'd had no idea. Sam had closed on the house days before she moved in. She'd signed the papers with him, but never really looked at the price. How in the world would she pay taxes on a property worth so much money?

She spied a goldenrod envelope with a return address of the county assessor's office, which piqued her curiosity. She tore it open. The letter said she owed eight thousand dollars in taxes for last year and the coming year.

Her options were outlined. Pay three thousand for the first quarter, and then one thousand a month for the next three months, and another two thousand to cover the last part of the year.

It said if she didn't pay the taxes in full, she could have her tax lien bid on in the upcoming tax lien sale. And if after five years she still hadn't caught up on her debt, the owner of the lien had rights to her property if the loan foreclosed.

The rest of the letter blurred as tears filled her eyes. Already Satan tempted her to doubt God's ability to take care of her needs. What would she do? Sam's parents had written her off after their son had died, so she couldn't ask them for help.

Bojan would probably help her if she asked, but would he even have that much money to just give away? She doubted it, and her pride wouldn't allow her to beg him for help. He'd already been way too generous with her and she didn't want to take advantage of his kindness.

Somehow she had to figure out a way to pay the taxes on her own. "Please Lord, give me strength. I don't want to lose my house, too. I've already lost so much."

You could sell.

Not sure if the Lord spoke, or the devil tempted her, she shoved the thought away. Even if someone bought her home it would take several months to ready the property and find another place to live. That required a lot of work and emotional fortitude. Work she couldn't do alone. She had no money to hire someone to assist her, either.

As she approached her front door, her heart stilled. The phone was ringing. Sprinting through the house, she reached for the phone and received a loud dial tone. Whoever had called had already hung up.

She pushed *69, but that number was unavailable according to the operator. Her last shred of patience snapped, and tears rolled down her cheeks. What if he'd finally called, and she'd missed him. When would he call again?

Trust Me, Daughter.

She trembled. It sounded easy to trust God, but in reality it took everything she had in her to not scream out her frustrations as she fell back on the couch. "Please, Lord, give me strength and help me to trust

You more."

If God had intended to use her current situation as an object lesson, she'd caught His meaning. God and God alone would be her portion. A sigh escaped her lips, and she forced herself to relax. "Okay, Lord. I'm listening."

The phone rang again. She snatched it from the couch. "Hello?"

Silence greeted her on the other end. She listened closely. A shudder snaked up her spine. Someone breathed into the phone and chuckled. With a shriek, she dropped the phone on the hard tile and ran to lock the front door and set her house alarm.

Returning to pick up the phone, she tried to find a dial tone, but no matter how hard she clicked, the phone wouldn't work. She even tried plugging and unplugging it several times. If she had only kept up on her cell phone bill... but she lost the service last week.

A groan wrenched its way from her throat. She hated being tested in her faith. Now she couldn't even call the police. "Lord, what am I going to do?"

Try your neighbor.

"Okay. I can do that." Grabbing her fur coat, she put it on, then knelt down and released Dude's leash. He darted up the stairs.

Checking her purse for her keys, she sucked in a deep breath and opened the front door. Though she didn't know the retired couple who lived down the road, necessity dictated that she would soon have to meet them. She had to find a way to call the police.

And she had another problem. How could Bojan call her if her phone was broken? She might ask her neighbors for a ride into town to buy a new one. Just thinking about riding in a car made her hands tremble, so she said aloud, "Perfect love casts out all fear. God, I'm glad You love me perfectly. I can do this. I know I can..."

The voice of doubt tried to wedge its way into her mind. *You can't do it. You're weak. You'll always be weak.*

"No. I'm strong because the same power that raised Jesus from the dead lives in me now." She shouted at the voice of doubt in her mind. "So stop tempting me, Satan."

Her neighbor's garage door stood open. Someone hunched over and checked under the hood of a car.

When she realized she'd just yelled, and how that must sound, she pressed her lips together and hoped her neighbor hadn't heard. She knew she wasn't crazy, and the last thing she needed right now was to have her neighbor turn her away. Swallowing hard, she approached.

*****

Bojan hung up the phone and frowned at the receiver. First the phone was busy. Then when he called back, no one answered. He wished she had an answering machine so he could at least leave a message.

Then it occurred to him. He could call Little Italy and leave a message. After dialing and waiting for what seemed like forever, he sighed with relief when the answering machine finally picked up. "Johnny? Is very important you give message to Laney for me, yes? Please tell her I arrived safe and am trying for reach her. Tell her I miss very much. Thank you."

He hung up and smiled. Surely Johnny would help him get the message to Laney.

Returning to the living room, he offered his uncle a grin, thankful he could speak to him in his native tongue. "I called Little Italy and left a message for Johnny."

"Johnny boy still works there? How is he doing?" His Uncle Alek patted his back, and they sat down on the couch to visit.

"Okay so far. Thanks for encouraging him to stick it out with me." Bojan nodded. "I really need a competent manager right now."

His uncle chuckled. "Who said he was competent? He knows what he's doing, but I still had to watch him so he wouldn't go off on his own and do things without checking with me first. Has this been a problem for you?"

"Not that I'm aware of. He had a small accident with the car, but that could happen to anyone."

Uncle Alek frowned. "Hmmm... I suppose."

An awkward silence ensued.

No one wanted to bring up the issue of Jovana's health. It had been many hours since her water broke and his parents had rushed her to the hospital. They were all worried and tired after pacing for many hours. The hospital staff finally sent them home after admitting his sister into surgery.

It looked bad. So much blood had come with her water, and she wasn't due for another six weeks. Bojan knew her life might be hanging in the balance, and it terrified him.

The front door opened, and they all jumped up. From the looks on his parents' faces, the news wasn't good.

"*Tate?* How is our Jovanichka?"

"She will live. But the baby did not." His face crumpled with grief. "I lost my first grandson."

Bojan's mother released a gut-wrenching wail. She held a bundle of blankets in her arms and lifted it to her chest. "We must have the service in the morning to bury this precious child who is no more."

Silence filled the room. His sister would live, but his nephew had died. Rejoicing mingled with mourning.

His parents' grief made them look so old. Bojan blinked, allowing his tears to drip from his chin. His father rarely cried.

It touched him deeply.

He would have to extend his stay. There would be a funeral for the baby in the morning after his mother prepared the body for burial, then a memorial service would follow nine days later. They would honor the short life of this innocent babe, mourning for the son who would never live to bless his mother.

"What is worse," his father said, intense grief lacing his words, "is our Jovanichka will not be released for seven days. She will not be there to bury her son. Only to join us for the ceremony."

Poor Jovana. She had suffered so much. Bojan couldn't imagine what his sister had endured for the past five years. When she was well enough to visit, he would see her. They would talk, and after listening to her story, he would share with her the hope that he'd found in Jesus Christ.

Since he would not be in Macedonia long, he must tell her soon, for he did not know when he would see her again once he returned to Arizona. And hope was all he had to offer her.

Chapter Twenty-Three

"Thank you so much. I really appreciate it," Laney said as she received the phone from her neighbor, Mary Crachet. "Are you sure you don't want me to pay you for it?"

"No, honey. We were just getting ready to donate it to Goodwill, and we're glad you can get some use out of it."

"Well, God bless you for helping me." Laney smiled.

Mary opened her arms. "You're more than welcome, dear. The Lord has blessed us, and we want to bless others."

Laney hesitated. "You're Christians?"

"Sure are." Mary's husband walked in the room and held out his hand. "Name's Alfred. Pleased to meet you."

"I'm Laney, your neighbor." She shook hands with him. He looked about Mary's age. He must be her husband. "Who was that man who let me in?"

"That's our oldest son. He's a mechanic and was visiting us over the holiday weekend."

"He seems like a nice man." Laney smiled and cradled the phone, eager to use it. "I think I'll be going now."

"Could I ask you a question before you go?" Mary smiled -- her face so warm and inviting, it made Laney's throat tighten.

Her grandmother would be about the same age had she lived. But she'd died of cancer when Laney was only ten. "Sure. I hope I can answer it."

She swallowed hard and prayed that God would calm her fears, and give her peace.

"Do you have a home church?"

Her throat tightened, but she told the truth. She had nothing to lose. "Not anymore."

"Would you like to go to church with us next Sunday?"

Amazingly, her pulse remained stable. "Where do you attend?"

"First Christian. It's off Route 92."

"I think I know where that is." Accepting the invitation would test her newfound courage. But she needed other people, and she knew it. God didn't want her to live alone, but to enjoy fellowship with other Christians.

"So will you come with us?" Alfred smiled. His baldness and pointy nose reminded her of her late grandfather.

"Sure. What time do I need to be ready?"

"We leave here at nine." Mary embraced her again. "I think the Lord brought you to us today. I feel His presence, His blessing upon you."

"Thank you." Laney sniffled, trying not to cry. "I'll see you next week. Thanks again for the phone." She walked out, marveling at how nice her neighbors were, and wondering why she hadn't bothered to meet them before.

Because you were grieving.

But she felt fine now. Life hadn't stopped just because she'd grieved the loss of Sam. It had been waiting for her all along. And now Bojan was part of her life. He'd been gone since Saturday, yet it seemed ages ago.

She could see his smile in her mind's eye and quickened her steps in anticipation of hearing his voice. Once she entered her house, she plugged in the phone. She heard a dial tone and decided to call Little Italy first. Maybe they would have news about Jovana and have heard from Bojan. They should know how to reach him.

"Little Italy. May I take your order?"

"No. I'm calling about Bojan. This is Laney. Have you heard from him at all?"

"Yes. In fact, he left a message here this morning. Said to let you know he was okay."

"Did he say anything about a woman named Jovana?"

"His sister? No, he didn't mention her."

Had she heard him correctly? "Jovana is his sister?"

"Yes. Who'd you think she was? His girlfriend?"

Laney pressed her hand to her forehead, heat blooming in her cheeks as she remembered Bojan's words... "*My sister is beautiful woman, but I want Laney for* devojka." At the time, she'd focused so much on the *devojka* part, the *sister* part never registered. Until now.

She decided not to answer that question, embarrassed that she'd been so worried about loosing Bojan to an old flame that she'd drawn such a conclusion. "Thank you for letting me know. If he calls you again, tell him I miss him."

"Sure thing." The man chuckled, and she recognized his voice as Johnny, the manager.

She started to hang up, then realized he might know Bojan's cell phone number. Then she could call him and tell him herself. "Um, wait! I almost forgot. Do you have his cell number?"

"He asked us not to give it out to anyone. Besides, it doesn't seem to be working. I've already tried to call him, and it keeps going to his voicemail."

"Oh. Thanks anyway." She swallowed the lump in her throat. She prayed the next time he called she'd be home and could get to the phone in time.

*****

The day following Jovana's surgery passed in a blur, for they had stayed up all night awaiting the baby's burial. Bojan had never felt such intense pain, at least not since his grandfather had passed away.

Seeing that tiny child prepared for burial, then saying good-bye. He couldn't imagine...

Yes, you can. Erika killed your unborn child.

He shook off the thought.

Back when his grandfather died, the entire village had honored their family and grieved with them. His grandfather had been a veteran of several regional wars, and well respected. So was his *baba*, for she had taken in many hungry and injured people during that frightening time when people didn't know whom to trust. Her reputation as the Florence Nightingale of Macedonia was known throughout the Balkans.

His *baba* entered the room. "We are ready."

The wailing began, and a heavy cloud of grief blanketed them. For the first time since he'd arrived, it really struck him how lost some of his family were. Some of them didn't know Christ. They had no hope, and it troubled him.

With his eyes closed, he prayed for each member of his family as the service proceeded. He prayed for Jovana most of all. Soon he would see her and would bring a light into the dark places. Hope was all he had to offer her, but it was more than enough, should she choose to accept it.

*****

Days after the mourners left, when Jovana was well enough to receive visitors, Bojan asked his *tate* if he could borrow the Fiat.

"Yes, Boki. But make sure you get gas before you return. The tank is low."

"I will, *Tate.*" Just like their spirits were low. He sucked in his breath and wiped his eyes one last time. He would bring joy and encouragement to his sweet Jovanichka, not sadness and weeping, for she'd had enough of that already. But if Jovana needed to mourn with him, he would be there for her.

He prayed as he drove through Struga to the hospital. Taking in the dark clouds, he thought of his sister. Since the tragedy had struck, the sun had not shone even one day. Overcast skies heavy with snow and sleet, the weather was atypically cold for this time of year.

The end of his nose felt frozen as he drove with the Fiat's heater turned off. He didn't need the heat in the vehicle to lull him to sleep on the long road.

Each night he'd tossed in bed, praying for sleep, but it didn't come easily. He'd start to drift off, and then he'd remember why he was here. What a sad trip this had turned out to be.

He detoured to a local bakery to get *bugatza* for Jovana before they were sold out for the day. She'd always loved the sweet cream pies. As he pulled up in front of the hospital, he prayed for peace. "Give me the words to say, Lord, for this will be hard for me."

He felt the Spirit of the Lord surround him in answer to his prayer and knew instantly that everything would be all right. Entering the room assigned to Jovana, he took small steps so as not to frighten her.

"My Jovanichka," he whispered, "*Kako si dobro*?"

She reached for him. "*Dobro, dobro* now that you are here, my *bratko*."

After visiting for an hour and sharing his testimony with his sister, Bojan asked, "Do you want to be free, Jovanichka?"

"Yes, I want to know this God of yours... The One Who makes your heart sing."

"Then I shall pray for you, and we will meet Him together." He took both of her hands in his and prayed with his sister. He felt warmth wash over them the moment the Lord touched her. Looking into her eyes, now streaming with tears, he saw them shimmer with hope.

Bojan enveloped his sister in his arms and rejoiced that she had come home not only in body, but in spirit as well.

For after years of suffering, Jovana's face now shone, bright and strong. Her heart was truly free, and he rejoiced with her that she had found salvation.

Smiling, he thought of one of his favorite scriptures. "For whom the Lord sets free, is free indeed."

His parents would be amazed when they saw her, and he could not wait to see their reaction. Surely after seeing a transformation such as he witnessed today, they would rejoice.

Chapter Twenty-Four

Exhausted after pouring out her story to the police, Laney said good-bye and closed the door. She leaned her forehead on the frame and exhaled.

As hard as it had been to relive the event, she was glad she'd given the police a thorough description. Maybe they would find him now. And after that scary phone call this morning, she wanted him caught more than ever. All day she could barely concentrate on her transcribing.

Though it was still early, she decided to bed down for the night. She would accomplish nothing tomorrow morning if she didn't get enough rest, so she trudged up the stairs, and readied herself for bed.

She lay down and caught sight of Dude and Baby snuggling close. With a groan, she turned over. Watching the Chihuahuas snuggling together did nothing to lift her spirits, and in fact, made them sink lower.

When would Bojan finally call her? She wanted so much to hear his voice. To let him know how much she missed him.

With that thought on her mind, she lifted him up in prayer. For some reason she sensed he'd need them, and she wanted so much to help him in any way she could.

Several days had passed with no phone calls. Discouragement weighed heavy on her chest, and she struggled to do mundane things, like eat.

"Lord, I'm trusting You. I am. But would it hurt so much to let him call me? I just want to talk to him, Lord."

Later that afternoon when she turned off the vacuum, she heard the phone ringing. "No! Not again!"

She sprinted toward the phone, praying it hadn't been ringing while she'd vacuumed the carpet. "Hello?"

"Elaine, I longed for hear your voice."

It was him! She giggled, deciding to use his proper name as well. "*S'agapo*, Bojan."

Silence lingered between them, and she worried that she'd said the wrong thing. "Boki? Are you there?"

His voice sounded tight and full of emotion. "I longed for you say those words, my *prijatelka*. I miss you." He sighed, and the sound made her heart sing.

"I've missed you, too. What took you so long to call me? I've been worried." She fluffed her bangs and sat on the couch, wondering if she had the right meaning of *s'agapo*.

"Did you not hear message from restaurant?"

"I did. But he only said you were okay."

"Johnny no tell how much I miss?"

"No. I don't remember that. Why?" She propped her feet up to lie back.

"Is nothing. I must keep phone call short. I call many times, but is *sekogash,* no answer, is always phone busy."

"I'm sorry. I've been a bit of a mess lately." She rubbed her eyes as several tears leaked out.

"Did you like gift I sent? Is beautiful, yes? You pleased?" The excitement in his voice convinced her to not tell him about the man attacking her. That would not help matters, and would only upset him.

"Yes, Boki. It was a very generous gift. I still can't believe you bought it for me."

"Is for selfish reason. I want for see beautiful smile and knew you be happy for gift."

"Well, it worked. Say, how are your parents?"

His voice lowered. "*Rotidels,* parents, are having hard time with family problems. Jovana lost her baby and we have done much grieving. Pray for family."

"I will. That's so sad about your sister."

"My grandmother is with her now."

"Boki? Do you want to talk about it?"

He lowered his voice. "I tell you later."

"Okay."

Silence reigned for a moment.

She nibbled on her lip to contain the joy bubbling from within. He'd called! He finally called... "I keep thinking about kissing you again."

"Ah, is very sweet. I think about much *baknuva,* too. What make you think for kissing me?"

"Let's just say that not only are Baby and Dude getting along, but if they keep it up they'll be parents soon."

Bojan laughed so hard she had to pull the phone away from her ear. "Dude is ladies' man, yes? I told him must show Baby respect. Dude show for Baby?"

"I suppose. But he sure likes to lick her a lot."

"Is funny. *Ljubov* is good, yes? Love is much good."

She swallowed hard. "Yes..." She hesitated, then blurted, "Please come home soon."

He sighed. "I have bad news for Laney. I must extend stay for funeral for my *vnuk,* my nephew."

"Why so long?" She rolled onto her side and propped her head on her hand.

"After burial, family has memorial nine days later. Is Macedonian tradition, so I must stay."

"I guess I understand. But I was hoping you'd be here for my birthday on the twelfth."

He groaned into the phone. "Is birthday soon? I no want for miss. We must celebrate when I return, yes?"

She sucked in her tears, refusing to cry while she spoke to him. "When will that be?"

"Return ticket is for December fourteen. Is only two days late. I am sorry. How old you be?"

"I'm turning twenty-six. When's your birthday?" She closed her eyes and blinked back tears.

"Is January thirtieth. I have twenty-eight years."

She giggled, a bit relieved. "I was wondering if you were older than me. Two years isn't too bad."

"Is very good."

She could picture him smiling. She loved his accent, his heart, everything about him. He was so wonderful that sometimes she worried she would wake up and find out he was just a dream.

"I must go now. Is very expensive for call across ocean. I call in few more days. Take good care for Dude."

"I will. And Boki, *s'agapo*. I know what it means. I really want to give you another kiss. A lot."

He chuckled. "*S'agapo* is Greek word. No mean kiss."

"It doesn't? Kiss is *bakni* in Macedonian. I knew that. I figured it was the same thing in Greek. If that's not it, what *does* it mean?"

His voice lowered and took on a husky tone. "Is secret, but promise for explain when I return home and kiss you."

"Can you give me a small hint?"

He sighed. "Is very small hint, okay? Laney, you is the apple of my eye."

"What?"

"I say no more. Goodbye." *Click.*

Laney kept thinking about what Bojan had said. It didn't mean I want to kiss you. So what did *s'agapo* mean? She logged onto the Internet and looked up websites with Greek and English translation dictionaries.

She started typing in the word the way it sounded but kept getting answers that looked nothing like English letters. Poor Bojan. Even their alphabets were different. No wonder he had such a hard time with English.

After searching several Web sites and wasting an hour, she gave up. With a sigh, she switched over to transcribing medical records. Within two hours her shoulder started aching, so she stood up and stretched. The phone rang.

It couldn't be Bojan again, could it? He called only three hours ago. So who else would it be? Only one way to find out. "Hello?"

Heavy breathing greeted her. The hair on her arms prickled.

"Who is this?"

A menacing laugh erupted, and the scratchy voice said, "Now I know where you live."

Fear squeezed her throat as she hung up the phone. Her hands shook. It couldn't be the man who tried to assault her. He had to know she'd call the police, so he'd probably stay as far away as possible. But the caller sure sounded like him. Who else would call and say something twisted like that?

She gasped. What if he planned to come back?

Running to the front of the house, she checked the lock and the alarm system. She peered through the blinds. No one had parked in front. The man must be toying with her. He couldn't be back. He wouldn't. Nobody was that stupid.

But just in case, she called the police. "I need to make another report. I think the man who assaulted me is making crank calls."

*****

After visiting his sister again, Bojan drove away from the hospital in silence. His *baba* had a serious look on her face. It almost resembled a frown. He knew that she wasn't unhappy with him, but merely thinking.

"Tell me what you said to our Jovanichka to make such a change in her eyes. I cannot explain it. She says she has peace because Christ understands her suffering, but I think it is more than that."

"I shared the Scriptures. The Holy Spirit of God touched her. He teaches all things from heaven above. Christ living in us is like a heart candle burning inside. It is He Who makes our spirits shine. He gives us hope."

A broad grin covered her wrinkled face. "Yes, *detto moya*. I think I understand."

Chapter Twenty-Five

Sunday arrived, and Laney walked to her neighbors' home to go to church with them. Her hands grew sweaty at the idea of riding in their car, then being around so many unfamiliar people, but she knew her heart needed the encouragement. She missed the fellowship she used to get at church when Sam was alive.

"I'm ready, Mary."

"Wonderful. Let's go." She turned to her husband. "Alfred, dear? Are you ready to go?"

"Ready and willing, I always say." He laughed and winked at Laney. She just smiled back, not sure how to take the old man's humor.

When they arrived at church, Laney exhaled slowly. She'd survived the trip without having a panic attack. Maybe soon she'd even be able to drive again.

Glancing around, she took in the stained glass windows and wooden pews. It was a small church, so she didn't feel so overwhelmed. The congregation consisted mainly of people over forty, but Laney liked that. She had no mother, so going to church with Mary made her feel surrounded by mothers. And the older women were so gracious and kind. She received enough hugs to last her weeks.

The service began. Laney cried through most of the sermon and the closing hymn. But it felt good to not stuff her pain deep inside. By the time they left, her spirit was refreshed, and her heart seemed filled to capacity.

Wiping the tears from her eyes as they headed to the car to leave, she asked Mary, "Will you do me a favor, please?"

"What is it you need, dear? Do you want to stop at the store before we go home?"

"I was thinking more about stopping at the cemetery. Would you mind taking me? I haven't visited my fiancé's grave in over six months, and I need some closure."

"I don't see why not. We can go visit our friend while we're there, right, Alfred?"

"Yes, dear." He nodded, but Laney wondered how much he'd paid attention. His mind seemed to be elsewhere.

Mary leaned close and whispered, "My poor husband is getting absent-minded. He'll probably forget what I said."

As they left the parking lot, his wife noticed the wrong blinker light was on, and corrected him. "Now, Alfred, remember. We are going to the cemetery."

"We are? When did we decide that?" He switched blinkers.

"Never mind. Just take us there."

"Whatever you say." He smiled and rubbed his forehead before pulling onto the main road.

Mary turned and looked at Laney. "Told you."

As soon as they pulled into the cemetery parking area, her mood turned somber. A lump formed in her throat.

Sam.

She could almost see his blue eyes shining as he looked at her and laughed. They had been so in love. Tears pooled in her eyes, and she blinked them away. She would be strong. Sam would want her to go on.

She approached his headstone and knelt on the soft, cool earth.

"Oh, Sam." Folding her hands, she closed her eyes and prayed, "Lord, help me to say goodbye."

Touching the cold headstone, she realized again that Sam was never coming back. He was in a better place, and one day she would see him again, but until then, he would want her to enjoy life.

In fact, if he were alive he would probably be friends with Bojan. Her throat tightened. "I love you, Sam."

She kissed her fingers and touched his name.

Several minutes later, she sensed Mary and Alfred behind her. She stood and exhaled. Turning to Mary, and with tears in her eyes, Laney nodded. "Thank you, Mary. I'm ready to leave now."

Mary opened her arms and embraced Laney, exactly what she needed. How did Mary know?

So far everyone she truly loved had died. Everyone except Bojan, and she was still discovering the depth of her new relationship with him.

Her sister and parents were buried in Tucson. She needed to visit their graves, too. Maybe when Bojan returned he would bring her to the site. He would do almost anything for her. She was sure of it.

*****

The last day of his visit had finally arrived. Bojan was due to fly back to the US. His mother had prepared a special meal for him. True to their tradition, she called it 'breaking the fast' to celebrate their relationship.

He inhaled the heady scent of his *mayka's* home cooking, wafting around the kitchen -- filling the house with heavenly aroma. Nobody could make a traditional Macedonian meal better than his mother could.

"Thank you for this wonderful dinner, *Mayko*. It makes me smile to know that my mother made a special meal to celebrate my last day here."

After making the sign of the cross and praying, his uncle passed the dish. Bojan inhaled deeply. Ah, he loved beef *lazagnia* with *beshemel* sauce. Nothing tasted more delicious. Except maybe Laney's kisses.

He smiled. Soon he would see her and would give her a kiss she would not forget.

"What is *detto moya* thinking about to make him smile so?" His father laughed and everyone looked at Bojan.

"I do not wish to share my innermost thoughts, *Tate*." He chuckled. "But if you insist. I was thinking of my girlfriend and how much I want to kiss her."

His father's smile faded, and he glanced over at Bojan's mother. She avoided looking at him.

Jovana smirked from across the table. They'd had many wonderful days together after she returned from the hospital. He would miss her very much. Maybe someday she would come to live in the United States with the rest of his family. Only his *baba* refused to leave their homeland. She said she has no desire to 'impersonate an American'.

Bojan would miss all of his family. Though full of heartache, the visit turned out to be a blessing. His sister had a new heart, and had bonded with their grandmother in spirit.

God had accomplished a work in their hearts above and beyond anything Bojan expected. And it felt wonderful to know that Jovana was in good hands. For the first time in years, he didn't need to worry. She was safe.

Jesus had brought her home.

*****

After the meal his *baba* cornered him. "We must talk before you leave, *detto moya*."

"Yes, *Babo?*" The look on his grandmother's face told him whatever she had to say meant a lot to her, for tears had pooled in her eyes.

"I have a special gift for you to give your *devojka* Laney. I can see in your eyes that you feel much *ljubov* for her." She held out her hand. "In case you ask her to marry you someday."

Her engagement ring rested in her palm. Bojan knew she'd treasured it since the 1930's when his grandparents were married. Tears rolled down her cheeks.

"This gift is too great for me to accept."

She pushed the ring into his palm and clasped his fingers so they fisted. "You must take it. This old woman has not many years left on this earth. Your grandfather is gone. I am no longer an *omazhena*, a married woman. I have no use for the ring anymore."

"It is a very generous gift, *Babo*. I am overwhelmed."

"That is why I give it to you, *detto moya*. I know you would treasure it *sekogash*, always."

Bojan thought about how he would see Laney the day after tomorrow. Then he realized the date and groaned.

"It is Laney's birthday today. I must call to give her best wishes." He remembered that he must take things slowly. "But I think I will keep this ring a secret. At least until I know for sure it is God's will for me to marry her. When the time is right, I will give it to her."

"That is all I ask, *detto moya.*"

Chapter Twenty-Six

The sweet smell of chocolate cake emanated from the oven. Inhaling the blissful aroma, Laney smiled. The scent brought back wistful thoughts from her childhood, when life was good.

Every year her mother baked her a chocolate cake just like the one she'd made herself today. Though alone tonight, she still celebrated, and had even set aside special doggy treats so Dude and Baby could join the party.

The sound of yips and snarls drew her attention. Dude and Baby played tug-of-war with the toy Chihuahua. She still hadn't found out who gave her the flowers.

A loud series of beeps from the timer told her the cake was ready. She grabbed a pair of oven mitts and pulled out the cake pan, then set it on a wire rack on the counter. Turning off the oven, she thanked God she still had enough propane for baking.

Her phone rang. Removing her mitts, she picked up the phone. "Hello?"

Heavy breathing. A low chuckle. "I know--"

Laney hung up the phone. She brought trembling hands to cover her mouth, and stifled a scream. That man had called at least once a day for the past week. If he was trying to terrorize her, he was doing a great job.

And she could swear a light had shined through her bedroom window more than once. At first she thought it might be people hiking in the dark, but now she doubted it.

Her nerves were frazzled from the stress of not knowing when, or if, the man who'd attacked her would return. She prayed he'd stay away. The Sheriff sent a car to patrol her street at least once a day to help keep him at bay. It seemed to be working. So far.

Her phone rang again. With a grunt, she grabbed the phone. "Listen, you sick--"

"Laney? Is Boki. Who you think this is?"

"Oh, hi." Her cheeks flamed. She'd almost given herself away. That would've been a disaster.

"I call for wish you happy birthday."

"Thank you. Hey, how do you say that in Greek?"

"*Xronia polla* is happy birthday." He chuckled. "Why you want for know how to say?"

"Just curious, I guess. I'm still trying to figure out what *s'agapo* means." She bit her lip. Maybe with that hint he'd tell her and put her out of her misery.

"I told you I tell you when I see beautiful face. I promise, my *devojka.*" His chuckle was deep.

The sound of his light laughter gave her the shivers. "Can you at least remind me what *devojka* means? All these foreign words are hard for me to remember."

"*Devojka* means my sweetheart, like my girlfriend."

She twirled a lock of hair around her finger, grinning like a goofy, love-struck teenager. "So you think I'm your girlfriend, eh? What gives you that idea?"

"Cause I no *bakni* my *prijatels*. I no kiss my friends."

"That's good to know." She giggled. "So how many *baknis* are you giving me for my birthday?"

"Oh, tradition say I should give many *bakni*. Maybe twenty-six for twenty-six years. You like, my *ljubov*?"

"There you go using fancy words again. What does that one mean?"

"Means same as *s'agapo*, only is Macedonian word."

"How do you spell it? Maybe I can look it up." She grinned. This time she would get the answer if it was the last thing she ever did.

"I no tell you. You must wait, my *shekjer* lips."

"Ha! I remember that one. That means sugar." She chuckled softly. "Are you calling me sugar lips? Hmmm?"

"Yes, you lips very sweet, like *med*. I must taste as soon as we meet."

"Okay, enough of the love talk. I'm lonely enough as it is. This mushy stuff is only making me feel worse."

"What is mushy stuff mean?"

"Love talk, kissy stuff. You know..."

"I like mushy stuff. Makes me *se zasmee*. Is good for soul." He laughed again. "I must go pack. Is late. Plane awaits. I must not miss flight tomorrow."

"I'll see you soon." She couldn't keep the wistful tone from her voice. Oh, how she missed him.

Never would she have thought she'd be in love with another man so soon. It had been a little over a year since Sam died, and already she'd moved on. But tonight the thought didn't make a lump form in her throat. Somehow she knew Sam would understand.

In fact, earlier that morning she'd taken the engagement ring Sam had given her out of the box. The enormous rock had to be worth at least six grand.

With any luck, she could pay some of her taxes with it and forestall having her tax lien bid on. It was worth a try. And she had to do it before Bojan returned. She had to take care of this problem herself.

Tomorrow she would sell her ring to keep her home.

*****

An hour later she took a bite of chocolate cake. The unexpected sound of the doorbell ringing sent her into a coughing fit. Dread washed over her. Wiping her mouth and eyes, she pushed her chair back and told the dogs, who curled up next to each other nibbling on their bones, "Stay right here, guys. I'll be right back. And be quiet, okay?"

The dogs stayed in the kitchen when she peered through the peephole. Honestly, their lovey-dovey attitude -- they were so into each other -- was starting to get on her nerves.

The man on her front landing looked familiar. Manuel, the border patrol agent who often stopped by just to chat, waited for her. He looked nervous.

She opened the door, hoping he wouldn't ask her out again. He couldn't seem to take 'no' for an answer. "Manuel. Hi. What brings you by?"

"I thought I'd report something that seemed odd to me. There was a man parked at the end of the road watching your house with high-powered binoculars. I only noticed him because I saw him turn on a flashlight when I was searching the road behind your place."

She reached for her throat. "What did you do?"

"I approached the man. He denied watching the house. Said he was bird watching. But the sun was setting, and he just didn't seem like a bird-watcher to me."

"W-what did h-he look like?" Her voice shook. The idea of someone watching her gave her the willies.

"He was pretty big, built, you know? And blond. Oh, yeah, and he had a mermaid tattoo on his neck."

She swayed on her feet. Manuel put a steadying hand on her shoulder. "Are you okay?"

Dude and Baby came barreling out of the kitchen, yipping and yapping at top volume. "Shhh..." Laney pushed her bangs out of her face and closed her eyes. "It's him."

"It's who?" Manuel shouted over the yipping.

"Hold on a sec, okay?" She shooed the Chihuahuas to the side door and shut them in the garage.

"Who do you think it is, Miss Cooper?"

She blinked. Manuel seemed genuinely concerned, and that worried her more. He wasn't even flirting with her, but all business. "The man who attacked me. He delivered furniture from *Finders Keepers Antiques* to my house, and then he tried to--" She couldn't get the words out.

He nodded. "I understand. I'm going back out to check the area and get a license plate number if I can. I'll contact the sheriff's office if I apprehend the suspect."

Still stunned at the idea of being watched, she shuddered. "Thank you, Manuel."

"Is there anything else I need to know?"

She swallowed hard. "He's been calling me. I'm scared. He just called an hour ago and said the same thing he always does. 'I know where you live'. Then he laughed and I hung up on him." A shiver caught her by surprise. "I've been setting my alarm, but if he's been watching me... Ooh, that creeps me out. I don't have blinds in some of my windows and I could swear someone shined a flashlight on my house the other night."

Manuel's neck reddened. "Let me go take a look-see and I'll report back to you." He touched her arm. "I'll watch out for you, okay?"

His kind smile was enough to clog her throat. Maybe he did genuinely care about her safety. "Thank you."

Fifteen minutes later, Manuel returned. "I scoured the area. He's gone. I didn't get the license plate, but I can tell you he drove a small, light blue truck. An old Datsun, I think."

"I'll be extra careful if I see any trucks like that, and I'll keep setting my house alarm."

"And stay away from the windows." He furrowed his brow. "I don't want anyone spying on you. It's not right, you know? It's twisted."

"I appreciate it, Manuel. I really do."

He stared at her for a moment. "Would you reconsider going out to dinner with me?"

"Actually, I met someone..." Her cheeks heated.

"I understand. Well, I better go. I'll keep one eye on your house whenever I'm in this area, okay?"

"That would be great." She bit her lip and wondered what to say next.

He made it easy for her by tipping his head in a brief nod. "*Adios, Se□iorita. Buenos noches.*" As he jogged back to his vehicle, she marveled at how polite he'd been.

If she weren't emotionally attached to Bojan, she might have reconsidered the invitation. But no one captured her attention like the Slavic man. He could steal her breath with one intense look.

If he found out about Tattoo Man, she worried he'd overreact. He seemed very protective. She decided to keep the harassment to herself so she wouldn't upset Bojan. He'd just lost his nephew. He didn't need more worries.

God would take care of her.

*****

Though dead on his feet when his plane finally landed in Tucson, Bojan detoured to a jeweler on his way back to Sierra Vista. He wanted to get Laney a nice necklace for her birthday. He chose a heart-shaped pendant set in white gold and surrounded by tiny diamonds.

The necklace would look so good on her. He couldn't wait to see her. Maybe she'd agree to go out to dinner with him and wear it. She did say she was doing better in regards to overcoming her fears.

He dropped the black velvet box into his pocket and called a taxi to transport him back to his home. A shower would sufficiently wake him, and would make him smell presentable.

He grabbed a cinnamon bun from Cinnabon and tucked the bag under his arm as he waited for the cab. If he hurried, he could get to Laney's before ten o'clock. But would she want to see him that late?

Flipping open his cell phone, he decided to ask.

"Hello? This is Laney."

"Hey, how is my *devojka* tonight? Would you like for have company? I miss you so much." His voice came out sounding more breathless than he'd intended.

"I-I don't think that's a good idea." She let out a nervous-sounding chuckle.

"What? I think is great idea." He smiled wide. Maybe if he assured her of his good intentions she would feel safe.

"No, we really should wait for morning. The idea of you coming over this late at night.... Well, it would be too... tempting. Know what I mean?"

While disappointed, he understood the potential danger. "In morning, then, my *omilen*, my favorite woman."

She giggled. "Wild javelinas couldn't keep me away."

Chapter Twenty-Seven

Laney hung up the phone and stared at the receipt again. Six thousand dollars. That's all the pawnshop gave her for a ring they said was worth over ten thousand. She understood they couldn't give her the full value, but it still stung.

At least the county accepted a partial payment and gave her an additional six months to come up with the rest.

As she brushed her hair for the evening, she smiled at her reflection. While not fully resolved, she was still proud of herself for all she'd accomplished that day.

First, she'd taken a cab to the pawnshop without having a panic attack. Then she'd parted with her engagement ring and paid most of the exorbitant taxes without crying. Yes, it had been a productive day.

Bojan would be proud. Except she didn't intend to tell him about her dilemma. He would want to help her out, and the tax issue was not his problem. She already owed him so much.

His friendship and faith had coaxed her from self-isolation. His obvious affection had breathed life into her dead heart. He'd given her a reason to have hope for her future.

Then there were those eyes... those heart-stopping honey brown eyes that melted her resolve to steer clear of relationships. And she was hooked.

Smiling, she climbed into bed and snuggled under the covers. Within minutes, she couldn't keep her heavy lids open.

A grin tugged at her mouth as she imagined the smile on Bojan's face when she welcomed him back. Yes, she would pour her heart and soul into every kiss. With a sigh, she drifted off.

"I must claim kisses now." Bojan nuzzled her neck and nibbled on her ear. She gazed into his eyes and he slowly coaxed her toward the couch. They fell back and she moaned. When she opened her eyes, she spied a mermaid tattoo within inches of her lips. A scream erupted. She punched the man above her. But he was too strong.

"Help me! No!"

Tears streamed down her face as she fought him until she had no strength left. "Why you hurt me?" Bojan gazed into her eyes, obviously saddened by her sudden attack.

"I thought you were..." She blinked. What had happened to the horrible man?

"Thought I was who? Tell me... Who you thought I was?" He grabbed her shoulders and squeezed them so tight she bit back a cry.

"You're hurting me. Please, stop!"

Sam peered into her eyes, gently tapping her cheek. "Laney? Are you okay? You keep screaming."

Her heart pounded. "Oh, Sam, I thought I'd lost you. I thought..."

"I'm here, babe. It was all just a bad dream. I won't leave you, I promise, I--"

She cut him off with a passionate kiss. When the kiss hardened, she started to choke. "Stop! I can't breathe. You're hurting me."

Bojan touched her cheek. "I am so very sorry. I never want for hurt Laney. Never. Please, forgive."

"Where's Sam? What happened to Sam?" she wailed. "Sam, where are you? Why did you leave me? Why?"

"I'm here, babe. I never left..." She glanced up and shrieked. Sam had become a decaying skeleton before her eyes, like something from a horror flick.

"Get away from me!" She fought him with everything she had, and won. He cursed and stumbled from the room.

A knock sounded on her bedroom door. "Laney? Is Boki. We must talk, my love."

She sat up. "Come in." With a smile, she scooted over and patted the mattress. "Sit down."

Bojan stumbled over to her bed and collapsed next to her. "This is very bad. I must confess..."

"What? What's so bad?" Panic lodged in her throat as she waited for him to speak. He looked remorseful with his head cast down and tears in his eyes. What had he done?

"I must leave again. This time not come back. I am sorry." He touched her chin. "I must says good-bye."

She awoke with tears streaming down her face. Laney sat up and wiped her eyes. After taking several cleansing breaths, her pulse returned to semi-normal. It was only a dream.

A horrible, frightening dream.

The phone rang. She sat up and grabbed the phone. "Yes?"

"Laney? Is Boki. I bring gift for you. You ready for see me soon?"

"Sure," she rasped. "Can you give me thirty minutes? I need to shower first. I must've slept through my alarm."

"Is no problem. I be at house very soon. In thirty minutes, yes?"

"I'll be ready." Hanging up, she sucked in her breath and muttered, "What could it mean -- if anything? No! I won't let it spoil my day -- not today." She shoved her bangs away from her eyes and leapt from her bed.

He was on his way, and she wanted to look her best.

*****

Bojan stared at the clock. When twenty minutes had passed, he climbed in his Hummer and started the engine. As his Hummer crawled up the dirt road, he spied a man on the road behind Laney's house, standing in the bed of an old blue pickup, watching something through binoculars.

At first he thought he was the same man he'd seen here earlier, but the vehicle was different, and this man had no goatee and wore his ball cap backwards. Strange that he was in the exact same place. Maybe it really was a place for birdwatchers.

He parked his Hummer in Laney's driveway and got out. Patting his pocket, he checked for the tiny box. He reached across the seat for the paper bag and grabbed it, then shut the door.

His heart hammered hard as he approached the front door, he heard his pulse echoing in his ears.

Before he had a chance to ring the bell, the door whipped open. Baby and Dude yipped and barked as they danced around Laney's legs. "Come in." She offered a shy smile and stepped back.

He entered and shoved one hand in his pocket. Offering her the paper sack, he grinned. "Is very special present for you. Please, look inside."

"Okay." With a smile, she accepted the bag. Peering inside, she sniffed the contents and tilted her head. "Is this breakfast?"

"Yes." He winked. "From Skopje. Is called *tiro-pitakia*, or cheese pie. Is kind of like cheese Danish. Sorry is not so fresh today, but is from my country and I promise for bring you gift."

She grinned. "So this is the special gift you brought me from home, huh? It looks tasty."

He watched her reaction, pleasantly surprised that she didn't seem in the least bit disappointed. His heart pounded double-time with anticipation.

"Before we eat *tiro-pitakia*, I give you traditional greeting and birthday *baknis*, yes?"

She paused, tipped her chin up, and slowly nodded, her eyes never leaving his. Such sultry, gorgeous blue eyes.

He inched closer, suppressing a cheer that the long-awaited greeting time had finally come. The thrill from her nearness and scent of her skin and hair made his pulse race. Jitters knotted in his gut and he felt like a kid on center stage with the spotlight pointed at him.

Her breath hitched and her pupils dilated a little as his shadow fell across her face. He could get so lost in those deep blue eyes...

With trembling hands, he reached for her face and cradled her cheeks. He closed his eyes and his head descended until he felt the warmth of her silky mouth under his. He deepened the kiss, and sensed her lips parting. His insides melted, and he stifled a satisfied groan.

Surely no woman on earth was more perfectly matched for him in every way. And she wanted him, too. He could taste it in her kisses, and felt the tension as he held her face.

He pulled away, breathless. "Only one kiss. Still have twenty-five more for later. *Baknuva* lasts for long time, yes? Is very... nice."

She flushed and whispered, "I can handle it."

The look in her eyes made him shudder. He knew he treaded on dangerous ground. One kiss threatened to undo him. Two might very well make him lose control. Never before had a kiss tempted him with such power, forcing him to call upon inner reserves he didn't know he had, to keep from plunging in without restraint.

Her hands reached for him and she pulled him into another kiss, one more powerful than the last. His blood heated until his pulse roared in his ears. Forcing his hands to stay on her face, he ceased kissing and rested his forehead on hers.

"Is enough kisses." His breathing came out in ragged puffs. "Must not continue." He stepped back. Peering into her eyes, he noticed tears collecting on her lashes.

"Boki, I--"

He touched her lips with the tip of his finger. "Shh... First I must give real gift." Reaching into his pocket, he pulled out the velvet box. "Is for you."

She stared, her mouth gaping. "For me?"

"Yes. Please, look inside." He rubbed his chin and watched the expression on her face soften.

She snapped the lid open, peered inside, and then burst into tears.

Oh, no, she hated his gift. A lump formed in his throat. Would he ever learn how to make her happy?

Chapter Twenty-Eight

Overwhelmed, Laney couldn't hold in the emotion threatening to burst from her, and she exploded into tears. What had she done to make him care so much? She would never understand it, but appreciated his affection.

Placing her hand over her mouth, she sucked in her tears and choked out, "It's such a beautiful pendant."

His tense expression melted and he sighed. "You like birthday present, yes?"

"I--" She swallowed hard. "I love it, Boki. It's the most beautiful necklace I've ever seen."

"Whew." He grinned and pretended to wipe the sweat from his brow. "I worry you not like gift when you cry.

She bit her lip and felt her chin quivering. "I'm just overwhelmed. I don't know why you care so much, but I'm glad you do."

"Come here," he murmured and pulled her into his arms. He rested his chin on her head and rubbed her back.

After several minutes of holding him, inhaling his spicy cologne, and listening to him breathe, she nudged him away.

"Thank you for the high boy dresser." She blinked back tears. "I still can't believe you bought it for me. Would you like to see it in my room?"

He nodded, his eyes flashing as he gazed at her and smiled. The dimple in his cheek deepened as his grin broadened. She resisted the urge to kiss it. He was so devastatingly handsome that bees swarmed in her belly whenever he drew near.

Maybe taking him to her room wasn't such a good idea.

She ignored the little voice of warning and ascended the staircase despite the additional twinge in her stomach telling her to keep their meeting downstairs.

He muttered, "Is tempting view here. Lord, give me strength."

Realizing what he meant, she suppressed a giggle. He was so honest about his feelings that it was downright cute. His verbal appreciation of her appearance only made him more endearing.

Opening her bedroom door, she gestured toward the dresser. "Isn't it gorgeous?"

He approached the antique, running his hand over the surface. "Yes. Now I must get antique couch."

"Oh, no... You've given me so much. I couldn't accept another thing. I already feel like you're giving everything in our relationship, and I'm just on the receiving end. I'm not sure I like that."

Bojan turned and faced her. He touched her cheek. "You listen, my *devojka*. I treasure time together. Is most valuable for me, more than things. Do not worry about how much cost for me. God blessed my restaurants and I have no things for to pay." He shrugged and spread out his hands. "RV paid for, and Hummer paid for. I owe no debt, so have money for spend. Is no big deal for me."

The sound of Dude yipping made them turn. He played tug of war with Baby over the stuffed Chihuahua.

Bojan chuckled. "I see Baby play with *igratcha* I buy for her."

"*Igratcha*? What's that?"

"*Polnet* Chihuahua. Is stuffed Chihuahua."

She gasped and stepped back. "You're the one?"

"One what?" He winked and reached for her hand.

"You gave me the flowers." Her eyes widened, and she bit the corner of her lip. "It was you."

"Yes, I must confess is true." He gave her hand a gentle squeeze. "Was surprise, yes?"

"You... you gave me those flowers, and you didn't even know me." She stared at him, pondering his revelation and what it meant.

"You like flowers?" He lifted her hand to his lips and kissed her knuckles. "Was much for please?"

"What? I don't understand--"

"Flowers make you happy for sad day, yes?"

She blinked back tears, and her throat tightened. "You did that for me? I'm...overwhelmed."

He furrowed his brow. "Is overwhelm good thing?"

Moisture blurred her vision, and she felt several tears roll down her cheeks. "Yes. It's very... humbling, actually. I'm not used to feeling this way, like I'm the recipient of unconditional love, or something."

He wiped the tears from her cheeks with the pads of his thumbs and cradled her face. "Is like Christ, yes? We not deserve love, but Jesus fill heart and forgive sins when we not deserve mercy, but death."

She nodded. "It's like that, and more. You're just a man, but you seem so perfect. Almost too good to be true. Have you ever done anything unloving or unkind, or is that not possible for you?"

His tender expression grew more intense. "Jesus change my heart, but before He save my soul, I not such good person." A shadow passed over his eyes.

"You mean you've actually had bad days? You aren't too good to be true?"

He rubbed his forehead and exhaled. "Sit." Easing on to the bed, he patted the space beside him.

Her heart clenched. His gesture reminded her of her dream. Hopefully what he planned to share wouldn't include leaving the country and never coming back. She reached for her throat and swallowed hard.

"Do I want to know this?"

"You may not like what I say, but you must know. I not keep secret from you. I must tell you truth."

*****

The look of fear in her eyes made him hesitate. *Are you sure I should say, Lord? What if she rejects me? I don't think I could handle that. I love her so much.*

The truth will set you free.

He reached for her hands. "What I say may hurt, but I not mean for to make sad. You understand? I must tell and risk hurt feelings. God told my heart for speak truth."

She nodded, her lips pressed together.

"In college I not have Jesus Christ as Savior and Lord of my heart." He swallowed hard. "I sin with women. But I sin most with Erika."

Laney didn't move, or flinch. Her eyes fixed on his, making his pulse race. He felt sweat beading on his upper lip. He rubbed his face and coughed.

Blinking back tears, he tried not to cry even though the pain of what he had to say still tore a hole in his chest. If he broke down now, he'd never get the words out.

"I tell her we must stop sinning. She tell me she got pregnant. I still grieve for baby I never know. Bible is true when says Jesus forgive sins and cleanses, but how do you say... hmm... consequences of sins... they still hurt me."

Laney took his hands. "Oh, Boki... that's so... sad."

"So I not so perfect as you think. But I try very hard to please Christ now with how I live."

"I'm sure He's very pleased," Laney whispered, her voice sounding tight, hoarse.

"Can you forgive?" His smile wavered.

"Of course, I can. You're a new person in Christ now. The old things have passed away. Behold, all things have become new." She squeezed his hands.

He gasped. "Is my life verse. How you know this?"

She shrugged. "I didn't." Averting her gaze, she released his hands. "Since you told me about your past, I should tell you about mine."

He forced himself to remain calm. Whatever she may have done, the Lord had also forgiven. So he must also forgive.

"I dated a man in college and thought I was in love with him. He gave me gifts, but with each one he expected more of me." She cleared her throat and stared at her hands. "We broke up before things got too out of hand, but I'm not totally innocent." She glanced up and captured his gaze. "But I have saved myself..."

Warmth fluttered in his chest. "Is very good. You have gift for husband as God intends, yes? But even if you not have gift, I still care for you." *You are my heart.*

*****

"I... uh... something like that." She offered a shaky grin.

His eyes shone with unshed tears. "I wish I could say same for me. I wish I not have sinned with women."

She felt his pain, for she'd come close once before. Thank God He'd provided a way out. "Have you... done that since you accepted Christ?"

"No. I not sin in same way since I become Christian."

"Then you have nothing to be ashamed of. He forgave you the minute you professed faith in Him."

He touched her cheek. "I know is true, but still hurts for me not have innocence for gift."

Drawn to him because of the repentant look in his eyes, she hesitated, then pressed her lips against his in a brief show of affection. She leaned back to gaze into his eyes. "I... I really... care for you, Boki."

A wry grin covered his face. "What you scared for say to me is meaning for *S'agapo.*"

She blinked. "What do you mean?"

"Ah, my *devojka. S'agapo* means... I love you."

Chapter Twenty-Nine

Laney opened her mouth, but the words refused to come. Her heart pounded as he gazed into her eyes. He looked so happy, and she didn't want to break his heart. But did she love him, too? Several times she suspected she might be falling in love with him. She'd be crazy to not be attracted to him, at least. He treated her like a princess.

"Now is good time for say something, my *ljubov*."

She blinked back tears. Her throat tightened. "I..."

A troubled look appeared in his eyes. "You not sure of feelings for me?"

Closing her eyes, she shook her head in frustration. "Sometimes I think--"

He touched her chin and tipped her head up so she had to look at him. "Look when you tell me, so I see eyes, my *devojka*. My heart hurts. I must know."

His eyes glistened and she saw pain flickering in their depths. "I think I do love you, Boki. But I don't know for sure. I know I think about you all the time. I miss you when you're gone. I want to touch you, to kiss you, all the time. Is that love?"

He closed his eyes and drew her into his arms. His voice grew husky. "Is hard to define love. I think if person loves, then person wants best for other person. Not think of self first, but other person's happiness. That is love."

She nuzzled him, burrowing into his chest. "Then you must love me. I know how you are. You're so honest and good. And I'm so... mixed-up." She bit her lip.

"Hey." He scooted over and peered deep into her eyes. She felt her inner soul being exposed under his perusal. "Is good for love, but I not pressure you for decision. No matter what you say for me, I still love you."

"I... don't..." She swallowed hard, not sure what to say.

His eyes darkened and skittered to her mouth, before returning to her eyes. "You are my gold."

"What?" Her breath hitched as he leaned closer.

"Means I love you in my language. You more precious than gold." He whispered against her mouth. "*Medeni usni*."

Her body tensed as she inhaled the masculine scent of his clean skin. She loved him, and though her heart shouted the truth of it, her mind rebelled. She feared she loved him even more than she'd loved Sam, and that scared her.

To love him meant she must trust that God knew best, and that trust was broken every time tragic accidents had snatched loved ones from her life.

But she couldn't deny her heart. "I think I do love you, Boki." Her voice wavered, "I'm j-just so afraid I'll lose you. It's s-so hard to trust God."

He nuzzled her neck, making her skin tingle.

She squirmed away from him. "Stop!"

Leaning closer, he inhaled and sighed. "I love way you smell. Remind me for vanilla ice cream. I must taste." With a chuckle, he nipped at her neck.

She laughed. "What does *medeni usni* mean?"

"Means lips sweet as honey." He growled low in his throat as he scanned her face, lingering on her mouth.

Plunging her fingers into his hair, she drew his head down. His slow, agonizing kiss turned her heart on full alert. "Ahhh... You're making me crazy."

He chuckled and nuzzled her ear. "You all ready say you is nuts for me."

Her chest pounded as she sat on her bed and thought about where they were. It would be so easy to keep up the teasing, the fun stuff. But it could also get out of hand, and she didn't think she could bear the guilt.

"Let's go back downstairs," she whispered a bit too breathlessly.

Laughing, he attempted to scoop her up. "I must carry you." His muscular arms surrounded her and he lifted her and carried her down the steps.

Her arms looped around his neck. When they reached the bottom step, she tipped her head toward the couch. "Go ahead and lay me down over there," she whispered, too emotionally exhausted to stand.

"Whatever you wish." He winked.

Stopping at the couch, he eased her down. She watched him closely, expecting him to crack a joke. Instead he caressed her with his gaze. "I love you so much, Laney. It hurts my heart if you not feel same, but I give time for you feelings to grow, yes?"

His lips were mere inches from hers. "I do. I really do love you. I think I was just scared to admit it. I do--"

He kissed her again, caressing her face with his palm. It was a good thing she was lying down, or she would have melted into a puddle. When his kisses grew more urgent, she started to nudge away from him. "I think we better--"

Ruffling his bangs with his hands, he released a shaky breath. "I must leave. Forgive for stupid thing. I put self between place and hard rock. Is not right for tempt you."

What he said made no sense. "What?"

He crouched beside the sofa. "I use idiom from book. Means I make bad situation with hard way out, yes?"

The meaning dawned on her, and she giggled. "Did you mean to say you put us between a rock and a hard place?"

"Is correct. Thank for help me explain."

She sat up and grinned. "Sometimes you're too much."

A wry grin tugged at his mouth. "Is too much so good?"

"You could say that." She winked.

The heating fan kicked on and hummed in the background as it circulated warmth into her home. "Is gas still full or you need more?"

"What? You mean propane? I think I have enough." Then it struck her, and she sucked in her breath. He'd paid for her propane, too. "That was you?"

"What was me?" His brow furrowed and he seemed truly puzzled by her question.

"At first, I thought I was losing my mind. But you did it. You filled my propane tank when I ran out."

A sly grin formed on his face. "Maybe so."

She marveled at his kindness and generosity. Didn't he have limits? "Don't you have to go to work today?"

"Not for five hours. Why you ask? You want for me go away, or something?"

"No. But I do think we need to set boundaries. I don't know about you, but I feel like we have far too much freedom with me living alone. I'm not sure I can handle it, you know?"

He stood. "I understand. I must not allow for tempting."

"We're in this together. Both of us." She touched his hand, and he pulled her up.

"I will be strong for us." He winked and stepped back. "Tell me what you want for Christmas. Is only weeks away."

She shrugged. "There isn't anything I need." Poking him in the chest, she snickered. "Except maybe you."

He grabbed her hand and pressed her palm over his heart. "Feel my heart beat? My soul agrees."

Her smile faltered. She loved hearing his words of devotion, yet a part of her worried that she loved him more from fear of being alone than from true, selfless love.

But she did love him, or at least she thought she did. Would the love she felt be enough? Could she let him go if God told her to? The answer to that question made her soul ache. Would Jesus be enough?

*****

An hour later, Bojan pulled up in front of his RV. He grabbed Dude and all of his belongings and hauled them into his house. After setting them down and letting his dog loose, he checked the time. The antique store should still be open. He searched through the phone book until he found the store on Main Street in Old Town Bisbee.

He remembered seeing a set of antique Victorian-era lamps, and wondered if they were still there. They would look nice in Laney's room with her new bedroom set.

Dialing the number, he tapped his foot and waited.

"*Finders Keepers Antiques and Collectibles.* How may I help you today?"

"Yes. My name is Bojan Trajkovski. I pay for antique dresser weekend after Thanksgiving holiday."

"Yes, I remember you. You're the man who bought the set and the spoon from Yugoslavia."

"Is me. I have important question."

"If it's about what happened to your girlfriend, I'm so sorry. We had no idea the man we hired used false identification. When the police came looking for him we found out he used an alias and fake social security card. Goes by John Smith, but who knows what his real name is."

"I no understand what you say. I call about lamps for bedroom for gift. What happened for my girlfriend?"

"She didn't tell you?" the woman's voice squeaked.

"Tell me what?"

"What he did. He tried to assault her. The police never found him. He seems to have just disappeared. He never even came to get his last check."

"What mean assault?" He swallowed hard. Had Laney deceived him? Why hadn't she mentioned anything?

"I guess he tried to kiss her, but her dog took a chunk out of his ankle and ran him off the property. At least that's what my nephew reported. He was working with John that day. My nephew is deaf, so when the police pulled him over, he was scared. John -- or whoever he is -- made Charlie drop him off so he could get away, I guess. Poor Charlie was terrified. Still is."

Much of what she said after that sounded hollow, like it echoed in a cave. Why would Laney not tell him something like that? He decided to call her and ask. She wouldn't lie to him, that much he knew. Or did he really know her?

Besides, the woman all ready had one fact wrong. No way could Baby have attacked anyone in her weakened state. It had to be Dude who had bitten the man. Bojan smiled at the thought. If his dog had done his job, he would thank Dude later for protecting Laney.

"So you want the lamps? You have very good taste. Shall I set them aside for you to come pick them up? We have late hours up until Christmas."

"Yes, I buy lamps. Thank you." He hung up, still stunned from all he'd heard.

*****

Laney's telephone rang. She hesitated, her hand hovering over the phone. What if it was that man who kept calling and making threats? Bojan had just left, so he would have no reason to call. But she couldn't let paranoia make her stop answering the phone.

"Hello? This is Laney."

"Laney, we must talk." The stiff sound of Bojan's voice made her chest tighten. He sounded upset.

"Sure. You want to come back over?" She offered a lighthearted laugh. "I knew you couldn't stay away long."

He cleared his throat. "Is not funny. I no *se zasmee*."

Okay, now his tone made her lungs constrict. "I'm sorry. We can talk over the phone. What's going on?"

"Tells me for what happen when gift come for house when I go for Macedonia."

Her pulse kicked up a notch. Though his English was confusing, she knew what he asked. How did he know? "What do you mean?" She swallowed and prayed for strength.

"I mean what happened for you?"

"Well, I, uh, had a little problem with the delivery man. He was flirting with me and wouldn't listen when I said I wasn't interested, so I let Dude bite him, and he left. Who told you?"

"Is not important. What I need for know is why you not says anything for me about man cause problem for you."

"I didn't want to worry you. I'm fine. No harm done." She forced a cheery tone.

"Is no more problem? You okay?"

She hesitated. How much should she share? The sick man hadn't called her in several days. "I-I think so."

"You must promise for tell me if you have problem. Must learn for trust me, my *devojka*."

"I do, Boki. Really--"

"No. You not trust. Is not good for us."

"But--"

"I must go. I call later. No more secrets, yes?"

She nodded, then realized he couldn't see her. "Yes, I promise. I'm sorry."

He sighed heavily into the phone. "Then I must choose forgive."

The statement should have eased her anxiety, but instead made it worse. Why did she get the feeling that this wasn't over?

"I must go. Good-bye."

He hung up before she could respond. No, things were not looking good at all.

Chapter Thirty

Bojan never mentioned that conversation again. She appreciated the closure, but still had the unnerving feeling the issue wasn't resolved.

She finished wrapping the few gifts she'd purchased on-line for Bojan, and smiled. While none of the gifts were expensive, they came from her heart. Somehow she knew he'd love every gift, regardless.

Ding dong!

Grabbing her purse, she opened the door and stepped into his arms. "Merry Christmas Eve." She kissed his cheek three times and smiled. "I've got some great stuff for you. Wait 'til you see."

He reached for her hand. "Come, I must take you for cola and get present."

"Okay. Give me a second to secure the dogs and set the alarm." She shooed the dogs into the garage.

After two days of pining after Baby and keeping Bojan up at night, Bojan had relented and decided that separating their dogs was too painful for everyone involved. So Dude moved back in with Baby. Then everything was all right in the world again. To top that, Baby's tummy bulged. They were fairly certain pups were on the way.

"Ready." She grinned and followed Bojan to his Hummer. So far she'd managed to go just about anywhere without getting nauseated. And though she enjoyed her neighbor's church, she couldn't refuse when Bojan asked her to join him on Sundays.

She loved his church and the people there. Everyone loved him. Even his manager, Johnny, and his family had started attending. Bojan said the holidays put people in the mood for church, but she sensed something more was going on with Johnny.

Now if she could just get up the nerve to drive again, she could think about getting a used car once she paid the rest of her tax bill. She had yet to figure out where the money would come from. God would have to provide.

Bojan pulled into a car dealership and grinned. "I gets you cola now, yes?"

Not sure why he picked a dealership, she assumed he would get her a drink from the machine in the lobby while he checked on the status of the company car. "Sure. That sounds great."

*****

Bojan's heart fluttered. She needed a *kola,* and he would buy her one today. Many beautiful, safe *kolas* surrounded him, and they were all on sale. He hoped to get her an SUV so she would feel more secure, even if in reality no vehicles were totally safe. Most of the four-wheel-drives stood high off the road, at least giving the illusion of being above the rest of the traffic.

He would do whatever he must to make sure she had more independence now that she finally seemed to be getting past her fear of riding in cars. He would ask her to drive the *kola* home today, while he drove the Hummer.

Then he would say Merry Christmas, and hand her the keys. She would probably faint, but he loved the idea of being in a position to help her that way. She couldn't afford a car on her own.

"Boki? I don't see a soda machine."

He hesitated. Why did she think he planned to look for a soft drink? "I not here for soda. I come for buy *kola*."

"You lost me."

Not sure what she meant about losing her, because she stood in front of him, he then realized she must have thought he meant a Coca-Cola. He chuckled. "I sorry I say in Macedonian. *Kola* is car or automobile. I want for buy *kola* for Christmas gift."

"Oh, that's nice. Who are you shopping for?"

"Is surprise. I need you for help me choose best one for gift. I needs woman for opinion."

"Okay." She furrowed her brow, as if confused.

As they walked around the showroom with the female salesperson, he noticed Laney examined the sturdier models and asked questions about safety. The appearance of the vehicle didn't seem to matter as much to her.

The tall brunette tried to get them to buy the more expensive models, but Laney kept going back to safety issues. Every time the woman spoke to him, he redirected her to Laney. "She make choice."

They finally settled on two brand new SUVs. When offered to take one on a test drive, Bojan insisted Laney choose one and do the honors.

Her face turned crimson. She pressed her lips together as she spoke. "You know how I feel about driving." Turning, she smiled at the saleswoman, and lifted her finger. "Give us a sec."

"I'm not driving," she said, her hands fisting.

"You look cute when angry. Please, do for me?" He offered his most endearing smile and placed his hand over his heart. When she hesitated and looked over at the vehicle, he knew he'd won.

"All right, but just for a short drive. I want you sitting next to me in case I need to pull over, okay?"

"Is no problem." He opened the door for Laney, then climbed in and handed her the key.

Though she paled at first, and her hands shook as she clutched the steering wheel and pulled onto the street, she eventually relaxed, and even seemed to enjoy herself.

Laney was all smiles by the time they returned to the dealership.

She declared with excitement, "I did it! I didn't pass out or get sick! I really am getting better."

She hopped out of the car, and he joined her.

"I told you if you face fears God can heal." He winked, and placed his hand on the small of her back as he ushered her to the office where they would complete the paperwork.

"Are you actually buying it today? I didn't think you were serious. You already have a Hummer."

"Hummer use too much gas. I want for you keep SUV in garage until I give as gift. I not have two spaces for park near RV. You have big garage and is how you say... hmm... is not used, is empty."

"True." She eyed him with skepticism, as if she didn't believe him. "I'm confused. Is this car for you?"

"No. Is surprise for someone. You help much. I thank you. Now you must wait for me." He tapped his lip. "No more questions."

An hour later, they approached the vehicle. "I need you for drive home. I not drive Hummer and SUV at same time. Is not possible."

"I can't drive this without you next to me." She frowned. "No way."

Bojan rolled his eyes and sighed. He approached her and touched her face. "You must stop say you can't do. You can do all things through Christ Who gives much strength. Is not what Bible says? Is Jesus not Son of God? He is not weak Savior, but strong. He can meet every need. You must believe, have faith, yes?"

With rounded eyes, she stared at him. "Sometimes I'm blown away by your insight. And to think you've been a Christian for only two years. I've been one for ten and you have more faith in your little pinky than I have in my whole body."

He clucked his tongue. "Is not true. You must stop saying such things. Come, we must pray. Then you drive in faith for home, yes?"

"Okay." Her shoulders sagged.

Taking her hands in his, he closed his eyes. "Lord Jesus, we believe You are Christ and have much power. You make fear leave. Perfect love, Scripture says, casts out fear. We ask for help for Laney overcome *stravs*. Please Lord, heal her heart. Amen."

She followed him back to her house and parked the SUV in the garage. When she got out, he approached her with a smile. "Have Merry Christmas, Laney." He dropped the second set of keys into her hand.

Dropping both sets of keys as if burned, she covered her mouth with shaking hands. "Ooh, you didn't..." Tears pooled in her eyes. "Why'd you do that?" She sobbed.

His heart twisted. "You not like gift?"

Swiping the tears from her face, she sniffled. "I can't believe it. Why would you buy me an SUV? I thought you were buying it for your family, like your mother. These things cost a small fortune. I could never repay you. I don't make that much--"

He touched her lips. "Say no more. God put on my heart for buy gift. You must accept. I not expect you pay back. God bless me, I bless for you. Is not wrong. Is good."

"But people just don't buy each other cars. Not even good friends. I can't accept it." She stooped down and retrieved the keys, then offered them to him.

"Is too late. Is registered with you name. I pay cash. No worry. I still have money in bank. I not starve." He gently pressed her hand back in her direction. "You must not reject gift, but accept. Is tradition in my culture. Never turn down gift from lover."

Laney's eyes widened. "I thought--"

"No, not means lover as bad word, but is like someone you heart loves. I love you. This is how I show love."

Her mouth gaped.

His eyes stung, and he blinked to clear his vision. She didn't want his gift. Maybe she didn't even want him anymore. Even so, he would not take the vehicle back. It was hers, and nothing could change that now.

With a groan, she leaned forward and pressed her forehead against his chest. "What am I gonna do with you?"

A thrill zinged through him. She'd accepted his gift, and it made him want to dance. He muttered, "I hope you marries me some day. Is what I hope you do with me."

She chuckled, and he joined her until they were both laughing. Suddenly her laughter turned to tears, and then a gut-wrenching wail.

"I saw Sam." She clutched his jacket and sobbed into his shirt.

He stiffened. She saw Sam? But he was dead.

"I should've told you before. When you were in Macedonia I visited his grave. I just had to see him and say good-bye, you know?" She finished through tears. "He's never coming back. What if I lose you, too?"

"Oh, my *omilen*, I not die unless is my time. Then I have no control. My life is held in God's hands, same as you."

She gazed up at him with woeful, swollen, beautiful eyes. "I do love you, Boki. I never planned to fall in love, but you... you..." She sniffled and glanced away.

"I what?" Tipping her chin up, he smiled. "Tell me."

Laughing through tears, she gave him a playful punch. "You're a thief. You stole my heart. I never wanted this..."

Grinning, he sighed, "Ah, my *ljubov*, but God not want alone for you. He want fill heart with joy and much love."

"Well, He must know what he's doing. I sure don't."

"He not want for waste beautiful eyes and sweet lips. God created you for me." He smiled tenderly.

She grew quiet, as if mulling it over. When she captured his gaze and locked on, he couldn't move. Good thing they were still in her garage. As vulnerable as he felt at that moment, going into her house was potential for disaster.

"Thank you," she whispered, lifting her chin for a kiss. "Thank you for every--"

He muzzled her words with a heart-stopping kiss, then said, "Merry Christmas Eve, my *ljubov*. I see you in morning for celebrate birth of Savior."

She nodded, glanced at the key in her hand, and sighed. With a tiny wave, she walked into her house. He stepped out of the garage as it started closing, and spotted that same blue truck at the end of the road. A shudder coursed through him.

He considered approaching the man to ask what he was watching, but shook off the thought. No sense stirring up trouble, for each day had enough trouble of its own. And he had a restaurant to oversee.

Chapter Thirty-One

Still overwhelmed the next morning by Bojan's extraordinary generosity, Laney prayed for peace. Tears filled her eyes. The Lord had shown her during her devotion last night that all good gifts came from Him. She found it hard to argue with a scripture like that backing up Bojan's claim.

The dogs started yipping, and she knew he'd arrived. She met him at the door and accepted the bag of groceries.

"Merry Christmas." She peered inside. "What's this?"

He grinned. "I make traditional chicken and nuts for meal. You help me cook?"

"I'd love to." Excitement filled her, and she took the items out of the bag. Soon, he would open his gifts. Though she hadn't gotten him anything expensive, she believed he would like the thought behind the presents.

One in particular she hoped he'd love. She'd found a book on Macedonian culture with color photographs, and had thought of him. It even included a history of the country going back as far as the New Testament.

While Bojan boiled the chicken, he chuckled. "What is big smile on face for?"

"Just thinking about the nice gifts I bought you. I hope you like them."

He inched closer and hooked his index fingers through the belt loops on her jeans, then tugged her toward him. "I like anything. You could give me smile, and would be enough for me."

She giggled and rolled her eyes. "You're too much."

The warmth from his skin heated her from head to toe. He drew near until she felt his breath on her forehead. Kissing it gently, he moved his way down her cheek with tenderness in each kiss, until their lips met.

After they indulged for several moments, he whispered against her lips, "Would you like song for Christmas gift?"

She couldn't imagine him singing. "Sure, why not?"

He winked and cleared his throat. "I sing first in Macedonian, then in English, yes?"

Nodding, she cringed and hoped he could carry a tune.

He began softly. His native tongue sounded so romantic, and his full, rich baritone tugged tears from her eyes even though she didn't understand a word of the song. She had all she could do not to sway on her feet as her toes curled in her sneakers. Then he launched into the English version.

"Your birth, O Christ our God, dawned the light of knowledge upon the earth. For by Your birth those who adored stars, were taught by a star, to worship You, the Son of Justice, and to know You, Orient from on High. O Lord, glory to You."

When he finished, he smiled. "Is traditional worship song in Orthodox church for celebrate Christmas."

Astonished by his beautiful voice as he sung praises to God, she felt humbled that God had chosen Bojan to be her soul mate. He complemented her in so many ways.

"That was beautiful, Boki. I didn't know you could sing so well."

"Is many things you still not know about me." He winked. "But is all good things." Taking her hands in his, he squeezed them gently. "I so happy for you are Christian. I could not love woman who not adore Christ."

When the chicken finished boiling, Bojan buttered a deep pan and lay the pieces in it. He added the special filling of nuts with breadcrumbs and unsweetened cookies and covered the chicken with the concoction. He sprinkled the remainder around the chicken, then poured rich, fragrant broth over it and placed it in the oven to bake.

"It looks and smells heavenly, Boki. Where did you learn to cook like that?"

"My *baba* teach me when I live with her."

"What's a *baba*?" She grinned. "Sounds interesting."

"Is word for grandmother."

She never would've guessed -- she still had so much to learn about him. "Can I give you your main present while the chicken is baking?"

"Sure." He winked. "I excited for to see what you buy for me. Is special day for showing much love, yes?"

Nodding, she jogged into the other room, and returned with the book.

"Thank you." He unwrapped the gift and stared at it. Tears filled his eyes, and he smiled. "Is wonderful gift. Thank you so much for special thoughts of me." He tipped his head down and kissed her.

Feeling suddenly shy, she whispered, "I didn't mean to make you cry."

He laughed. "Is not cry for sad, is tears for joy. Is gift from God for cry when He fills with much happiness."

That made sense. The tender look in his eyes told her he truly loved the book and hadn't just said that to make her feel good. "I'm glad for your tears of joy, then."

She reflected on the day when she'd first seen him cry tears of joy over Jovana, who she now knew was his sister. She remembered wishing he'd feel such emotion for her someday. It appeared her wish had come true. It terrified her to be the recipient of such powerful affection. Now if she lost him, it would hurt that much more.

*****

The days sped by until New Year's Eve was upon them. Bojan had to wait to see Laney after he closed the restaurant at one in the morning. She agreed to wait up for him so they could ring in the New Year together.

In her garage.

And he could hardly wait.

Lost in thoughts of Laney, Bojan parked his Hummer in front of Little Italy with a satisfied grin on his face. Love felt so awesome. As he stepped out of his vehicle, he noted a light blue pickup outside resembling the one he'd seen near Laney's house. *The bird watcher...*

His chest tightened as little warning bells rang in his head. He found Johnny and asked, "Who does blue truck belong for?"

"Our new guy. I had to fire Tom for sneaking money from the register this morning. I caught him red-handed and made him put it back. He swore he'd never stolen cash before, but I don't believe him."

"What has red hand to do for stealing money?"

"It's just an expression. Anyway, this guy walked in today looking for a job, so I hired him under the table to do deliveries."

"What is man's name?"

"I think he said John Smith. Why?"

"You check for references?" He hoped Johnny hadn't hired another criminal. He kept telling Johnny to leave the hiring up to him. A lot of people paid folks cash, or "'under the table', and though illegal, it was a common practice. But not one he knowingly allowed.

"Is not okay for pay cash under table. I must see his papers."

"He didn't fill them out yet. We got busy, so I told him he could fill them out later."

Panic washed over Bojan in a tidal wave. What if it was the same guy? What if Laney hadn't told him the whole story about this man? He had a sinking feeling and asked, "Did he tell you where he work before?"

"I think he said someplace in Bisbee. Oh, and Laney ordered the usual, but since I didn't know when you were coming in, I sent him to deliver it."

Bojan felt panic rising in his chest. He was the boss. He was responsible for his employees. If the man hurt Laney, it was his fault.

Nausea made his head swim, and he felt an urgency to call her. Flipping open his cell phone, he dialed her number. It rang and rang. The longer it took her to answer, the more worried he became. As far as he knew, she had planned to stay home. So why wasn't she answering the phone?

*****

Laney heard the phone ring when she turned the hair dryer off, but right before she grabbed it, it stopped ringing. Seconds later, the door bell rang.

Running a comb through her now-dry hair, she approached the front door. Her dinner had arrived on time, for once. Peering through the peephole, she checked. The man had his head down, but she read the logo on his hat and could see the delivery car in her driveway. "Just a sec."

She set the comb down and reached for her purse. The moment she opened the door, she sensed danger -- smelled it, but it was too late. One glimpse of the mermaid tattoo and she knew her instincts were correct.

Pizza Man wedged his foot between the door and frame. "You dinner, ma'am."

With all of her strength she shoved the door in a futile attempt to shut him out. Her feet slid on the tile as he shoved his way inside, and then locked the front door with a *click*.

"Don't be rude, now." He grinned and thrust the boxes at her. "I brought you dinner... on the house."

"I don't want it." She shoved the food away.

Prying the takeout box open, he stuffed it under her nose. "Look what we have here. Pizza, loaded with onions."

She glimpsed inside the box. He lied. It was her usual order. But she didn't dare challenge him as she inched toward the cordless phone.

With a snicker, he threw the pizza to the floor. "I've lost my appetite. I think I'd rather have something sweet. What do you say, sugar?"

He pulled off his ball cap and removed his sunglasses, revealing a scar -- like a Z -- next to his eye. Immediately, she recognized Sam's cousin though many years had passed since she'd last seen him. His ice-cold eyes gave him away as the poor, crazy guy who had a crush on her, who tried to force himself on her when she was in Junior High. The one she had cut with a piece of glass she'd found on the ground when she fought him off. "Oh my God. Richard?"

"So you haven't forgotten me, eh, babe? I know I've never forgotten you. Not like you forgot Sam." He stroked the scar with his finger and leaned so close she felt the heat from his body. "Too bad I ran him off the road."

A shudder wracked her spine as she caught the sour stench of his onion breath. "You sick--"

That moment, the phone rang. She dove on it, pressing the *answer* button. Before she got a word out, he swatted the phone away. She shrieked, hoping whoever called would sense danger and call the police.

*****

Bojan tried the number one more time and someone picked up the line. He heard a blood-curdling shriek.

Then the phone went dead. He stared for a second at his cell phone and flew into action.

"Johnny, you must call 9-1-1. Man you send with pizza attack Laney. Sheriff is looking for arrest for crime."

Johnny's eyes widened. "Are you serious?"

"Yes. Call now. I must go."

Darting into the parking lot, he glanced at the other delivery car, then at his Hummer. The car would get there more quickly and had a much quieter engine. Reaching for his keys, he scrambled into the car and sped toward Laney's house. Minutes later he heard sirens in the distance. Thankfully, the police weren't far behind him.

Slamming on the brakes, he shoved the gearshift into park. He raced for the front door to her house and twisted the handle. It was locked.

Bojan searched frantically for another way inside, and remembered the glass doors at the back of the house. Jumping up, he scaled the brick wall leading to her backyard patio.

He tested the door. Locked. A sharp scream came from inside the house, and movement caught his eye. Inside, a man had pinned Laney's arms behind her as she struggled against him.

Rage surged through Bojan, and he grabbed a log and threw it at the glass door. The glass shattered, sending shards crashing to the floor.

The man holding Laney turned and swore. He shoved her into the wall and lunged to grab a butcher knife from the counter.

Laney screamed and ran from the room.

The man emitted a guttural yell and charged. The knife he held sliced the air near Bojan's head. Dodging the weapon, Bojan rolled to the side, and the attacker slammed into a cabinet door. The knife pierced the wood.

As the man tried to yank it free, Bojan glanced around the kitchen and searched for anything he could use to defend himself and Laney. He hoped she would get out, get somewhere safe while she had the chance.

Laney charged back in through the door, screaming like a madwoman. She swung a fireplace poker at the attacker.

He twisted the knife free.

"Laney, no!" Bojan threw himself in front of her.

The man intercepted the iron rod before the implement connected with his head, wrenching it from her hands.

Bojan tackled the man, knocking the knife and poker away as both men hit the floor with a thud. The sour stink of the man's sweat assaulted Bojan's senses.

Laney lunged for the knife and kicked it, sending it spinning and clattering across the tile floor. She scrambled for the poker and positioned to swing it at her attacker like a golf club, but hesitated.

"Move!" she screamed at Bojan, the poker wavering in her hands as she aimed it at the man.

Bojan glanced up. His attacker cursed and clipped Bojan in the jaw. The metallic taste of blood filled his mouth.

The man's face contorted and turned crimson. He growled as he flipped and tried to buck Bojan off like an angry bull.

Red-hot rage coursed through Bojan. He clamped one hand over the man's tattooed throat, punching him repeatedly with the other hand until his knuckles bled.

The man writhed, groaning, then spit blood on the tile floor. Veins bulged in his neck. "Get off me!"

Police sirens wailed louder, breaking into Bojan's blind anger, and he paused, panting, his fist raised.

A pounding on the front door sent Laney running to open it. He heard her sobs as she let them in. They followed her to the kitchen, guns drawn.

Bojan pinned tattooed man down. The raging man twisted and butted Bojan's face as he tried to wrest free. Groaning, Bojan winced and applied more pressure.

"Police! Don't move!" They aimed their guns at Bojan, then at the man beneath him, as if they weren't sure whom to arrest. Both men were splattered with blood.

One of the sheriff's officers approached with handcuffs as another pried them apart.

"He's the one..." Laney wailed and pointed to the attacker. "The one with the tattoo. He -- he tried to r-rape me. Twice." She sobbed into her hands.

Bojan reeled at her words, his arms hanging limp at his sides. The man with the tattoo had tried to rape her once before? He blinked and wiped the blood from his mouth with his sleeve.

Laney squatted before him. "You're hurt." Grabbing a kitchen towel, she dabbed at his lip.

He grimaced and turned his head away. After he'd showed how deeply he'd cared for her, she still hadn't told him the truth. But he quickly reconsidered his response. Thankfully Laney didn't seem to notice. She must've been hurt and embarrassed to keep such details from him. Hadn't Jovana done the same at first?

"Isn't your face sore?" She followed his movement with the rag. "Just let me--"

"No. Please. Just give me second for catch breath."

She blinked as if stunned. "What's wrong?"

He could tell by her expression, she hadn't a clue. Since she said she appreciated his honesty, he held nothing back. "I worry for you. What is this you say about man tried to rape twice? When this happen?"

She bit her lip. "When he delivered the furniture he cornered me, but I got away."

"Is whole story? He not hurt more?"

"He did force himself on me, sort of. But I got away before anything happened. He just..."

Bojan raised his hand and looked away. "Is enough. Say no more. I must think."

"But--"

"Ma'am?" An officer approached. "Is this the same man who made threatening phone calls?"

She nodded. "I just found out he killed... he killed..."

Bojan frowned. "He killed who, Laney? Who this man killed?"

"He killed Sam..." She sobbed into her hands.

Bojan frowned as the officers arranged to take Laney's statement the next day and led the handcuffed man from the house. How could she do that to him? How could she put herself in danger and not confide in him? He didn't understand. "Is not just attack you? Also phone calls? Why you not trust me? Why not tell me?"

"I didn't want you to worry. I'm sorry, I was wrong to keep that from you. Please..." She burst into tears all over again, making Bojan feel regret over his harsh words. After all, she'd been hurt by the wicked man. He'd killed her fiancé Sam. Bojan didn't want to make things worse.

His vision blurred as he blinked back tears. "I forgive. I am much sorry I not think of your hurts first. Is wrong for me to think for myself before think for you."

"O-okay." She nodded, her chin trembling.

"But please promise you never keep from me things like this again." Reaching for her cheek, he touched it. Her hand clasped his, and he sucked in his breath.

"Oh, I'm sorry. You're hurt. Your hand is swelling. Oh..."

"Is okay. Need ice for swell. Can get later. Now promise you not scare again and you tell truth."

She fell against his chest, and he wrapped his arms around her. "Oh, Boki, I'm so sorry. I do promise, I promise I'll never... Ooh..." Clinging to his shirt, she sobbed, "I'm sorry I hurt you. I'm so sorry."

He kissed her hair, and groaned low in his throat. "Is not about me. I worry for you. I must help keep you safe. Is my duty as man who would care for you, my *ljubov*."

Peering into his eyes, she softened. "I love you, too, Boki. I promise I'll never hurt you again."

"Then I must believe you and trust." He offered a wry grin, but stifled his smile when the pain from his bleeding lip and chin radiated through his face. Touching his jaw, he cringed. He'd have a bruise tomorrow, for sure.

"Oh, is your mouth sore?"

He winced and nodded.

Before he could speak, her soft mouth touched his. She gently massaged his lips with her tender kisses.

164

The fine line between ecstasy and pain blurred as he met her kiss for kiss.

Chapter Thirty-Two

Easter weekend Bojan coerced Laney into traveling to Peoria to meet his parents after the Orthodox service. She forced herself to keep her hands steady. The idea of meeting his parents frightened her more than driving over two hundred miles. "Will they mind that I'm not Orthodox?"

"Parents did at first. Now is okay. They understand my feelings for you and wish to meet."

Several hours later, they arrived at the Macedonian Orthodox Church in Peoria. The service had already ended, and people flooded the parking lot. It sure seemed like a long drive just to go to church, but Bojan had said his parents had limited options in Arizona.

Bojan touched her arm. "See people over by red truck? They my parents. Come, let me introduce."

He nodded at his parents. They stared at her, looking just as tense and nervous as she felt.

Laney decided to help ease their anxiety, and stepped up to Bojan's mother, grabbed her shoulders, and kissed her cheek three times.

"It's good to meet you, Mrs. Trajkovski. I'm Laney Cooper."

His mother's face registered surprise. She opened her mouth, then snapped it shut. Laney repeated the same greeting toward his father, and he gave her a hearty hug in return.

Tugging at her shirtsleeve, Bojan pulled her aside. "Excuse, please." He nodded toward his parents, then whispered, "What you kiss parents for?"

"I gave the traditional greeting. Did I make a mistake?"

A wry grin tugged at his mouth. "Is funny. Hope you not embarrassed, but I trick you on traditional greeting. Is only done in Macedonia. Not for people in America."

Her neck heated. She covered her mouth and assessed what he'd said. "You... I don't believe it. You tricked me?"

"But was good surprise, yes?"

A sheepish grin formed on her lips, and this time she offered her hand to his parents. "I'm sorry if I embarrassed you. Your son told me that was the traditional greeting, so I thought..."

His parents' eyes darted toward him.

Bojan shrugged. "I knew I must get for to know Laney. I need for find a way -- and tradition worked for me."

She hugged him. "Don't worry. I'm glad you took a chance on me, my *ljubov*." She winked. "I'm glad you did."

A yipping noise captured her attention. "Oh, I almost forgot. This is for you." Laney lifted the box from the concrete, and removed the screen lid.

Two adorable Chihuahua puppies peered up at them. The larger of the two, a brown shorthaired Chihuahua, stood straight and regal, like Bojan had the night they met. The smaller dog wrapped her front paws around the brown Chihuahua's legs and trembled, her eyes squeezed shut.

While his parents cooed at the dogs, she had to laugh. The puppies reminded her of the grace of God in her life. With a grin, she thanked the Lord for unconditional love.

*****

Laney smiled at Bojan from across the candlelit table. The soft glow against his golden skin made the evening that much sweeter. The look in his eyes, all dreamy and tender, made her heart thump.

Her gaze fixed on the tiny scar on his chin. She still marveled at his heroic rescue of her a few months ago. She shuddered at the memory.

The moment Onion Boy had removed his cap and glasses she realized the delivery guy had come back like an apparition. To finish what he'd started years ago. She'd screamed, but he'd forced his way inside.

"Don't fight me, and it'll be over soon," Onion Boy had said when he'd attacked her the first time. She had only been in junior high. He was older and in high school. They had been neighbors.

A shudder snaked through her as she remembered those chilling words. Sam had saved her then. If Bojan hadn't come this time... she forced the horrid memory away. She couldn't dwell on that now.

"I have important question tonight." He winked.

Her mouth went dry. "Okay..."

"But first, tell me about mortgage and taxes for house."

"What? How did you know about that?"

He pulled a section of the paper from his back pocket and unfolded it on the table before her eyes. "Says here taxes up for tax lien auction and listed you home as address Please, explain."

"Okay." She nibbled on her lower lip. "I found out in December that my taxes were due. I owed eight thousand dollars on the property."

Bojan whistled. "Is much debt. Why not ask me for help?"

"I didn't want you to bail me out. I... I sold my engagement ring, and that brought in most of the money I needed. They said if I paid the rest by June then I wouldn't have a lien on the property tax."

He ran his fingers through his hair. "I check on this. Is big mistake. You owe three thousand for this year and three for next. County made clerical error, so is wrong."

"That's wonderful! I was so worried I wouldn't have the two thousand I need by June."

He leaned forward and whispered, "But not enough for you to tell me so I can pray for you and help."

Her cheeks heated. "I didn't want to burden you with my problems. We aren't married, so there's no reason for me to expect you to bail me out of my tax crisis."

"Is time for change tonight. Now is question." He took her hands and kissed her fingers. His eyes shone, and he blinked several times before coughing into his hand. With a sigh, he scrubbed his face, then exhaled again.

"Elaine Cooper, I must tell you of my love and ask for you as my wife and best friend. Please, say yes."

He pulled a small velvet box from his pocket and set it in front of her. "Look."

She cracked it open and gasped. A gorgeous emerald ring surrounded by diamonds lay on the velvet bed. Removing it from the box, she slid it onto her finger. With tears rolling down her cheeks, she squeaked out, "It's beautiful. Where did you get this ring? It looks like an antique."

"*Baba* gave for me before I leave. But you not answer my question. Will you marry me, my *ljubov*?"

Glancing into hopeful eyes, she smiled. "Yes, I will. I want to be your wife."

He stood and reached for her, pulling her into his arms. Mumbling foreign words into her hair, he squeezed her tightly.

"You make me happiest man in world." Stepping back, he gazed into her eyes and said, "Now we must find way to get back ring you sold for taxes."

She tipped her chin up. "No." She kissed him deeply, then drew in a ragged breath. Smiling, she whispered, her words thickly accented, "Is in past, my *ljubov*. Boki, he is future."

He chuckled, nuzzling her neck. "Laney need English lessons. I must help teach." And he sealed his statement with a kiss.

The End

Read Jovana's Story

In Plain Sight

About Michelle Sutton

Michelle Sutton has been reading since she was in kindergarten but never enjoyed writing, and she certainly never expected to be an author herself. However, in 2003, she felt God calling her to write. Once she got started she discovered she has no desire to stop. Now she is a multi-published, award-winning author of numerous romantic fiction titles. She still reads a lot of books and in her spare time writes reviews for a variety of blogs and websites as a media reviewer. Michelle lives with her husband and two sons on a four-acre ranch in sunny Arizona.

Read more about Michelle at: http://www.MichelleSutton.net